LEFT

TO

HIDE

(An Adele Sharp Mystery—Book Three)

BLAKE PIERCE

Blake Pierce

Blake Pierce is the USA Today bestselling author of the RILEY PAGE mystery series, which includes seventeen books. Blake Pierce is also the author of the MACKENZIE WHITE mystery series, comprising fourteen books; of the AVERY BLACK mystery series, comprising six books; of the KERI LOCKE mystery series, comprising five books; of the MAKING OF RILEY PAIGE mystery series, comprising six books; of the KATE WISE mystery series, comprising seven books; of the CHLOE FINE psychological suspense mystery, comprising six books; of the JESSE HUNT psychological suspense thriller series, comprising seven books (and counting); of the AU PAIR psychological suspense thriller series, comprising three books; of the ZOE PRIME mystery series, comprising three books (and counting); of the new ADELE SHARP mystery series; and of the new EUROPEAN VOYAGE cozy mystery series.

An avid reader and lifelong fan of the mystery and thriller genres, Blake loves to hear from you, so please feel free to visit www.blakepierceauthor.com to learn more and stay in touch.

BOOKS BY BLAKE PIERCE

EUROPEAN VOYAGE COZY MYSTERY SERIES
MURDER (AND BAKLAVA) (Book #1)
DEATH (AND APPLE STRUDEL) (Book #2)
CRIME (AND LAGER) (Book #3)

ADELE SHARP MYSTERY SERIES
LEFT TO DIE (Book #1)
LEFT TO RUN (Book #2)
LEFT TO HIDE (Book #3)
LEFT TO KILL (Book #4)
LEFT TO MURDER (Book #5)
LEFT TO ENVY (Book #6)
LEFT TO LAPSE (Book #7)

THE AU PAIR SERIES
ALMOST GONE (Book#1)
ALMOST LOST (Book #2)
ALMOST DEAD (Book #3)

ZOE PRIME MYSTERY SERIES
FACE OF DEATH (Book#1)
FACE OF MURDER (Book #2)
FACE OF FEAR (Book #3)
FACE OF MADNESS (Book #4)

A JESSIE HUNT PSYCHOLOGICAL SUSPENSE SERIES
THE PERFECT WIFE (Book #1)
THE PERFECT BLOCK (Book #2)
THE PERFECT HOUSE (Book #3)
THE PERFECT SMILE (Book #4)
THE PERFECT LIE (Book #5)
THE PERFECT LOOK (Book #6)
THE PERFECT AFFAIR (Book #7)
THE PERFECT ALIBI (Book #8)
THE PERFECT NEIGHBOR (Book #9)
THE PERFECT DISGUISE (Book #10)
THE PERFECT SECRET (Book #11)

ONCE SHUNNED (Book #15)
ONCE MISSED (Book #16)
ONCE CHOSEN (Book #17)

MACKENZIE WHITE MYSTERY SERIES
BEFORE HE KILLS (Book #1)
BEFORE HE SEES (Book #2)
BEFORE HE COVETS (Book #3)
BEFORE HE TAKES (Book #4)
BEFORE HE NEEDS (Book #5)
BEFORE HE FEELS (Book #6)
BEFORE HE SINS (Book #7)
BEFORE HE HUNTS (Book #8)
BEFORE HE PREYS (Book #9)
BEFORE HE LONGS (Book #10)
BEFORE HE LAPSES (Book #11)
BEFORE HE ENVIES (Book #12)
BEFORE HE STALKS (Book #13)
BEFORE HE HARMS (Book #14)

AVERY BLACK MYSTERY SERIES
CAUSE TO KILL (Book #1)
CAUSE TO RUN (Book #2)
CAUSE TO HIDE (Book #3)
CAUSE TO FEAR (Book #4)
CAUSE TO SAVE (Book #5)
CAUSE TO DREAD (Book #6)

KERI LOCKE MYSTERY SERIES
A TRACE OF DEATH (Book #1)
A TRACE OF MUDER (Book #2)
A TRACE OF VICE (Book #3)
A TRACE OF CRIME (Book #4)
A TRACE OF HOPE (Book #5)

CHAPTER ONE

The team leader glanced at the notification scrolling across his satellite phone. *Vermisstes.* Missing persons. The notification came direct from the BKA. A strange thing for the German intelligence agency to take an interest so quickly. Then again, these two weren't the usual missing persons.

The team leader adjusted the zipper on his faded red and green overcoat and gestured toward the three other members of his unit. Volunteers—all of them. Their logo in crisp black letters: *Bergwacht Deutchsland.* Mountain Rescue, Germany. They stomped through the snow in the fading evening. Only an hour left before they'd have to turn back. No sense searching at night and risking his team as well. A gorge dipped from slipping ravines on their left, and to their right, the mountain only protruded higher, threatening to pierce the clouds in their grayish gloom.

The Bavarian Alps were a long and intricate mountain range. And two cross-country skiers as experienced as the missing persons were could cover a significant distance from the *Wolfsschluct Resort* in the time they'd been missing.

Sasha, the local guide, pointed off into the distance. The team leader paused at the sound of an approaching buzz. He turned, chill wind cooling his exposed face as he regarded the orange helicopter whirring through the blue sky. An echoing hum from the chopper blades resounded in a continuous loop against the backdrop of mountains encumbered with snow.

"*Kapitän,*" said Jerome, the youngest team member. He huffed a bit, approaching the team leader with quick steps, flicking snow as his boots plunged and lifted from the burdened trail.

"Hmm?" said Luka Porter, the unit captain.

Jerome leaned in, yelling to be heard over the chopper. "No more ski tracks. *Scheisse!* Think we should double back."

Luka regarded the young man and breathed, allowing a trail of vapor to twist up past his cheeks and probe toward the evening sky. He also responded in German. "*Nein.* We go back, you know what

1

happens, then?" he asked, quietly.

Jerome hesitated. "It's—it's growing dark, sir. Just that, I thought one of the rules was to return before nightfall."

Luka scratched at the stubble on his chin. He'd been roused early that morning without a chance to shave. These *Vermisstes* were important people. Underscored by the BKA agents who'd personally shown up at his home to drag him to the office beside the resort.

"An hour," said Luka. "Then back. But an hour more."

Jerome looked disappointed, but disguised it well enough. Both of them trudged through the snow along the trail, following Sasha as she led them along the trajectory of the last known direction the Italian couple had followed.

"I hear… I hear they were wealthy," Jerome said, gasping in between words now. Some of his eager energy was beginning to fade the deeper the snow became.

Luka grunted again, limiting his words, saving his strength. "Twenty-four hours missing. In this weather, in November, wealthy or not, they'll freeze all the same."

"Or worse," Jerome muttered.

Luke frowned but didn't reply, doing both of them the favor of conserving their breath.

Just then, Sasha held up a hand from further along the trail. The light trickle of snowfall had stopped and started a few times over the last few hours, disguising any further ski tracks they might have found. Yet Sasha motioned rapidly, drawing Luka's and Jerome's attention.

"What is it?" Luka called out.

Sasha was pointing toward the sky, and the two men followed the indicating gesture.

A single beam of blue light extended faintly in the evening horizon, originating from the helicopter, but swishing and circling around a small grove of trees at the very top of the gorge, near the slope.

"They found something!" Sasha shouted.

Luka nodded and picked up the pace, feeling the sting of the cold now and the quick freeze of his breath vapor against his cheeks. He bowed his head, following Sasha's footsteps as they rushed toward the grove. The Italian couple had set out skiing from the resort more than twenty-four hours ago. Yet, still, there was a chance they'd survived. Properly garbed, perhaps carrying shelter, they'd be in a bad way, but death wasn't a certainty. Many of the people their *Bergwacht* unit was

2

sent after ended up being recovered. Many, but not all.

They neared the grove of trees, following Sasha, who had skis strapped over her shoulder. The snow here was too fresh, too light for skiing to be optimal. Luka frowned—so why was the helicopter indicating this grove?

A scattering of coniferous larch and spruce trees circled the indicated beam of blue light, which only seemed to strengthen the more the evening darkened.

"Lights!" Luka called.

The other members of the search and rescue team hit their headlamps, and Luka withdrew his well-used one-hundred-thousand-lumen aluminum safety light. He clicked the switch and pointed the large flashlight toward the trees. Luka blinked a bit at the bright glare, like the headlights of a police vehicle. He nodded at the others to approach.

Care was in order. Jerome, their law enforcement volunteer, drew his sidearm. One could never be too careful in the Alps. All sorts of creatures lurked in these mountains.

"I see something," Sasha called as she moved toward the trees. Snow crunched underfoot, suggesting new snowfall had been blocked, mostly, by the trees, leaving only residue and whatever had been dislodged from the branches.

"Careful," Jerome called, his weapon in his gloved hand.

Sasha nodded but waved away the caution, stepping toward the indicated portion of the forest. She pulled up sharply.

Luka could see it now too. It was hard to miss. Dark shapes against the snow. Dark stains.

Jerome's gun lowered slowly as they approached through the coniferous trees. Then the young volunteer cursed and his arms went limp. "*Oh mein Gott,*" he said, murmuring a quick prayer before crossing himself.

Luka stepped past Jerome and came up level with Sasha, beneath a giant fir. He brushed aside an extended branch with one hand and stared into the snowy grove, his eyes fixed on the scene.

"The tourists?" Sasha asked in a low, trembling voice.

"Call it in," Luka said, sharply. "Now."

He heard Sasha at his side fumbling with her SAT phone, followed by the quick beep of buttons in response. He listened to the helicopter still whirring overhead, like a vulture circling a carcass. Jerome tried to

3

move closer, but Luka held out an arm, pressing back against the young man. "Don't," he said, quickly. "Can't disturb it."

"What—what do you think did *this*?" Jerome murmured, staring.

Luka returned his attention toward the grove, difficult as this was. He'd seen victims of animal attacks before, but *nothing* like this. Bear attacks weren't common in the region—or, at least, hadn't been in a long while. Recently, though, in the past few years, there had been a resurgence of brown bear sightings in the Alps.

Now, the proof lay before him.

Two bodies—at least, what remained of them. Bloody, frozen, scattered like impressionistic art in droplets and spray around the area. A few streaks had even speckled the trees. Pieces of human flesh also ornamented the ground. An entire foot was caught in a young sapling, the tree's growth stunted by lack of sunshine.

Bloody furrows and cuts laced the bodies. So much blood. Too much, suggesting the victims had been alive for a good portion of the carnage.

Luka simply stared, arm extended, braced against Jerome as he listened to Sasha. "Yes... yes, is the agent still there? The one with BKA? No, Franz, no time—*now*. We—we think we found them." A pause. A staticky voice on the other end. Sasha swallowed. "Dead," she said. "Definitely dead."

CHAPTER TWO

Another vibration on her desk. Adele glanced down and resisted the urge to roll her eyes. Angus. Again. He'd been texting her for three days now.

She pushed her phone out of sight beneath a stack of papers balanced on a metal tray. Late. She'd pushed off the paperwork for too long already. Agent Grant, her supervising officer in San Francisco, was a patient sort, but even she was getting tired of Adele's procrastination.

In fact, her last comment had gone something like, "Stay the hell in your office. Lock the door, and don't leave until you get the forms on my desk. Understand? Christ, Adele, I have bureaucrats breathing down my neck as it is."

Not the most comforting of words to have echoing in her head as she filled out the overdue forms. Adele wrinkled her nose and glanced at her empty mug. The faint odor of coffee hung on the air of her small office. Really, it was little more than a walk-in closet with an opaque glass door. Windowless, with a single desk and chair and an overhead yellowish light, it served well enough.

She lifted another file, dropped it in front of her, and began flipping through the pages. Her eyes glazed as she did, and the hand holding the pen went limp, pressed against the desk. Only fifty more documents to go.

The joys of corresponding between multiple agencies couldn't be overstated.

At last, she found the portion of the document requiring her attention and moved to fill it out.

More vibrating.

"Damn it!" she shouted, launching her pen at the stack of papers now shielding her phone.

She grabbed the phone, lifted it, and read, "4 New Messages." All of them from Angus. The handsome, curly-haired coder had broken up with her a few months ago. At the time, she'd thought they were on the verge of getting engaged.

She glanced at the pile of folders, then at her phone. Then, quietly muttering to herself, she unlocked the screen and scrolled through Angus's messages.

Hey Adele, have a sec?

A sec? Quaint. Cute. To the point.

Don't know if you got my last message. Can we talk?

She scanned the times the messages were sent. Only two hours in between. Was it just her imagination, or was Angus getting desperate? What could he possibly want anyway?

Adele, look—I'm sorry for how things ended. I've been thinking a lot. Do you think we could hash things out this week?

Adele's eyebrows inched up and she tapped her pen against her whitened teeth. Interesting. Was... was it possible Angus wanted to get back together?

She read the last message, which simply said:

Please.

She sighed and pushed her phone back beneath the pile of papers in the metal tray. No sense sorting it out now. She was swamped. Hurting Angus's feelings a little was nothing in comparison to what Agent Grant would do to her if she postponed filling out the forms another day. Besides, Angus had done his share of hurting last time they'd interacted.

Adele squared her shoulders and tried to return her attention to her paperwork.

No use.

She leaned back, emitting a quiet sigh that extended toward the ceiling as if encapsulating the yellow light and blending with the illumination. Though he'd hurt her, she wasn't interested in hurting Angus. He'd been a good boyfriend—a solid boyfriend. Predictable? Maybe a little. Reliable, though? Certainly. Honest, too—though sometimes too nice, too hesitant.

Safe. Perhaps the best word to describe him. Rich now, too, if what she was hearing about his last tech company was anything to go by.

Her left hand inched toward the phone again, but she paused, allowing it to linger on the soft surface of the paper beneath her fingertips. All this paperwork could have been avoided, at least— *mostly*—if she wasn't forced to spend so much time in airplanes, or moving between agencies. When she'd agreed to work with Interpol as

6

a correspondent between BKA, DGSI, and the FBI, she'd thought she'd known what she was getting into. But now…

She wrinkled her nose again at the pile of folders in front of her.

Perhaps it was time to set down roots. Moving, constantly moving… It wasn't conducive to a happy life, was it? Recently, Adele had read an article in *Psychology Meritus*, a journal that the FBI Behavioral Unit swore by, which said that people who constantly moved in their youth, and continued to do so as an adult, often found it difficult to connect to others. The threat of uprooting and leaving could sometimes even have a traumatic effect on a child.

Adele frowned at the memory. Could it be true? It wasn't like she had many friends.

She thought of Robert, and a small smile played across her lips. Even Agent Grant, despite being her boss, was someone she could confide in.

Her smile faded a bit as she thought of John Renee. Crack-shot, wisecracking asshole extraordinaire. Nothing safe about John. The anti-Angus in many ways.

Frowning now, she reached for her phone, intent on calling Angus. A call couldn't hurt, could it? Especially if he wanted her back. What would she say? Would she even know before hearing his voice?

As she picked up her phone and felt the smooth weight, it began to ring. Not vibrating this time, but a shrill chirp. The only number in her phone set to make a sound came from upstairs.

Adele's frown deepened and she could feel the furrowed lines gouged into her forehead as she pressed the phone to her ear. "Agent Grant, I'm working on the files. Not done yet, but I should—"

"Adele, forget the files," said the voice on the other end. "We need you upstairs."

"Are you sure? If you give me a few more hours, I'm sure I could—"

"Forget the files, Adele," said Agent Grant's voice. It sounded strained, reluctant, but certain. "Hurry. Something came up."

"I'll be right there."

Adele waited for the silence on the other end before lowering her device and staring at her desk for a moment. *Something came up.* The way Grant had said it sent a tingle along the back of Adele's arms.

Well, roots—at least for now—could wait.

Adele pushed from her chair, pocketed her phone, and—trying not to smile *too* widely—distanced herself from the pile of paperwork, pushing out the door and heading upstairs to Agent Grant's office.

CHAPTER THREE

As she stepped into Agent Grant's office, Adele was surprised to see Ms. Jayne sitting in front of the desk, her hands clasped over her knees in a prim, patient posture. Adele hesitated and tried not to frown in confusion. She surveyed the room, half expecting to see Executive Foucault show up as well, but—this time—there was no sign of the French head of DGSI.

Ms. Jayne, on the other hand, worked for Interpol. She was an older woman, with bright, intelligent eyes behind horn-rimmed glasses. She had silver hair and was a bit heavier than most field agents. Adele knew from experience that Ms. Jayne spoke without an accent, suggesting she'd mastered the English language, but it didn't seem as if it were her native tongue.

As the door clicked shut behind Adele, she stepped further into Agent Grant's office. If Ms. Jayne had seen fit to come herself, something had *come up* indeed.

Agent Grant cleared her throat behind the desk. Adele's supervisor brushed a hand through her medium-length hair and pressed her lips into a severe expression. She was only a few years older than Adele, but had premature wrinkles around her mouth and the corners of her eyes. Lee Grant had been named after the two generals from the Civil War, and was well-known among the San Francisco field office for her forays out of the building and onto crime scenes whenever she had the opportunity or excuse to stretch her legs. Secretly, Adele suspected that Agent Grant missed the field work. And, though she'd never say it, Adele believed Grant's skills were wasted behind a desk.

"Sharp," said Agent Grant, nodding across her desk.

"Agent Sharp," Ms. Jayne said, nodding with a curt bob of her perfectly trimmed hair.

"Ms. Jayne," Adele said, hesitating. She'd never been given a first name. She nodded toward Grant as well. "How can I be of assistance?"

She waited, letting the silence linger between them as the commanding agents glanced at each other. Agent Grant broke the silence. "We have a... *delicate* predicament."

9

Ms. Jayne's eyes narrowed almost imperceptibly behind her glasses. A brief crack in her proper, prim facade, but Adele caught it before it slipped away behind bright eyes and a placid expression.

"Delicate?" said Adele. "Well, anything to get me away from that paperwork…" She chuckled weakly, but when the mirth wasn't reciprocated, she fell quiet again.

"The locals," Ms. Jayne began, in her normal crisp, precise tones, "believe it was a brown bear attack."

Adele tried another smile, and once again abandoned the half-hearted attempt to lighten the atmosphere. "Didn't know there were any brown bears in San Francisco," she said.

Agent Grant shook her head. "The Alps."

"The… the Alps?"

"An extensive mountain range, stretching across eight countries in Europe," said Agent Grant in manner of explanation.

"Oh, er, well, no—yes, I mean. I know what they are. So there's a case in the Alps?"

Adele thought about Angus's texts. She thought about her desire to set down roots. But at the same time, a quiet, prickling chill of excitement probed up her spine. This time, she fought to suppress the smile threatening to curl her lips.

"Yes," said Agent Grant. "As I mentioned, locals think it was a bear attack. A wealthy Italian couple vacationing at a ski resort. Both of them accomplished cross-country skiers. Both of them found dead, mauled."

Adele nodded once. "But not a bear?"

Grant glanced to the third woman in the room. Ms. Jayne kept her hands folded over her knee and peered from behind her spectacles up at Adele. "The local search and rescue mentioned the possibility of a brown bear to the media. They've been running with it."

Adele nodded. Ms. Jayne's English, as always, was perfect, though clipped and sterile. The Interpol correspondent continued. "We are currently allowing the narrative to play. For now."

"But you know it wasn't a bear?" Adele hesitated. "Why the pretense?"

"It is not a pretense," said Ms. Jayne. Again, her eyes narrowed, just *barely*, behind her glasses, and again the gesture was gone before the average person might spot it. Adele, on the other hand, spent a good deal of time paying attention to details. Ms. Jayne's irritation wasn't lost on her. But she kept her peace, allowing the older woman to continue. "A *delicate* situation," she said, repeating the words Grant had used. "A wealthy Italian couple dies in Germany. And given the couple's political connections back in Italy, well... you can understand if Interpol would like to handle this with care, to the satisfaction of *all* parties involved."

"I'm... I'm confused," said Adele, slowly tracing her finger along the edge of Grant's desk. She kept her eyes downturned, listening but no longer watching, following the thin trail of dust dislodged from the underside of the table. "You said this has to do with the Alps. Not just one resort, not just one mountain. But the range of mountains... Am I right?"

Ms. Jayne nodded. "Yes. Astute. The Italians weren't the only incident. Another couple—Swiss—also went missing. A couple hundred miles away. A week ago—we still haven't found them."

"Let me guess, also in the Alps?"

"Just so. The French Alps, to be exact."

Adele resisted the urge to heave a sigh, doing her best to keep her expression and breathing neutral. "I see... And you're here in person because...?"

Ms. Jayne uncrossed her legs and delicately placed both feet on the floor, before leaning forward and peering up at Adele. "The Italian couple and the Swiss couple show no connections, besides where they went missing—and even then, they were separated by nearly two hundred miles. And yet..."

"Let me guess; the Swiss family is also wealthy and important?" Adele said.

Ms. Jayne bobbed her head. "It's important we handle this carefully. Already there are too many cooks in the kitchen. We'd like to avoid spoiling the broth entirely."

"I'm guessing you're not here to borrow a recipe, though."

Agent Grant snorted softly and Adele looked up, meeting her supervisor's eye. "They're looking for another cook," Grant said with a nod toward Ms. Jayne.

This time, Adele did sigh, though she tried to disguise it as a yawn, but halfway through, decided this might seem more inappropriate, and covered by quickly asking, "So you want me in the Alps to investigate an unconnected missing persons case where the culprit might have simply been frostbite or a famished grizzly?"

Ms. Jayne got slowly to her feet, adjusting her tailored suit. "Brown bears. And we have strong reason to believe the killings had nothing to do with wildlife. I wouldn't have come if this wasn't important. Well, Ms. Sharp—can we count on your aid?"

Adele quirked an eyebrow at Agent Grant, who grunted and nodded. "Not my say-so. Higher-ups already gave the nod. Your call, Adele."

There was something significant in her supervising agent's gaze as she waited, watching the younger woman. Adele looked back, but then glanced away. Another case, more traveling. She would be well within her rights to refuse…

And what?

Go back to paperwork? To Angus? To safety.

Was that really so bad?

"Please," said Ms. Jayne. And for the first time, Adele detected a note of unease in the woman's voice. Was this case personal to the Interpol correspondent? Why the emotion?

She hesitated, but then looked directly at Agent Grant. "As long as you get someone else to complete the paperwork, I'm in."

Grant's eyes narrowed, and unlike Ms. Jayne, she made no effort to conceal her annoyance. But at last, it was her turn to sigh and she waved a hand airily toward the door. "Your wish is my command. Besides, your flight is already booked."

CHAPTER FOUR

Adele approached the third parking level with a slight skip in her step. It had been more than two months since she'd last been abroad. Her stride felt sure-footed, and thought the parking structure was walled, it felt like there was a wind ruffling her hair. Roots could wait—now that the opportunity presented itself, she felt a sudden relief at the prospect of travel. A distraction from considering her time and place in life? Perhaps—or, perhaps, some people simply weren't meant to stay put for too long.

She cleared her throat and adjusted her sleeves as a couple of colleagues maneuvered past her, through the sliding glass security door toward the metal detectors and posted guards. Adele nodded in greeting, but then moved toward the back of the parking structure where she'd parked her sedan.

And pulled up short.

Someone was standing by her car.

Her hand inched toward her service weapon on her hip, but her fingers froze as she recognized the curly-haired silhouette. He'd been working out; his arms were at least an inch larger than last she'd seen him, and his waist an inch smaller. She eyed him up and down, enjoying the view a moment before making her presence known.

"Angus?" she called out.

Her ex-boyfriend turned suddenly, blinking out at her. He no longer wore glasses either. Contacts? Lasik? His hair was longer than she remembered, and he had a new scar on his upper lip, barely visible.

"Oh, jeez, hey… Adele," he said, clearing his throat. In the past, he often would call her by pet names, but now he pronounced her name exactly, as if fearful he might have forgotten it.

"What are you doing here?" she said without returning the greeting.

Angus shifted uncomfortably, leaning against the hood of her car. Adele eyed where he sat with a severe expression, and he coughed and quickly pushed off the car, raising his hands apologetically. "Oh, sorry—er, sorry," he said, quickly. "I just… was just in the area, and I wanted to make sure that…"

13

"I got your messages."

"Oh…" He trailed off. "Oh," he repeated in a hurt voice.

Adele inhaled through her nose, trying to refocus and switch gears from thinking of murders in the Alps to an awkward ex-boyfriend. "Look, Angus, I wasn't ignoring you—I was swamped. You wouldn't believe the amount of paperwork they shoveled onto my desk."

Angus nodded, still communicating a hurt look in his eyes. "I get it," he said, slowly. He glanced out over the third level of the parking lot at the afternoon sky. Then he lifted a brown paper bag. "I brought you something—they had it at the store next to work. Well, actually, it was a few blocks down. Took me a few stores to find it… But, yeah, here you go."

He gave a lopsided smile and pushed the paper bag toward her.

Reluctantly, Adele accepted the gift if only to calm him. She glanced in the bag, and part of her smile turned authentic. "Oh, Angus," she said, in a soft, sad voice. "You shouldn't have."

"I remember it's your favorite—right? You'd eat it every morning. I like chocolate cereal too, but, haha, never as much as you did." He nodded toward the discount box of Chocapic cereal. "It's from Germany right?"

She lowered the cereal, gripping the bag in the same hand that had strayed toward her hip when she'd first spotted him by her car. Angus, of course, knew about her triple citizenship—American on her father's side, French on her mother's, and German based on their family's relocation. But while he knew it, it sometimes struck her how considerate Angus was. Sometimes *too* considerate, and sometimes, in her quiet opinion, to *too* many people. She knew it made her selfish, but there was something Adele liked about being the only one allowed into the softer side of her partner. Angus, on the other hand, was like a golden retriever—he would expose his belly to everyone. Growing up, Adele had always preferred pit bulls. Dependable, intelligent, and fiercely loyal to only one person.

"France," she said.

"Come again?"

"The cereal, it's from France. Never mind—thanks, Angus. But you didn't come all this way to drop off a box of breakfast."

He scratched the back of his head, tousling his curly hair. She could see the indents along his cheeks where he used to wear glasses, just barely, faint—perhaps simply from sun marks. They hinted at a

14

history—a memory.

"I—I wanted to talk," he said, cautiously. "I've been doing a lot of thinking... And really taking some time..." He began to speak faster, louder, mustering up courage as if he'd rehearsed these words before.

Adele watched him patiently, quietly, allowing him to speak, but dreading what came next. Did he want to get back together? What was this about? Did she even want to know?

Roots. Roots were safe. Roots were reliable, dependable. Roots were home—somewhere to go back to.

Adele glanced out over the parking lot divide and studied the horizon, glimpsing the distant sky. A small, tiny voice—a part of her that she pretended wasn't there—gave voice to its own opinion. Roots were restrictive. Roots were like chains. Roots kept you trapped.

"Look, Angus," she said, cutting him off mid-sentence. "We can talk. I promise, we'll talk. But now isn't a good time."

His face fell as she moved past him toward the car. She clicked the locks and tossed the paper bag with the Chocapic into the backseat. She turned and smiled apologetically, wincing. "I promise," she repeated. "Soon. I'm heading out of town for work. After I'm back, okay?"

Angus paused, mouth half open. He really had always been nice to her. The look of hurt on his face made her feel a bit like she'd just kicked a puppy. She felt a clawing sense of guilt in her chest and desperately tried to suppress the emotion. She knew, looking at him, if she stayed longer she would change her mind. She would hear him out. And then... words had a way of convincing people. And Adele wasn't sure she wanted to be convinced. Besides, he was the one who had broken up with *her*. Just because he'd sorted his shit out, didn't mean she had too.

With quick motions, she stepped into her car, flashed another apologetic smile at her ex, and began to close the door. The haunting sense of loneliness, of guilt, of confusion chased her into the front seat and propelled the words from her mouth, "Later. I promise. I'm sorry, Angus. Really, I definitely want to talk. Just not right now. Is that okay?"

He nodded, a sad look in his eyes. "I'm sorry, Adele. I shouldn't have come here, you're right. Does next weekend work?"

She paused, then winced. "The job is going to take a while. It's in Europe. I'll let you know when I'm back. *Really*. I will."

And with that, she gunned the engine and eased away from the spot,

15

waving at Angus as she pulled out and turned down the row of parked cars. As she crawled out of the parking complex, she refused to look over her shoulder, and her eyes fixed on the trail ahead, avoiding any efforts to glance in the rearview mirror.

There was a killer in the Alps. Perhaps a serial killer. Two couples missing—two hundred miles apart. Priorities. She had to focus. Adele gripped the steering wheel, pushing thoughts of Angus from her mind and cataloging every item she would need to pack for the trip. As she drove, pulling out of the lot, she began to pick up speed, a smile stretching her cheeks.

The hunt was on.

***

First class, no layovers. This was the life. Or, at least, it would have been if not for the bloody pictures of carnage splayed across her upright tray. Adele studied the crime scene photos, listening to the hum of the jet engines and—every so often—glancing up to make sure flight attendants weren't passing by. She'd learned the hard way, a few years ago, the impact some of these photos had on the general public.

Causing another flight attendant to faint over the Atlantic? Not ideal.

Adele shifted, sliding along the cushioned backrest to shield some of the photos from view. Mr. and Mrs. Beneveti had been found two days ago, pieces scattered around a grove of trees. Mr. and Mrs. Hanes, the Swiss couple, had disappeared nearly a week before that, and had yet to be discovered.

Hundreds of miles separated the two missing couples. Their only connection: wealth, influence, and the Alps.

Adele's brow wrinkled and she reached out, taking a sip from her ice water, then returning it to the cup holder. She issued a long breath, the sound lost in the whir from the overhead air conditioning nozzle. She tapped her fingers on the edge of her tray, bending one of the photos that refused to sit flat.

"A bear attack?" she murmured to herself, allowing the question to permeate her atmosphere.

It didn't seem so. Not according to the prelim report—though they were still waiting on the medical examiner. And yet, a quick online search made it abundantly clear that the public was still convinced

16

brown bears had returned in force to the Alps. But there were no bite marks, and a few portions that looked like they'd been caused by raking claws could easily have been caused by a hatchet or an axe as well. Some of the cuts were jagged—true… a rusted axe, perhaps. A blunt machete?

Adele winced at the thought of the couple huddled together in the frigid woods, out for a daytime ski trip, only to be set upon by…

By what? By whom?

Adele scanned the photos again, cataloging the information. There were FBI agents much smarter than her, others who were more connected, and still others with a greater natural talent. But there were very few who worked harder than she did; who paid attention to the details.

The devil was in the details. And, by the looks of things, also in the Alps.

CHAPTER FIVE

The vehicle they'd sent for her pulled up to the *Wolfsschluct Resort*, and, thanking her driver, Adele stepped out of the car, grateful for the opportunity to stretch her legs and take in the fresh air. From within, the driver called out. "Need directions?"

Adele glanced back and gave a faint shake of her head. "No, thank you—I have someone coming to meet me."

The driver waved, already turning back to face the road. Adele retrieved her own luggage; she'd never liked making her driver do it, though some agents thought of it as a perk.

With her rolling suitcase gripped in one hand, she stood in the roundabout at the heart of the resort. When she'd first heard of the *Wolfsschluct Resort,* she'd initially pictured a hotel with a couple of ski slopes, maybe an indoor pool or two. But what confronted her now seemed more like an entire village peppered with snow and surrounded on all sides by the most pristine scenery she'd ever laid eyes on.

As she stood at the edge of the roundabout, just below the curb of the largest hotel, she took in the array of blue glass windows and quaint buildings lining the street, leading up to the mountain pass where cottages and hotel wings and outbuildings were cradled by the snow-tipped mountains and spattering of greenery. There was even a chapel made of stone, and an insulated water tower proudly displaying the resort's name.

Her father would've called it a *God moment.* The beauty alone was mesmerizing—the perfect blend of human endeavor and natural art.

Adele glanced down at her suitcase, realigning her thoughts, trying to focus on why she was here.

"Hello!" a voice called from within the heart of the hotel before her. The building seemed to be made more of glass than walls, as if the architects hadn't wanted to waste any opportunity to display the beauty of the Alps.

Adele turned toward the sliding doors which had opened to reveal a young woman—no older than twenty-one—standing in the doorway and waving cheerfully at Adele.

Adele smiled, recognizing the woman. Her hair was much shorter than the last time they'd met—almost shaved, in fact. Everything about the young woman suggested cleanliness and order. She wore a black suit and boots that seemed to glint from the sheer amount of polish. Her eyes were bright and eager and she waved at Adele, but then stopped the gesture halfway through the motion and nodded in greeting, as if worried her eagerness might be perceived as unprofessional.

"Hello," the woman said again as Adele approached, stepping onto the sidewalk and trundling her suitcase in one hand while hefting her laptop bag in the other. "I'm Agent Beatrice Marshall," she said with a dip of her shaved head. She spoke nearly perfect English, with only the faintest hint of an accent.

Adele nodded in return. "I know," she replied, also in English. "We've worked together before."

Agent Marshall's smile returned at this. "I remember! I just wasn't sure if you did, Agent Sharp. It's a pleasure to be working with you again."

"Likewise. So…" Adele's tone turned somber and she paused in the glass doorway of the impressive hotel. The atrium was a combination of lacquered wooden beams and natural stone. A small waterfall spilled with gentle ripples into a pond by the counter. A man in a gold and maroon uniform nodded politely at the two women in greeting, but then returned his attention to a computer behind the check-in counter.

"So…?" Agent Marshall echoed. "I can show you to your room if you like."

Adele paused. "That would be ideal. This is the resort where the couple went missing, yes?"

The BKA agent's nose wrinkled and she nodded once. "They were found only a couple miles from here by one of the mountain rescue teams. They're on standby if you wish to speak with them."

Adele considered this, gnawing on her lip, but then decided against it. "Not yet," she said, carefully. "Soon, perhaps. But I'd like to touch base with DGSI and make some calls, if that's all right."

"Agent Renee!" exclaimed the young agent. "I remember!"

Adele frowned. "Not just John, er, Agent Renee. I have others I need to speak with as well."

"Of course, yes, of course. I didn't mean to imply anything."

Adele's frown deepened, and Agent Marshall seemed to realize she was treading on thin ice. "It's good to see you came packed for the

19

weather," she said, nodding at Adele's overcoat. "Obviously, the hotel is kept comfortable. I'll show you to the room, shall I? Hotel staff have been advised not to bother you and to avoid your room. We have a temporary lock on the keycard readers to prevent any snooping."

Adele followed the younger agent as she led them past the small waterfall and toward a staircase of stone and curving, polished wood.

Her room was also an affair of glass and wood, with magnificent views of the valleys and precipices beyond. Her eyes trailed the snow-tipped mountains and whitened forests as she placed her suitcase by the bed and withdrew her phone.

She cycled to John's number, frowned a bit, and instead dialed Robert.

No answer.

She huffed impatiently and returned to John's number, shielding her phone with her body from Agent Marshall, who stood by the door, waiting patiently. Muttering to herself, Adele lifted her phone, waiting for John to pick up.

A few rings later, she heard static, then Agent Renee's voice, speaking loud and angry French. "I told you to stop calling me. I swear, I'm going to hunt you down and burn your world down—do you hear me? I don't want your shitty moisturizer, and whoever put my name on your call list is going to have hell to pay!"

Then before Adele could say a word, John hung up and she stood listening to dead air. Adele inhaled through her nose and out through her mouth, counting slowly in her head.

Then she dialed again and waited, her impatience growing. Agent Marshall watched her curiously from the doorway.

"Holy shit!" John started with a vengeance. "Do you think I'm *joking*, because—"

"John, it's me," Adele snapped in English. "Adele. Shut up for a minute."

A pause. Then a gently cleared throat, another pause of embarrassed silence. Then, in a clipped, forcibly calm voice, now also speaking English, John said, "Adele? How nice to hear from you."

"The one and the same." A small smile began to twist the corners of her lips, but then faded just as quickly, and she frowned. "Hang on— why isn't my number in your phone?"

John grunted on the other line. "I only have two numbers in this phone. Work and my mother."

Adele rolled her eyes, but out loud, she said, "Figures. And moisturizer, huh? What sort of subscriptions do you have?"

"Funny. So I hear you caught a case on this side of the pond again."

Adele nodded, then realized John couldn't see her and sidled closer to the floor-to-ceiling window, her breath fogging the glass as she stared into the wonderland of the Alps. "In the mountains, yes," she said. "Actually, it's why I'm calling. There was a second couple— Swiss. They also went missing."

"The Haneses, yes," said John. "Disappeared in France. Also in the mountains."

Adele cleared her throat, tilting her head slightly. "Ah, so you're aware already."

"Not just aware," said John, speaking slower now that they were in English. "I'm working it, with Robert."

"You are? Perfect—I was wanting to coordinate with DGSI anyway. Do you think—"

"Well, actually, Adele, the executive wants the cases separate. Doesn't want to get mixed in the German situation. Right now, we're treating the cases as unconnected." There was a slight pause and an apologetic tone to his voice.

Adele felt herself shaking her head. "We can't know whether or not they're connected yet," she said. "Surely Foucault knows that."

Renee sighed on the other end, blowing into the speaker so loudly it hurt Adele's ear. She winced, but waited as the Frenchman continued. "I know that. You know that. But there are politics involved." He said "politics" like uttering a dirty word.

"Oh? What politics?"

"Let me put it this way. Who is your babysitter?"

Adele glanced surreptitiously toward the young German agent in the doorway. She cleared her throat and delicately said, "An old acquaintance."

"Right. But BKA though, hmm?"

"Affirmative."

"So that's the politics. You've got BKA boots on the ground, along with the locals, and—because of our case—the French are sniffing around, and Interpol too. The Italians, I'm told, also want a hand in the investigation due to the nationality of the victims."

Adele scratched at her chin. "Ah. So what are the odds of getting DGSI involved?" she said with fading hope.

Another grunt on John's end. "No dice. DGSI is steering clear. Foucault said something about too many cooks spoiling something or other. Didn't understand. Basically, I think he gave me a metaphor for being chicken."

Adele sighed, passing her free hand over her eyes and slowly moving away from the large window toward the small kitchenette at the start of the hall. She grabbed a glass from the lowest cupboard and began pouring some water, though turning the knob only partially to avoid making much noise.

"Okay," she said once John was finished. "But the Swiss couple—you're looking into it?"

"Right. Robert and I are paired up on this one. Gotta say, your old boss is what the boys back in the unit would've called a sleeper."

"Sleeper?"

"Not much impression up front, but got a hell of a kick once you start riding around. Smart fellow. Weird. I like him."

Adele smirked at this description of her old mentor. She pictured Robert in her mind; a short, prim, proper man with hair plugs and two missing teeth. He'd been a father to her, and the best detective she knew.

"Hey, ah, shit, I've gotta go, American Princess. I'll shoot you a message if I have anything. Actually, scratch that—Robert will."

"Don't tell me you're still not going to save my number," Adele said playfully.

John chuckled. "Maybe one day, eh? One other thing... Hang on." John's voice grew quieter, suggesting he'd pulled the phone from his cheek. Adele heard him call out, distant, "Be right there—don't get your cufflinks in a knot! Hang on!" Then, louder again, he said, "Gotta go. But Adele, be careful."

Adele held her glass of water, staring at the expensive wooden cupboards in the kitchenette. "Always am. Why in particular?"

"Not talking about the murdering grizzly bears, or whatever it's supposed to be. I mean your babysitter—the media. The *politics.*" He doubled down on the word, filling it with venom.

"I'll be careful there too." Adele took a sip from her glass, her eyes refusing to travel toward where Agent Marshall waited patiently in the doorway.

"Yeah, but I'm serious. Higher-ups want to avoid any connection between the missing couples leaking at all costs. Understand? We're talking career-enders here if you let it out. Now, normally, I don't give two pigeon shits what their splintered asses want, but you're more the career sort, yeah?"

"I'll be careful. Thanks, John."

Without so much as a goodbye, John clicked off, and Adele once again listened to dead air. She wrinkled her nose and pocketed her phone, taking another long sip from her glass of water and trying to process what she'd been told.

"Ah, excuse me?" Marshall called from the door, jarring Adele back into English. The young agent waved a hand.

Adele glanced over.

"Excuse me," Marshall repeated in English, "but, ah," she cleared her throat. "Who was that?"

Adele raised an eyebrow. "Pardon?"

Marshall winced in embarrassment, but pressed on, pointing at Adele's pocket. "Who were you talking too—just, it's important that we keep a lid on some of the case details. Actually, very important. More important than…" She frowned and trailed off, but shook her head and winced again, waiting expectantly for Adele to reply.

She'd been about to say *more important than solving the case.* Adele was sure of it. She gave a weary little shake of her head. "Just law enforcement. It's fine." Frowning, she stowed the glass and turned back toward Agent Marshall. "Anything I should know about the context of the case?"

Looking relieved, Marshall smiled politely but quizzically from the door. "Context?"

Adele nodded. "Right—everyone seems to have a bit of a bug on this one. Mind telling me why?"

Agent Marshall gnawed her lip, and Adele's eyes narrowed. The younger agent gave off the "innocent and inexperienced" vibe, but one didn't become a BKA agent without a level of shrewdness and discipline. Whether it was an act, or simply a personality trait, she couldn't tell, but she'd be silly to let her guard down around an operative from another agency.

"Okay," said Marshall, clearing her throat. "This isn't common knowledge, but one reason the locals are intent on having this a bear attack is to keep eyeballs off the papers. A bear attack? Forgettable. Two missing couples, though? Possibly murdered—less so."

Adele kept her gaze fixed on Marshall, unblinking. "Why?" she

23

said, simply.

"I don't know the extent of it myself. But from what I'm told, I suppose you might need to know." This time it was Marshall's turn to lower her voice and glance over her shoulder. She stepped further into the room, closing the door behind her as she did. "There's another resort—in the *Wettersteinspitzen* region. The resort is called Wetter Retreat."

"So?"

"So," she replied, extending the word past its usual due. "The resort is opening tomorrow. Understand?"

Adele blinked. "A resort like this?" She glanced toward the window again, at the many buildings surrounding the main hotel.

"Actually, even bigger. And more expensive," said Marshall. "We're talking hundreds of millions invested, see. And if it were to get out before the opening that a murder took place on their back porch... you can imagine the press and the economic disaster, yes? Thousands of jobs, tourism, infrastructure. Lost." She shook her head.

Adele stared at Marshall. She felt a cold chill along the back of her hands as she eyed the younger agent. Was Marshall there to help solve the case? Or to prevent Adele from stirring up trouble?

She whistled beneath her breath. "Multimillion-dollar project opening tomorrow... Let me guess, all sorts of politicians and celebrities etc.... The whole nine yards?"

"I'm not familiar with the nine yards," said Marshall. "But yes, there are going to be important people there. Understand? We have to be quiet on this one."

Understand? Yes, Adele thought to herself. She was beginning to understand all too well. They didn't want Adele to solve the case, they wanted her to brush it under the rug; to keep a lid on things. Or to solve it quietly, behind the scenes.

"Fair enough," said Adele in a clipped tone. "Can we at least speak to search and rescue? See the crime scene? I heard it was in the woods—figure that ought to be remote enough to not raise any eyebrows."

Marshall smiled, though it seemed half wince. "Yes, of course. I'll place the call for the team leader to meet us there. Do you need refreshments? Food? I could order a—"

"I'm fine," Adele cut her off. "I'd like to see the crime scene. Do you have a car?"

Agent Beatrice Marshall nodded again and, without word, turned, pushing open the hotel room door and exiting into the hall, beckoning for Adele to follow.

CHAPTER SIX

Adele remembered why she chose San Francisco stateside. Some people simply weren't built for the cold.

She pulled her hood low past her ears and tugged on the drawstrings of the thick, flannel jacket to further secure her throat. She winced against the faintest of frigid breezes, and resented the quiet crunch of the snow beneath her boots. The trail had been packed down not long before, and Adele was grateful for this. Despite her boots, she suspected trudging through the snow for the two miles it took from where they'd parked would have been an endeavor in misery and frostbite.

Ahead, Luka Porter—the leader of the volunteer mountain rescue team—guided the two agents along the snowy ski trails.

"A fresh fall," he called over his shoulder in German, waving a gloved hand through the air in front.

"I see ski tracks; are they fresh?" Adele called out. She cleared her throat, swallowing a couple of times and finding not only her lips chapped but her throat dry.

She missed the Golden State. Grumbling inwardly, but refusing to communicate weakness to her German colleagues, Adele followed Luka into a grove of trees at the end of the packed trail.

He waved a hand toward the grove. "Found them here," he said, quietly. A somberness tinged his words. "Ripped to pieces—real nasty work. Lotta blood," he added. "Probably alive for a good part of the mauling." He winced, his face pale.

Adele nodded, scanning the trees. Besides faint ski tracks, which she guessed were from search and rescue crew, there was little in the manner of physical evidence. No footprints had been found according to the report, and the bodies had long since been recovered—at least, what had remained.

"What's your theory?" she asked, breathing slowly and allowing her fogged breath to usher toward the prickly tree leaves sheltering the ground in scattered patterns from view of the sun.

Luka scratched at an ear beneath his thermal hat. "Brown bear, most likely," he said, knowingly. "They were gone from the Alps for decades, but a couple years ago, some sightings occurred. We're only"—he glanced over his shoulder and then down at a smart watch on his wrist—"about two miles from the resort they were staying at."

"The same one you're at," Agent Marshall supplied quietly from Adele's flank.

Adele nodded to show she'd heard, but maintained her silence, allowing Luka to fill it.

"Didn't see bear tracks," he added. "But the snow disguised most of that." He shrugged. "Pity, really—not quite sure what the pair of them were doing out in this grove. My guess; Mr. and Mrs. Beneveti were on a cross-country ski trip, and the bear spotted them—gave chase. They deviated from the main trail and tried to hide in the trees." He shook his head. "Didn't end well."

"No," said Adele. "Guess it didn't. So you think it was a bear?"

Luka paused, frowning as he turned fully and regarded her. "You're saying it wasn't?"

Agent Marshall cleared her throat and hastily inserted herself between Adele and Luka. She rubbed her gloved hands together and puffed a breath into them as if to warm them. "We can't discuss the details of the investigation, I'm afraid," she said. "Is there anything else you found? You saw?"

Luka's eyes squinted in thought, but then he said, "No—nothing. Though I hear those folks are rich, powerful types. Pity this happening to them. Just goes to show money can't buy everything, I guess."

"Thank you," Adele said in a polite tone. Then she moved through the crime scene, slowly, delicately, her eyes higher than the ground. The snow-covered floor provided little in the way of physical evidence. The crime scene photos she'd studied on the plane were far closer to the timeframe of the attack, with less fresh fall. But the trees… the trees were still exposed, visible.

She spotted no cuts or breaks along the trees—or near the small branches at the base of the saplings. She didn't know much about bears. But she did know it was strange for the trees themselves to be untouched if a two-ton ball of muscle and fur had come barreling in here hunting two fleeing skiers.

No. The crime scene photos suggested a hatchet, or an axe. Rusted, perhaps—blunt. But human—definitely human. Whoever the killer was, though, had to know his or her way around the area. The ski trail was known, but not obvious. Whoever had killed the Benevetis had been waiting for them, watching.

Now, it was up to Adele to discover why.

"See anything?" Agent Marshall asked.

Adele glanced back and gave the faintest shake of her head. "Nothing new. When did you say that new resort was opening?"

"Tomorrow," Marshall said, tone clipped, her eyes darting to Luka and back to Adele.

"Millionaires, politicians, and murder," Adele said with a humorless smile. "Sounds like the start to a movie."

And following another scan of the trees and snowbound floor, Adele and the two Germans turned and began their long hike back up the trail toward the resort. Vaguely, Adele could only hope John and Robert's case was faring better back in France. She hoped the Swiss couple hadn't met the same horrible fate as the Benevetis.

CHAPTER SEVEN

"Second gate so far," John muttered in French. "What are they guarding in here, *hein*? A pile of gold?" He glared through the front of the faintly tinted windshield as the automatic gates opened before the DGSI vehicle, and his partner guided their car up the path.

"It is a very exclusive resort," said Robert, patiently. "They take their security seriously."

John glanced at the much smaller man, raising an eyebrow. "Friends of yours?"

Robert guided the vehicle along the quiet path toward the resort in the distance. The French resort was impressive in its sheer size. Few other nations could compete with the acres and acres of ski trails and lifts—nor the small villages interconnected by cable cars lounging through the air, or the ski trails moving along the mountains.

On all sides, the trail they currently used was lined with ornamentation—including sculptures and quaint glass and wood gazebos beneath ancient, towering trees. A couple of guards—with their weapons hidden out of sight—smiled politely from beneath blue berets and nodded as the approaching vehicle rolled by. One of the guards cast a longer look toward the DGSI car. Likely, he hadn't seen a regular sedan in months of wealthy tourists in flashy coupes.

"*Bonjour!*" the soldier called out, tipping his flat cap. Even the guard was sipping a cup of vin chaud, and looked to have quickly lowered a cigarette into an ashtray as they'd approached.

John could spot a military man from a mile away. And the last six guards they'd spotted all had the look. Ex-military private security didn't come cheap. Then again, nothing in this gated resort looked cheap.

Robert cleared his throat. "Not everyone who has means is related," he said.

"Means? You mean stinking rich, *oui*?"

Robert frowned a bit, his hands clasping the steering wheel in the perfect ten and two position, his eyes glued dutifully on the road ahead. His hair was slicked back and, when he spoke, occasionally John

29

glimpsed two missing teeth in the front of the older agent's mouth.

He still wasn't quite sure what to make of the small man. Robert's old partner, Adele, had a fondness for him, and the investigator was a bit of a legend around the DGSI, but half the time it was nearly impossible for John to discern what the other Frenchman was thinking.

"Where do we park?" John asked as they pulled into a roundabout beneath old stone pillars set across from four wide glass sliding doors at the top of a gently curving marble stairway.

"We don't," Robert said, primly.

He pulled off his driving gloves and turned off the engine. Then he switched to a couple of mittens he had in the backseat, daintily pulling them on. John watched all this with mild amusement.

"Nice mittens," he said.

"Thank you. And, thank you." The second thank-you was directed toward the valet who had hurried up and opened the door for Robert.

"Mr. Henry!" the valet called. "It is good to see you!"

Robert refused to look at John as he returned the greeting and stiffly exited the vehicle, handing his keys to the valet. The young man in the red cap and crimson outfit smiled politely at John as a second helper hurried over and opened the door for the tall DGSI agent.

John scratched at the scar along the underside of his chin, then with more than a little discomfort, he exited the vehicle.

Robert adjusted his sleeves. He'd insisted on wearing a suit and a pea-coat for warmth. John, on the other hand, wore two hoodies, one on top of the other. Robert had offered to buy him a jacket, twice, on the drive up to the Alps, but John had refused. Mostly, though he hadn't told Robert, because of sheer enjoyment at the look of discomfort on the older agent's face every time he saw the hem of one of John's sweaters poking out beneath the other.

"Luggage?" asked the valet who had opened John's door.

The tall Frenchman grunted, stretching his leg as he exited the car. "Old guy has some. I don't."

The valet gave John a strange look, but nodded to show he'd understood before hurrying to the trunk and grabbing Robert's *three separate* suitcases.

John watched in wry humor as the attendant carried the suitcases up the marble steps one at a time. John wasn't sure *what* Robert had needed so desperately that it took three suitcases. John was relatively confident he'd never packed a single suitcase in his life. They would only be here a few days—what he couldn't buy in a gift shop, he could likely borrow from lost and found. All fancy hotels had them.

John eyed the sliding doors with the severest of distrust as Robert walked stiff-legged up the marble steps and waited for the attendant—still lugging the investigator's final suitcase—to pause, lower the suitcase, and open the door with a smile, before entering into the resort's atrium.

For a moment, in the cold, Robert paused, grimacing and coughing. John called out, "Are you all right?"

But Robert simply waved him away and moved into the hotel.

John followed after Robert, bunching his hands into the pockets of his hoodie and stalking up the marble steps. On either side, jutting turret-shaped towers framed the stone, glass, and log building. Even John, who had never developed a taste for the finer things, paused to admire the architecture. He also noted three windows, tinted blue, which would serve as a perfect lookout spot for a sniper.

Useful information given their circumstances? Perhaps not. But John could little afford to put his instincts behind him. They'd served well on more than one occasion.

"We need to speak to the manager," Robert said, quietly, as John joined him in the expensive atrium. Marble, glass, ornamental lights, and tastefully arranged plants and art gave the resort entrance an impressive feel.

John grunted. "Where's the manager?" he asked the attendant who was now lodging Robert's three suitcases onto a trolley.

"Ah, *excusez moi*?" said the attendant, hesitantly. "Manager Pires is most likely indisposed at the moment. But I'm sure there are clerks who would be more than happy to—"

"Surely, there's some way we can change your mind, hmm?" said Robert, a purr to his voice. He extended a hand, and John glimpsed a hundred-euro note secreted in the old investigator's palm.

The attendant cleared his throat, glanced at the note, and his eyes flicked toward the low, marble counter circling the far wall of the atrium. "I, I don't think I can arrange that," he began, hesitantly.

"Come," Robert wheedled. "I'm certain we can reach an arrangement, *monsieur*."

The attendant still looked reluctant. John's patience had worn thin at this point. While Robert tried a third time, in quiet, cajoling murmurs, John turned, faced the atrium, and, at the top of his voice, the

31

tall scar-faced French agent shouted, "DGSI! We're here to speak with the manager. *Now!*"

The attendant wilted, and seemed to want to shrink into the floor and disappear. Robert sighed with resignation in his partner's direction, but reluctantly stowed his money and crossed his arms over his neatly pressed suit and jacket.

"Well?" John shouted, louder now. "The manager?"

"I'm sure, if we're patient, and just wait—" Robert tried to say, but before he could finish, there was a flurry of movement from through a doorway behind the long counter. A few customers and a couple of clerks were looking in John's direction, but pretending not to.

Through the doorway, a woman in a neat red uniform appeared, walking quickly toward where the agents stood. She took in Robert, in his neat suit and combed hair, and then her gaze flicked to John and his two hoodies and disheveled appearance. At John's appearance, her eyes slid along the atrium toward where two security personnel were standing near the doors. She hesitated, but then addressed the DGSI agents.

"Hello," she said, pressing her lips together. "May I help you? I'm Maria, assistant to Manager Pires. I'm afraid he's not available right now. How might I be of assistance?"

"Excuse me, mademoiselle," said Robert, stepping forward and taking Maria gently by the hand. He held her hand in greeting and gave a slight bow of his head. "We are in need of some information—if you'd be gracious enough to bless us with your time, we'd be eternally grateful."

John watched the strange exchange, feeling an itch somewhere in the vicinity of his collar. He'd been told in the past he had a face like a lazy pit bull when he was impatient. The person who'd said it had ended up in the hospital with a broken nose and bruised eye. Yet, in this moment, John bit his tongue and waited for Robert to take his shot.

The assistant manager Maria looked taken aback, even flustered by Robert's demeanor. When she acknowledged the wealthy investigator, though, she almost seemed to ease up. Some of the distrust and worry she had displayed at the sight of John faded.

"You say you're with the DGSI?" she asked, politely, still extending her hand and allowing Robert to gently guide her toward the clerk counter.

"Yes, dear child," said Robert. "A delicate matter, I'm sure."

John remained forgotten as the two moved arm-in-arm to the back of the atrium. The expensive, polished floors winked up at glinting lights in ornamented brackets throughout the ceiling.

"Yes," the manager said, quietly, her eyes darting to a couple of customers checking in at the front. Their many bags and luggage rested on a dolly, pushed by another crimson-uniformed attendant. Robert's own bags now awaited them by the elevator, the attendant patiently standing with his arms crossed by the three pieces of luggage.

John hefted his own small laptop bag—where he'd stowed a shirt and a change of boxers—and stomped after his smaller partner. Anyone who looked his way received a glare and a half. He managed to catch up with the smaller investigator and his captive audience with two long strides.

He reached the counter with them, hearing Robert finish a sentence with, "... Perhaps somewhere more private?"

Maria leaned one arm on the counter, giving a significant look to the clerk at the computer hidden behind the marble partition. The clerk nodded in greeting, then hurried away, moving to the opposite side of the long divider.

For her part, Maria dropped her voice and quietly said, "Mr. and Mrs. Hanes have been coming here as long as I can remember. Once a year."

"Ah," said Robert. "But you are so young! It couldn't have been too long, no?"

Maria tittered a bit and John felt his stomach turn. "I've been working here nearly fifteen years," she said. "Started as a waitress and worked my way up. We only serve the most *prestigious* clientele. As I'm sure you're aware."

Robert smiled and patted her on the shoulder, looking her deep in the eyes with his warm gaze. "Yes, yes," he said, "very impressive. I wish you all the more blessing on your hard work. Fifteen years is an impressive commitment. I hope they reward your loyalty?"

Maria hesitated, her nose wrinkling. But she coughed and smoothed the front of her pristine uniform with her free hand. "I have no complaints. The Swiss couple, though—this is why you're here?"

Robert nodded once, his eyes fixed on Maria as if there were no one else in the room. His every nod and smile, every gesture, responded to Maria's words or posture, mirroring back her excitement, interest, curiosity all in rapid synchronicity. To John, it was like witnessing a chess match of body language, which the assistant manager didn't even realize she was a part of.

John knew, though, from the little time he'd spent with Robert, that the older investigator wasn't a manipulator. He knew how to react, to respond, but he also meant the things he said; he had an annoying knack of *caring* about everyone they interacted with.

"Bigwigs in oil," Maria was saying, softly. "Though," she frowned, "I don't know if I was supposed to say that."

"No—do not worry. You're being honest. I can tell you're an honest person, *oui*," said Robert, nodding. "It's in the eyes, yes. And their room, where did they stay?"

Maria cleared her throat. "They had their own chalet on permanent reserve. Fifteen years now; probably more. Search and rescue has been looking for them, but found nothing."

"And when did Mr. and Mrs. Hanes arrive to this lovely establishment you run so wonderfully well?"

Maria frowned in thought, but then nodded again. "I remember all our customers. They're part of the family. Mr. and Mrs. Hanes arrived before first snowfall. They went missing four days ago."

John spoke for the first time, and his presence, followed by a grunt, seemed to break a sort of spell. Both Robert and Maria glanced at him, their eyes narrowing somewhat. "*Before* snowfall," John said. "Means the bodies might be covered."

Robert's eyes widened nearly imperceptibly in alarm. Maria gasped, staring white-faced at John. "Bodies?" she said. "You think they're—they're…" She swallowed.

"Dead?" John provided. "Probably. Been gone a while." He glanced toward Robert, who had passed a hand over his face and was massaging the bridge of his nose as if against a sudden headache.

"They may very well be fine," Robert said, patting Maria on the arm again before lowering his hand and turning toward John.

John grunted. "Probably not. Probably dead. We should go looking though—soon."

"I—I can tell you the trail they usually hiked," said Maria, clearly holding back a sob. "Like I said, they were family to us here."

John shrugged. "Probably were lured somewhere quiet. Whoever got to them wouldn't have wanted them on familiar ground when they struck. What?" he demanded of Robert, who was now glowering at the larger man.

34

In a clipped, long-suffering tone, Robert said, "We don't know they're dead. Nor do we know the context of their unfortunate disappearance. All of this is conjecture."

John eyed the smaller man. "Conjecture? I don't know what this word means."

Robert sighed and smiled one last time at Maria, before bidding farewell and then moving toward the elevator. As they approached Robert's luggage and the attendant in waiting, Robert muttered, beneath his breath, "Don't you have a jacket? Something besides those greasy sweatshirts?"

John kept his eyes straight ahead. "Not all of us packed three closets for a couple days in the snow."

"Oh? In a place like this, my friend, you might want to pay attention. Appearance matters more than character in these halls."

John paused, turning on Robert and looking him straight in the eye. "I'm aware of the appearance I'm portraying," he said, quietly. "Not all bees are caught with honey, yes?" Then he turned once more and strode toward the elevator.

They would unpack, claim their room, and then set out in search of Mr. and Mrs. Hanes. The search and rescue team were treating it like a missing person's case—as if they'd gone hiking and fallen into a gorge. But John knew better. A killer was on the loose, and to find the Swiss couple, he would have to think like a murderer.

CHAPTER EIGHT

Adele heard a knock on her door. She held up a single finger, then realized the person on the other side of the threshold couldn't see her. "One moment," she called out.

Adele turned back to her computer, and her eyes flicked to Agent Marshall, who was sitting on the opposite side of the circular wooden table. Adele inhaled deeply, gathering her thoughts. "So you're telling me the Benevetis were deeply invested in fracking operations," she said.

Agent Marshall nodded once, her short-cropped hair catching the light through the window beyond in a strange pattern, like a smudge around her forehead.

"What were these two doing up here? Do you think they were involved in the opening of the new resort?"

Agent Marshall shook her head. "I don't know. That information is protected. Even to us. Where there's money at play, power comes too."

Someone knocked on the door again, politely, but a bit louder this time.

"Almost," Adele called. She returned attention to the German agent. "An Italian bigwig in the oil industry goes missing in the Alps. There's a headline for you."

Agent Marshall smiled politely at Adele, her arms crossed in front of her. But she held her tongue. Adele studied the younger woman, trying to read her expression. Was Marshall here to help on the case, or was she there to prevent Adele from meddling?

Before the person outside could finish their third knock on the door, Adele called, "Come in, please."

The door opened with a click and swung in, hesitantly. A man in a valet uniform shifted uncomfortably in the door.

"Hello?" Adele said curiously.

"Yes," said the man in the doorway, hesitant. He took a shuffling step into the room, but then seemed to think better of it, and just as quickly retreated. He waited uncertainly in the threshold, glancing from Adele to Agent Marshall.

Adele turned her own quizzical countenance on the young agent. Marshall, though, stood to her feet and gestured at the man. "Thank you for coming, Otto." Marshall shot a look toward Adele. "You had mentioned you wanted to speak with some of the employees about the Benevetis."

Adele's eyebrows inched up in understanding.

"This is Otto Klein," Marshall said. "He's been working in the resort for nearly five years. He often interacted with Mr. and Mrs. Beneveti."

Adele's expression softened, and she glanced at the man. "Are you a valet?"

Otto nodded once and cleared his throat. "Yes, I am," he said, in crisp German.

"And the missing couple, you knew them?"

Mr. Klein was still standing in the door, but at a gesture from Adele, he reluctantly entered and came to the edge of the table. The door behind him was still open, and Adele knew from experience that people in flight-or-fight situations would often try to manage the quickest point of exit. Those who preferred flight wouldn't shut the door. Those who preferred to fight would.

She examined the valet from her chair, and he didn't sit, looking down at her with a nervous expression. He was quite handsome, as most the employees of this resort were. Adele knew that one thing her case had in common with John and Robert's case was the level of clientele. Most of the people in this resort were extraordinarily wealthy. In fact, she would've doubted that anyone outside the millionaire's club could've afforded the stay.

She caught a whiff of cologne from Otto—a fragrant, flowery smell melded with the odor of a fresh car. A sudden thought came to her; vaguely, she remembered her own childhood. Memories surfaced, for the faintest moment, like the knell of a whisper. She pictured herself, her father, her mother, before the divorce. She pictured snowbound hills, sliding down bunny trails. She pictured hot cocoa by the fire, and she pictured throwing snowballs at each other, as they rushed from the outdoor hot tub into the indoor heated pool. She smiled faintly, but then the smile faded as other memories also surfaced. Memories of arguments, of anger.

She wrinkled her nose and pushed the emotions, the thoughts aside.

She fixed her gaze on Otto. "What did you think of Mr. and Mrs.

Beneveti?"

Otto hesitated. The valet scratched his chin, adjusting a slight, thin strap that looped into the hat perched on his head.

"They were excellent clients, and tipped well," he said.

Adele's eyes narrowed. Clients. Tipping. Both comments about the customers' financial situation. Low-hanging fruit. But also telling.

"Did you like the Italian couple?"

"As I said," Otto said, hesitantly. "They were generous. Tipped very well."

"Yes, but did you like them? If they didn't tip well, would you have gotten a beer with Mr. Beneveti."

Otto paused. "I don't think Mr. Beneveti drank. Not that I was aware of. They were never in the bars."

"The resort has its own *bars*? Plural?"

"Yes," Otto said, hesitantly. "Four of them. And a couple of the more expensive rooms have their own."

Adele tried not to let her surprise show. Perhaps she needed to reassess exactly how high-end this facility was. "All right, but Mr. Beneveti, let's start with him. What did you think of him? Aside from the tipping."

Otto held his hands up defensively and rocked back on his heels, as if moving toward the door, but then readjusting and standing steady. "I didn't know the man well," he said.

"You didn't like him, did you?"

Agent Marshall's eyes darted to Adele, the wraith of a frown inserted across her face. But Adele kept her gaze fixed on Otto.

The valet scratched at the corner of his chin again, adjusting the strap to his hat once more.

"I had a couple of interactions with Mr. Beneveti," Mr. Klein said, carefully, "that weren't particularly pleasant."

Adele nodded. "You're a very polite man, Otto. I respect that you're doing your job even now. But this is an investigation. A murder investigation."

At this, for the first time, Otto's demeanor shifted. Quiet, nervous, hesitant—the mask faded to be replaced by horror, fear. He stared at her. "Murder? I thought it was a bear attack."

Adele narrowed her eyes. "The local news said that, right?"

Otto nodded. "The resort owners, too. The managers. Everyone is saying it."

38

Adele shook her head. "*Nein.* I'm not convinced yet. We haven't received the medical examiner's report."

Otto nodded. "*Oh Gott!* That's terrible. No one deserves that, not even..."

"Even?" Adele said, jumping on the word.

Mr. Klein blushed slightly, his cheeks taking on a similar hue to his uniform. But he eventually coughed and said, "Mr. Beneveti could be rude, arrogant sometimes. He once threw a drink at a friend of mine. Said he didn't *imbibe*, to take the swill away. Doused the young busboy in vodka and tonic. The boy had simply got the order wrong. Taken it to the wrong room. Received a reprimand. Mrs. Beneveti went to the manager and tried to get him fired."

"Was he fired?"

Otto shook his head. "No, but they moved his shifts. Cut back his hours so he wouldn't interact with them. Cost him rent for a couple of months. The rest of us helped him out as best we could. Mr. Beneveti had a temper. He had wealth, lots of it. And he knew it."

Otto fell silent, realizing he'd spoken more than perhaps he wanted to. He shrugged bashfully, his cheeks reddening again. "But like I said, they were generous."

Adele tilted her head, steepling her forefingers beneath her chin as she examined the valet. "Anything else? Any other interactions? Anyone else who might've had a grudge against the Italian couple?"

Otto quickly shook his head. "I have no grudge. Like I said, I have nothing personal against him. He was rude and obnoxious, Mrs. Beneveti could be a bit overbearing. Protective. But a lot of the clientele here are like that. They're wealthy, and with that comes some paranoia. They never know what people actually want from them. It's a pity when you think about it." Otto nodded once with certainty, as if trying to convince himself, then his head bobbed again, with less certainty, and he scratched the side of his face.

"All right," said Adele. "There's nothing else you can think of?"

Otto shook his head. "No, but," he hesitated, "that busboy, the one who delivered the vodka and tonic. He might know some more. He's only a teenager, nineteen. But he still on staff."

"Is he here now?" Adele asked.

"Yes, should I fetch him?"

Adele shook her head. "No; I will go speak to him. Where is he? We won't take any more of your time, I know you're on the clock."

39

"All right. His name is Joseph Meissner."

"Joseph Meissner?" said Beatrice Marshall.

"Yes. He's working at one of the bars now. Called the Respite in the Cliffs. Beyond the indoor golf course."

"There's an indoor golf course?" Adele asked, flat-toned.

"Next to the heated pool." Otto smirked. "Welcome to the one percent."

He regarded them each in turn with a practiced, professional smile, then hesitantly moved back toward the door and disappeared, leaving the two agents alone in the room once more.

Adele shared a look with Agent Marshall. "Did you hear that?" she said, quietly.

"I heard a lot," said Marshall. "What do you mean in particular?"

"The story about the bear attack. The owners were repeating it; the managers. Almost like they'd rather there be a rampaging bear in the slopes than a murderer."

Marshall whistled. "It would make sense. The clients here pay good money. *Good* money. The owners wouldn't want to scare them away."

Adele regained her feet, closing the lid of her laptop and heading for the door. As she did, she gripped her jacket.

"Do you know where Respite in the Cliffs is?" she said.

"Honestly, I'm kind of in the mood for a drink."

"Yes, but we need to speak to this Joseph Meissner fellow. Sounds like he might've had a grudge against the Beneveti couple."

"You don't really think a busboy killed them, do you? We still don't even know if it was murder. The medical report hasn't come in yet."

Adele shrugged. She didn't say it, but in her bones, she knew what this was. Like a bloodhound with a scent, she knew. "All right," she said, "do you think there's someone who can take us to the bar?"

Marshall also gathered her jacket, pulling it on as she too moved after Adele. "They have golf carts moving all around; keys are at the counter downstairs."

Adele resisted the urge to roll her eyes. Golf carts on demand. Private swimming pools warmed next to golf courses. Private bars in the rooms. It all sounded amazing. But at the same time, it sounded so alien and strange. A foreign way of living. Still, Adele could remember her own memories on the ski slopes. They had never come somewhere this nice. Her family had never been able to afford it. But she could remember the ski slopes. The warm conversations by the fire. The

40

arguments at night. She remembered it all.

CHAPTER NINE

Respite in the Cliffs was placed at the very edge of the resort. The building was three stories of glass and circular wooden platforms. It seemed to be situated on stilts, extending high enough to graze the tops of the trees around, and presenting a view into the valley below. Adele and Agent Marshall exited the golf cart they had been allowed to borrow and moved up the many wooden steps, which were glazed with small bits of glittering stones that reflected the light above.

Adele had her hands in her coat pockets, and her nose had reddened from the cold, but she still couldn't ignore the sheer beauty of the scene surrounding the elevated bar.

Mountains as a backdrop, a valley in the foreground, windows all around displaying nature's allure. Adele marched up the steps, with Agent Marshall in tow.

She pushed open the door to the establishment and was confronted by a few tables already occupied by clients. One of them even had a family. The children were sipping on Cokes while the parents had glasses of wine.

The tables themselves were fascinating. They were made of glass, with small stones, polished or put through a tumbler, encased in a resin. The single bulbs set in concave casings in the ceiling illuminated and cast sparkling designs across the tables. The ceiling itself was dark, and with the reflected colors looked like the night sky. Skylights above suggested that on the darkest nights, with clouds gone, visitors would be treated to a glorious vision of the heavens as well.

For now, it was still early evening, and night had yet to fall.

Adele approached the bar with Agent Marshall behind her. She felt a bit out of place as she maneuvered up to the counter and leaned over. "Excuse me, I'm looking for Joseph Meissner."

The woman behind the counter glanced over, and she placed a drink in front of a burly man wearing a brown overcoat. She smiled at the man, making chitchat before approaching Adele and Agent Marshall. "Joseph is out," she said, curtly.

"You know where he is?"

"Resupplying. Why? Who are you?"

"My name is Agent Sharp. I'm looking into the disappearance of Mr. and Mrs. Beneveti. I heard Joseph had some run-ins with them."

Sometimes the most direct approach was enough to dislodge people's distrust. Or so Adele hoped. She studied the barkeep, and the woman's eyes narrowed. "Joseph is a good kid. He didn't have anything to do with it. Besides, I thought it was a bear attack."

"So I keep hearing," Adele said. "You know when Joseph will be back?"

The woman crossed her arms. She had no tattoos on display. But Adele could see small holes, vaguely covered with a dusting of makeup, in the woman's ears and nose, suggesting that when she was off hours, she had at least three piercings.

"Like I said, Joseph is a good kid. Besides, the Benevetis were assholes."

Adele blinked. Agent Marshall leaned in closer.

"How forthright of you," said Adele. "Mind expounding?"

The woman behind the counter snorted. She turned away, grabbed a couple of glasses, moving over to the far end of the counter, and pouring something from a long brown bottle with golden filigree. No sooner had she finished pouring than two of the clients at the furthest table raised their hands, and one of them called out, "Another round. Please."

The woman smiled, grabbed both the drinks, walked over, and placed them at the table before returning.

Adele waited patiently, watching as the woman approached again. The barkeep rubbed her hands against the small towel behind the counter. "They were assholes. Loud, obnoxious. Felt like they owned the place. Mr. Beneveti made more than one pass at me. Obviously, I wasn't allowed to make too big a deal of it. But he got handsy. Mrs. Beneveti has tried to get more than one of us fired. Joseph too, from what I remember."

Adele nodded. "So I heard. You say Mr. Beneveti assaulted you?"

The woman snorted. "Don't use your words for my problems. No. I said he got handsy. Obnoxious. I work in a bar. Low inhibitions and wealthy clients. It tips well, but some of my dignity," she nodded toward the door, "I leave on those front steps. Otherwise I'd never make it."

Adele stared at the woman. "All right, so you didn't like the

Benevetis."

The barkeep shook her head once. "Not much to like. Rich assholes. They tipped well; that's fair. But, if you're making as much as they are, it's easy to tip and hope your problems go away. Not saying it wasn't good of them. But yeah, I didn't like them. A lot of people didn't."

Adele tapped the counter. "I'm beginning to get that sense. Well, I'd like to thank you for your time. There anything else you might've noticed? Anything strange? Anyone you know who might've had a grudge against the Benevetis?"

"I thought it was a bear attack," she repeated.

Adele shrugged. "Just crossing our t's and dotting our i's. Anything you can think of?"

The woman began to answer, but just then, her carefree expression and candid attitude shifted. A mask of worry quickly faded to a docile, obedient expression. She stood straighter, her shoulders back, and smiled politely. "Will that be all?" she said in a pleasant, careful tone.

Adele frowned, then heard the quiet jingle of a bell behind her and glanced back.

A man in a gray suit was standing in the door. He hadn't even worn a jacket. He was round and small and balding. One jacket hung over the arm of a busboy behind him. The man was shaking his head, and his face pulsed red. "Excuse me," he said, sternly, "excuse me, you two!"

It took a moment for Adele to realize the man was indicating her and Agent Marshall. She turned. "Yes?"

"Are you harassing my employees?"

Adele realized a second later, the man holding the coat was Otto. Mr. Klein winced sheepishly and shook his head, mouthing, *Sorry.*

Adele looked back at the shorter man. "And who are you?"

"I'm Manager Adderman. I run this establishment. I hear you're bothering my employees." He spoke sternly, but quietly. With the practiced ease of someone in authority. Loud enough for Adele to understand his distaste, but quiet enough for most clients not to overhear. He approached, his voice following his footsteps. He was shorter than Adele by a good head. Even Agent Marshall was taller than him.

"I need to ask you to leave immediately," the manager said.

Adele quirked an eyebrow. "I'm afraid you can't do that. This is a criminal investigation."

Manager Adderman's face turned even redder. "Keep it down," he said, sharply. He reached out as if to grab Adele by the wrist and drag her toward the door.

Adele stood still and twisted her wrist out of his grasp. She glared at the manager. "I'll advise you not to touch me again. We'll leave when we're ready. We don't answer to you."

"This is private property," he said, wagging his finger at her.

Agent Marshall shook her head. "It doesn't matter. We're investigating. If you'd like, you can take it up with my boss."

"And who is your boss?" demanded the manager.

"Director Baumgardner," she said without batting an eyelid.

Some of the steam seemed to fade from the manager. "BKA? And you? Where are you from?"

Adele shrugged. "FBI. Interpol. We're investigating the disappearance of Mr. and Mrs. Beneveti. We heard they were regulars at this place. Is that true?"

The manager's face was even redder than before. He shook his head. "Just stop harassing my employees. Leave the clients alone. You have to investigate, fine. I can't stop you. But stop ruining my business."

"How might we be doing that?" Adele said, frowning.

Now, dropping his voice even more, the manager leaned in and hissed, "This was a bear attack! That's what search and rescue said. That's what we're going with. Stop scaring the clients. A couple of them have already been asking questions. If you chase out my business, God help me, I'll sue you. I'll sue you until there's nothing left. Understand?"

Adele studied him and shook her head. "Is the resort perpetuating the story? Pushing the narrative it was a bear attack?"

The manager studied her, shrewd. His reddened cheeks seemed flushed from both anger and the cold. He stepped back and shrugged. "We're just going with whatever the search and rescue team reported. The investigating is up to you. But stop bothering my employees and my clients. Thank you."

He stepped aside and gestured toward the door in a sweeping fashion.

Adele glanced at his hand. Out of spite, she wanted to stay. Part of her thought of what John might've done. He'd likely order a drink and down it right in front of the manager, enjoying the ever-increasing red along the small man's face. But Adele wasn't John. She wasn't someone who let her pride make all her decisions. The manager didn't want her here. He was rude, obnoxious. Scared. Scared of losing business. Another resort was opening up nearby, just as expensive, and perhaps that was what had him on the fritz.

A lot of money in places like these. More than she'd suspected. And where there was money, there was motive.

Adele trailed her hand along the counter. Something about the cold wood beneath her fingertips made her glance past the manager toward the windows displaying the snowy slopes beyond.

Again, she was only ten. Again, she pictured her father and mother, sitting across from her in... the dining room? No, not a dining room. A restaurant. Also on the slopes. She remembered skiing as a child. In the Alps. Adele paused, frowning.

Beautiful memories, but splintered by scenes of anger. Arguments. Shouting.

Adele shivered, wanting to retreat from her thoughts.

She shook her head, as if to dislodge a headache, and got up, moving away from the counter. She nodded in gratitude toward the barkeep and gestured stiffly in farewell toward the manager. Agent Marshall followed along behind. The two agents exited the bar and moved down the steps.

"Well, that was eventful," said Marshall beneath her breath.

"Yes," said Adele. "The manager has a vested interest in stopping the investigation."

"What are you thinking?" Marshall asked, quiet now.

Adele took another few steps, making sure they were out of range of earshot from the bar. "I'm wondering if there's anything else they might've covered up. Anything. There's a lot of money on the line here."

Marshall frowned. "You don't think the manager had something to do with the killing, do you?"

Adele lifted her shoulders. "I can't be sure. There are a lot of suspects here. It's our job to narrow the list."

"That Swiss couple in France, any news on that front?"

Adele shook her head. "I haven't had a chance to catch up with the investigators."

"You know them, though? I know you worked with the French before."

"I'm part French. American too and German."

Marshall whistled as they approached the golf cart. "Three citizenships? Impressive. You speak the language very well."

"Thank you. But no, no further information about the Swiss. I'll talk to the investigators when I have a chance."

Adele got into the golf cart with Marshall, and the younger agent began to drive them back toward the main part of the resort.

Adele frowned as they moved, her face pawed by wisps of wind and cold. She studied the cliffs and the trees beyond, her eyes tracing the snowy trails. The Benevetis had been murdered. She was sure of it. The medical report couldn't come in soon enough; that would confirm it. But conjecture was nothing without clues. A gut instinct meant little without direction. If she was going to get others on board with her instincts, she would have to come up with solid proof.

CHAPTER TEN

Adele reclined in the cushioned chair by the fireplace. Many stones stippled the walls, placed in the fire pit, and circling up into a chute that led through the ceiling. At her back, the walls of glass remained bare, the curtains open, allowing starlight to twinkle through. The soft, white glow from the sky melded with the flickering orange radiance from the hearth.

Adele vaguely thought of Robert and his mansion. She thought of sitting by the fire with her old mentor, studying the flames and their case notes. Adele had her hand extended on the armrest, her knuckles just barely brushing the circular wooden table upon which sat her phone.

She waited.

The medical examiner's report was due any minute now. It would confirm her suspicions. It had to.

Already, she had pissed off the manager and riled up a couple of the employees. This was a political game. Agent Marshall's presence proved that. What she'd been told about the situation only further underscored the need for answers, and soon. Tomorrow, the new resort would open. Thousands of jobs, hundreds of millions of dollars. An entire industry flush with cash.

And in the mountains, two couples, missing. One of them found dead, ripped to shreds.

Adele glanced at her phone, but the screen was dull gray, stagnant. No notifications just yet. She leaned back, crossing her hands over her stomach and staring into the fire.

Flames had an entrancing quality that demanded attention. Some memories were similar. Emotions fueling the flames of thought, and hearkening back to a different time. Just such memories inserted themselves across Adele's mind.

A specific scene played out in her mind. Her father was a stern man, but at the time he'd been smiling. He rarely smiled nowadays. But then she pictured him reclining in the outdoor hot tub of the resort they'd stayed at. Banks of snow all around him, with a slight separation between the edge of the bubbling, steaming hot tub and the start of the snow. The heat from the water and the bubbling jets extended toward the snowflakes, catching them and turning them into just another droplet in the hot water.

Adele remembered her father grabbing a handful of snow from outside of the bath and launching it at her mother. Playful, silly. She remembered her mother grabbing some snow and throwing it back, underhanded, and pegging the sergeant in the side of the face.

She remembered laughing so hard that she had fallen off the edge of the hot tub and tumbled into the water.

The laughter had faded. Her parents' smiles had disappeared. They both had rushed to her side and pulled her out, making sure their young daughter was okay.

The one thing her parents had in common until the very end. Their daughter. Adele. They had expressed their feelings in different ways. The sergeant was always cold, demanding, expecting better. His greatest fear, she suspected, was that she end up in a dead-end job, as he had. He never advanced beyond sergeant. Her mother, though, had been gentle, quiet, encouraging. She'd gone out of her way to see the best in Adele, even when it was unwarranted. She would drive Adele to any sport, activity, or friend's house. Anything her daughter had wanted. She hadn't been a pushover. She hadn't let things slide, but her corrections had been kind, soft. Gentle.

Her mother had died right after Adele had left college, more than a decade ago. The killer was gone, escaped. No clues. Once upon a time, Adele thought she might've unearthed a new lead or two, but as always, they'd faded into the background. Little more than stagnant, white noise.

She thought of her father. There were other memories circling in her mind around the same time. Many memories of fights, of arguments. What sort of arguments? She thought she remembered her small self pressing an ear to her parents' bedroom door at the resort. She thought she remembered screaming. It didn't make sense. Why couldn't she remember fully? Her hand inched toward her phone, hesitant. For a moment, her fingers hovered over the device, and her body seemed caught, stuck between two choices.

Then her brow narrowed, and she grabbed the phone, her motions quicker all of a sudden. The hesitation faded. The focus returned. She pressed the phone to her ear after dialing her father's number.

Her father still lived in Germany. Only a couple hours away. He still worked as a sergeant in the local police force. He'd been a military man for a while, but no longer.

He had investigative skills. Perhaps nothing as impressive as Robert, but he was a smart, shrewd man. And he had answers. Answers to the memories. She wasn't sure why she did it. But as the phone rang, she didn't feel cold feet. She didn't back down. Instead, she felt an increase in zeal. She needed him here. She wasn't sure why, but the thought struck her as imperative.

A few rings later, a crystal clear voice grumbled, "Hello?"

"Dad?" said Adele. She spoke in English, but then, a second later, switched to German. "Hello, Dad? It's Adele."

A pause, perhaps her father turning off the TV, arising from his table. Or maybe turning off the stove while he boiled some soup. Her father always liked soup.

"Adele?" he said. Not Sharp. He didn't call her by her last name this time. Mild improvement.

"Dad, I'm in Germany. The Alps."

"Oh?"

"Yes. In fact, I was wondering, but what are you doing this weekend?"

A longer pause. "Nothing planned. Nothing important, at least. Why?"

"Would you..." She hesitated, the word stuck in her throat. This felt uncomfortable. She didn't want to ask him. Vulnerability. The sort of thing he had often thrown right back in her face. The sort of thing he had been unequipped to deal with. Her father was an emotionally stunted man. A man who hadn't accepted emotions as a fact of life. A man who would see them as weakness. But in his own way, it had locked him in his own cocoon of coldness. Indifference. A trait she'd seen in a lot of people of her father's generation. Not one that she blamed them for. Life was different back then. But now, the divide, the gulf between them only expanded, it seemed. And yet, at last, she summoned the words with what little courage she had. "I was wondering if you'd like to come up. To help in the case," she added quickly. Nothing too vulnerable. No, she couldn't afford it. Rejection would just hurt too much then. "If you could just come up and give me your insight. I know you know the area. We used to go skiing when I was a kid. I was wondering if maybe you'd like to pitch in a hand."

50

A crackle, a deep breath. "When?"

"As soon as you can make it, honestly. Tomorrow if you want. If not, then Saturday."

"I can make it. All right. I'll see you then. Just send me the address."

Then her father hung up.

Adele felt equal parts relief and annoyance. She would have to work with him on farewells. It was a jarring thing to simply be hung up on. But at the same time, she felt elated. Her father had agreed to come. And if there was one thing that could be said for Sergeant Sharp, he was a man of his word. An honest man. One she could trust. If he said he would come, then he would.

She stared at the fire. Again, her phone lowered back on the armrests. Sergeant Sharp would be coming. And while it was true she needed help in the case, honesty wasn't Adele's strong suit in the same way. She wanted his help, but she also wanted his memories. She wanted answers.

Why was it pressing all of a sudden? Why now?

She couldn't be sure. But something was nagging at her mind. Something niggling at her consciousness. Something she'd forgotten. Something important.

She shook her head, trying to focus, thinking. When her father came, he would provide answers. Just then, the phone beneath her hand began to buzz against the armrest.

Jarred from her thoughts, Adele glanced back at the device. Was it her father? Calling to apologize for hanging up so abruptly? Her father hated apologies. But maybe he was learning.

With a kindling of hope in her heart, she turned her phone over, but realized a second later that it wasn't her father. Just a notification. An email.

The medical report was in.

Quickly, Adele scrolled to the contents of the file. She opened the tabs and glanced at the pictures, scrolling past to the medical findings. She stared, reading the file. She reread it.

The fire seemed to have died a little bit, as if the fuel were suddenly vapor. She looked away from her phone, blinking, processing.

She'd been right.

Not a bear attack.

A blunt weapon. Sharp once, but no longer. The medical report said

51

most likely a hatchet or an axe.

Someone in these mountains had stalked the Benevetis, hunted them down, and chopped them to pieces with a rusted axe. Someone had killed the millionaires and disposed of their corpses by the ski resort.

Adele clicked her phone, putting it back in her pocket and steepling her fingers beneath her chin.

Was the motivation money? Did it have a connection to the Swiss couple who had died in France? And why in the Alps? Was it something to do with the new resort opening tomorrow? A political motivation perhaps?

Adele stared into the fire, allowing the cycle of thoughts to rip through her brain again and again and again.

CHAPTER ELEVEN

"We're getting close, I can feel it," said Robert. He nodded and patted his hands together in a small clapping gesture.

John, who had had it up to *here* with the small man's chipper attitude, growled, "Close?" He gripped the end of his shovel, glaring. "Explain to me exactly why I was left on digging duty?"

Robert pressed his hands daintily together and nodded over the tops of his folded fingers at John, as if conceding this was a good question. The two men stood within sight of their resort, beneath the first beams of morning sunshine, scanning the nearest ski trails and overturning fresh snowfall, looking for the missing persons. Robert was coughing again—but seemed to be trying to hide it. John frowned.

"I understand your frustration," said Robert, his face paler than it had been before. Something about the weather didn't seem to suit him. "But you're just so big and strong. And I am old and frail."

"Don't start with that shit," said John, growling again. He began to shovel with renewed intensity, throwing pile after pile of snow over his shoulder. There were three other digging teams the local search and rescue had provided them at the government's insistence. Each of the teams was out in a square grid, all of them shoveling in a checkered pattern to cover the most distance possible. There were gaps between the squares, but small enough so a body couldn't be hidden.

"Well," said Robert, "I feel like you're doing a splendid job."

John grumbled again, trying to keep his frustration at least somewhat in check. He could feel his phone buzzing against his pocket, but couldn't be bothered to take off his gloves and answer. Besides, he figured it was likely Agent Sharp again. The medical examiner had confirmed it last night. Murder. An email had already been forwarded to them.

John felt his fingers numb beneath the gloves he'd bought from the gift shop, and the two hoodies he wore instead of a jacket were starting to prove insufficient against the insistent chill. Still, he refused to show it. He wouldn't give Robert the satisfaction.

The small man with the slicked hair and missing teeth stood snug as a bug in his oversized coat. In John's assessment, the old investigator looked like a stuffed potato. He also never stopped smiling, a facet which was starting to wear on John, especially since he'd started digging. The coughing, the paleness, though, seemed suspect. John wondered if Adele knew about Robert's declining health.

John heaved another shovel of snow, his large muscles straining beneath his sweaters.

"Wait, look," said Robert.

John pulled up sharp. He stared at the end of his shovel, where he dug, but spotted nothing. Just more snow, and hardened ice beneath.

He looked over at Robert and saw the investigator pointing toward the trees.

"What?" John said.

"An Alpine chough. See the crest feathers and the yellow beak? It's beautiful. They're rare in these parts. They mate for life, did you know that?"

John stared incredulously at the investigator and thought, for the briefest moment, there was a twinkle in the man's eye. Was he having a go?

John felt cross at first, but the humor of the situation settled on him and a crack in his façade allowed a grin to slip along his lips. Robert's eyes, still twinkling, surveyed the trees. Again, glancing away from John.

The brief flash of amusement faded in the face of the chill seeping through John's lackluster clothing, exacerbated by the blisters forming on his fingers as he continued to dig. Mentally, he felt the wear of inevitably being out here all day, looking for two needles in a frosted haystack. The mountains were covered with snow, and the location of the Swiss couple couldn't be determined. They would have to dig, and do it the hard way.

And so John set to one shovelful at a time.

**

Three hours into the digging, Robert wondered if he should mention something. He'd already determined the unlikelihood they would find the bodies. The Swiss couple had been missing for almost a week. If animals hadn't found them first, then the snow would have covered them. Robert continued to glance to the trees. The birds were

54

beautiful, yes, but really, his attention was caught by the structures beyond, in the mountains just past the resort.

He frowned.

He could hear John grumbling every time he shoveled another heap of snow and found nothing.

Robert supposed he should tell John his theory, but then decided the large man needed to get some of that pent-up aggression out. Toil and labor was good for exhausting an angry bear. Robert nodded to himself, trying to hide his amused expression as he moved past John and said, with a slight wave, "I'll be right back."

"Where are you going? Out for a stroll while the rest of us dig?"

Robert pretended like he hadn't heard and moved toward the leader of the French search and rescue team. He approached the woman, a local who knew the mountains better than anyone else. She'd grown up in the Alps, skiing and hiking and living with her family in cabins.

He approached the woman and nodded politely, catching her attention.

She was also digging with a partner who carried a shovel. She said, "May I help you?" The words came gasped, and her face was slick with sweat from the effort. She had a chipper disposition though. John approved of this. He quite liked happy people.

"Pardon me, *mademoiselle*," he said, "you are doing a splendid job. Just one question. What is that?"

He pointed over his shoulder in the direction of the structures he'd spotted.

Her eyes narrowed. She had blonde hair, just like Adele. Robert smiled fondly at the thought of his young protégé. Adele Sharp was one of the brightest minds the DGSI had ever seen. Though they were too stupid to realize it sometimes.

He glanced back toward John and then returned his attention to the leader of the rescue team.

She wiped her gloved hand over her sweaty brow, pushing back the hem of her hood, and then said, still breathing deeply. "Old cabins. From the last resort. Before the new one bought the land."

Robert frowned. "There used to be another resort here?"

"Yes. A family affair. Not nearly as expensive. The cabins aren't in use anymore, though. Dusty, broken down." She shrugged. "Sometimes squatters find their way in there, or high school kids. For the most part they're just locked up."

55

Robert bobbed his head. "Thank you. You have helped immensely."

He turned and moved away, his feet crunching in the snow as he approached John once more.

He watched the large man shovel for a few more minutes, impressed by the sheer industry of Agent Renee's musculature. Despite his grumbling, he moved more snow than the next two search teams combined.

"Excuse me," Robert said at last, waving a little hand toward John.

Agent Renee grunted and slammed his shovel back in the snow, glancing up once more. "What?"

Renee had never been one for pleasantries.

"I think we're looking in the wrong place," said Robert.

John cleared his throat and tried not to roll his eyes. He didn't try very hard. "What do you mean?"

Robert smiled pleasantly again. "You know the birds I showed you?"

"We're not on about the bloody birds again, are we?"

"Give me a second. The birds, they like to follow tourists. They hope to find discarded food."

"What's your point?"

"The investigators, the search and rescue team, they wanted us to search along this path. Why?"

John stared at him, dumbfounded. For the first time, it was Robert's turn to feel a bit of irritation. He missed Adele. She had never been slow on the uptake.

"Why are we searching here?" he said, slowing his words a bit, just in case John couldn't keep up.

The tall, scar-faced agent grunted. "Near the ski trails. Most likely place to find the missing couple."

"Yes, if they were attacked by a bear. But…" he said, patiently, allowing the silence to extend. He wanted John to reach it on his own, if only to give the man some of the joy of stumbling upon the conclusion. But John just stared back at him, his expression blank. The man wasn't stupid. Robert knew that well. John was not a stupid man, but he did a good job pretending.

Testily, Robert said, "If they weren't killed by a bear and they were murdered, like Adele's victims—you got the email right?"

John nodded again. He let go of the shovel now, and it tilted over, still lodged in the snow, splattering into the white frost, disappearing

56

from sight. "I have a feeling you're going to tell me something I don't want to hear," he said, expressionless.

Robert smoothed his mustache. "If they were lured away by a murderer, I don't think they would be near the trails."

"Let me guess, you know where they are."

"I say we check those buildings."

John turned, following the direction of Robert's pointed finger. The tall man and the small man both looked through the trees, standing in the snow, the backdrop of the resort outlining their silhouettes. They stared in the direction of the wooden structures, just hidden past the row of trees in the periphery of the forest nestled by the mountains beyond.

"What are those?" asked John, dispassionately.

"Abandon structures," said Robert. "Old homes. Used to belong to an old resort."

"How long have you known this?"

"It just occurred to me," said Robert, lying.

John's eyes narrowed suspiciously, but he didn't return to retrieve the shovel, and instead began stalking back toward where they'd parked their vehicle. He grumbled all the while, muttering to himself beneath his breath about *grinning monkeys* and *old farts*.

To be honest, Robert couldn't discern half of it as his hearing had been going in the last ten years.

Robert moved over to where the shovel had fallen. He dusted it off a little bit, and then walked primly over to where the nearest search and rescue team was. He extended the shovel, nodding apologetically, and, once the bemused worker retrieved the tool, Robert turned and followed after John toward where they had parked.

CHAPTER TWELVE

John's frown only deepened the closer they got to the old, abandoned outbuildings of the dilapidated resort. "Outside," John said. "They just kept telling us to look outside. But what if they're inside? No one thought *inside*," he muttered. He shot a sidelong glance at Robert. "How do you think of this shit? *You* didn't kill them, did you?"

As they pulled to a crunching halt on the side of the trail, John put the vehicle in park. He glanced down at Robert's hand as the smaller man reached out and affectionately patted him on the knee. "It's called investigating, my dear." Robert wasn't so petty as to add, *You should try it.* But his tone implied it well enough.

Robert unlatched his car door and stepped out. A split-second later, the old investigator loosed a strangled cry.

John looked sharply across the seats at Robert. He was waist deep in snow, stiff as an icicle, wide-eyed as he regarded John through the car. "Renee," he said, urgently, "Renee, stop looking at me like a yard sign. I can't move in this." He wiggled his arms, causing some of the snow to splash around, but he stayed stuck.

"A good deduction," said John, nodding seriously. "Do they call that investigating too?"

Robert stared crossly at the larger man. "I think you're going to have to help me."

John stared. "You want me to carry you?"

Robert crossed his arms where he stood waist deep in the snow. "No one's been this way for a while. Things will only get worse. You need to help me."

While Robert might have been the sort to avoid pettiness, John prided himself on it. "What's the magic word?"

Without blinking, Robert said, "Would you please do me the favor of helping me to the cabins?"

John chuckled a bit and pushed open his own door, hearing the scrape of snow being shoved aside by the metal wing. He stepped out and immediately found himself sinking up to his thighs.

He felt the chill through his pants, but resisted the urge to tremble or yelp. He stomped over with giant loping strides toward where Robert was on the other side of the car. He took the man beneath the armpits and lifted him up like a child.

"John," said Robert, "if you ever tell anyone about this, I will murder you in your sleep. It'll be poison; it will be untraceable. Understand?"

John paused for a moment, still lifting the man, and he felt, for the first time, a chill that he couldn't quite dislodge creep down his spine. He glanced up to Robert, whose head was higher than his. For the first time, the older man wasn't smiling. His eyes were cold, black, and fixed directly on John's face. "Don't test me, Renee."

John swallowed and readjusted his grip. He mimed zipping his lips and throwing away a key, and then, helping Robert along, he headed for the elevated steps at the end of the trail which led to the first row of cabins.

He placed Robert on the lowest steps. Here, trees shielded the stairwell from much of the snow. The snow would fall on the branches, and the wind would brush it away before it could tumble down. Still, large clumps of frost had made it through the branches and pockmarked portions of the wooden stairway.

John pointed immediately. "Footprints," he said.

Robert, dusting himself off from where John had placed him, followed the large man's attention. He noted the disturbance as well. "Good eye."

John felt a flash of pride. He wasn't sure why. It wasn't like Robert's opinion mattered to him, did it? The footprints faded eventually, disappearing due to either wind or weather. But there had clearly been a disturbance in the snow.

"Do you think the killer lured them here?" John said, quietly.

"I think," said Robert in a spurting whisper, "if there's a killer in these mountains, an abandoned cabin would be the perfect place to hide out."

Another shiver crept up John's spine and he reached his gloved hand toward his pistol at his hip. Together, the two of them, mismatched as they were, moved up the creaking steps toward the wooden cabins, doing their best to remain as quiet as possible.

***

59

They checked three of the cabins. Only a fourth remained. The other three had been locked with a couple of windows broken, suggesting perhaps animals or vagabonds. But Robert and John had peered in, using the flashlights search and rescue had provided, and hadn't spotted anything untoward. One of the cabins had a pile of raccoon droppings in the middle of the floor, but besides that—which had elicited a chuckle from John—they had been empty.

Still, Robert was confident in his hunch.

The two of them approached the final wooden cabin.

"Hang on," John said, suddenly. "Look."

Robert followed his gaze. The door was ajar.

A slow chill fell across his shoulders, and Robert shifted uncomfortably. He could tell the larger man had been freezing for the last few hours, but his pride had prevented him from going back to retrieve a coat from the gift shop. Robert wasn't one to interrupt a fool in their foolishness. Now, though, he wished on his part he'd thought to bring a weapon. Robert took a slight step back, allowing John the lead. For the first time, Robert felt a flash of gratitude Agent Renee was with him. The tall man had already snapped into a combat posture, his weapon appearing in his hand faster than Robert could blink. John adopted a shooter's crouch, and he approached, stepping sidelong toward the door, with rapid pace, but also cautious motions.

Robert witnessed, impressed, as the handsome man neared the wooden cabin. John moved quieter, somehow. Before, he had seemed a lumbering giant; now, like a snake moving through tall grass, unnoticed, but deadly. Robert followed along behind, careful where he stepped, careful not to alert anyone who might be inside.

John reached the door and glanced back, just briefly, his weapon trained in front of him, his shoulder pressed against the wooden trim of the doorframe.

Robert mouthed, *Caution.*

John nodded once and then inhaled and gestured with his head slightly to the side. Robert frowned. John rolled his eyes and gestured again. It took Robert a bit longer than he would ever admit, but at last he realized what the agent wanted, and stepped out of the line of fire from the doorway.

John returned his full attention to the cabin.

The fourth cabin. The final one. Old land, brought by the new resort. Everything else torn down, or built over. Except for these four

60

cabins. What were the odds?

John moved all at once, with the powerful and yet controlled motions of someone who'd breached doors hundreds of times before. His shoulder went first, his foot followed, his posture steadying, his body squaring up behind his weapon, his gun raised into the black at the same time as his body moved through the threshold.

He kept his crouch as the door slammed open. John pulled up short, standing, his chest still in the threshold of the old cabin.

"Do you see anything?" Robert called.

The cabins weren't large. They didn't even have bathrooms. Only a scattering of outhouses provided any form of potential relief. "You better come look," said John, checking the cabin once more and then slowly holstering his weapon.

Robert took this as indication it was safe to approach. Hesitantly, he stepped up the final two stairs, and then neared the dark threshold of the cabin. Inside, the cabin was dark as well. He stared, and then spotted them.

Bodies. Two of them. It had been hard to tell at first, from the many pieces scattered every which way. Bloodied, but frozen. One of the heads had tumbled into the fireplace. A hand, in a pool of frozen blood, lay just beyond the threshold, a single frostbitten finger curled into the laces of a discarded, ripped shoe.

"I think we found our missing persons," John murmured.

Robert swallowed, suppressing a sudden urge to vomit. He focused on breathing, his breath fogging the air and trickling up, disappearing into the darkness of the ceiling as he stared at the scene of carnage.

CHAPTER THIRTEEN

Adele watched as the Sergeant walked across the trail leading from the taxi. Granted, her father was round of belly these days, and he more waddled than walked. He had wide shoulders and arms that suggested he spent a good amount of time in the weight room, despite his age. He had a long, walrus mustache, which he was very proud of, but the hairs on his face seemed to have been contributed by those once on his head. He was balding, a facet of his appearance he wasn't proud of. Currently, the source of mild embarrassment was covered by a baseball cap beneath an upturned hood.

Adele's father had a backpack slung over one shoulder, and he wore a tan sweater. She'd texted him earlier to avoid presenting anything that might associate him with the investigation. She knew her father liked wearing his sergeant's uniform in public. It gave him pride. But now, they needed him to go incognito.

She waited, sitting at the circular table before opening hours of Respite in the Cliffs.

She glanced across the bar toward where the woman from the night before was cleaning the counter and preparing for the early customers.

It had taken some convincing, but Adele felt confident her father's identity would remain shielded from the local law enforcement. Not even Agent Marshall knew about his arrival. Adele had told the young German agent she was out for a run.

"You're sure there's a place here for him?" she asked, still watching her father through the windows.

The woman behind the counter continued to clean and nodded as she did. She didn't look up, but said, "If you say they were murdered, then I'm happy to help. Just so long as you keep your end of the bargain."

Adele tapped her fingers against the smooth, lacquered surface of the circular table, admiring the many polished stones set in resin beneath her fingers. "I'm going to do my due diligence," she said. "I'll make sure this doesn't land at anyone's feet who wasn't involved."

"That includes Joseph, right?" said the barkeep. This time she did look up, lowering her hand from where she'd been maneuvering a few glasses and arranging them for the day.

Adele inhaled. "Like we discussed. He just needs a place to stay for a couple of days. Let him blend in as a tourist."

"Who is he exactly?" the woman asked.

Adele smiled, shook her head. It would've cost too much to get a room for her father. She also hadn't wanted to go through the German authorities and tip them off to his arrival. He was the ace up her sleeve. She watched as her father took the steps, approaching the stilted bar overlooking the valley beyond. For a moment, she saw him pause and survey the forests and the mountains. The faintest wisp of a smile curled beneath his drooping mustache. *A God moment*. That's what he called it whenever they were in nature.

Seeing her father happy made Adele happy. A rare occurrence.

Adele glanced back toward the barkeep. "Look," she said, "I'm going to go where the clues take me. But I do owe you for this. As long as you keep your bargain, I'll keep my end."

Adele wasn't sure why, but she trusted the woman. The barkeep had said her name was Heather. She had a dimpled smile when it was displayed, and a cynical view of the world which Adele understood. Her father would be staying in a room above the bar, pretending to be a tourist along with the others, mingling with the customers and seeing what he could find.

Heather continued to arrange the glasses, and then turned to cleaning out the sink from the night before.

"He's a detective is all," said Adele. "A specialist. Don't worry about it, just make sure no one knows he's here. If they do, just tell them he's a distant relative, a tourist. Just like everyone else."

"I have a suspicion that's exactly what he isn't," said Heather. She shrugged again. Currently, she still had the two piercings in her ear, and the one in her nose. When work hours came she would remove them and cover the holes with makeup. A rigid structure. Common rules of the resort had to be followed, or it was grounds for termination. Adele had sensed some of the discontent exhibited the night before. Adele didn't like manipulating people, but Heather, in her cynicism, didn't seem the sort that could be manipulated. Just the sort that might be trusted. In a country like Germany, with politicians and wealthy folk involved, in the Alps, there were very few Adele could rely on. Even with Heather, it was a risk. But right now, Adele had a murder to solve.

And she was running out of options.

The small bell jangled over the door, and it swung in as her father stepped into the well-lit room. He grunted, nodded toward his daughter. "Adele," he said.

"Sergeant," she said in return.

Her father smoothed his mustache.

"You'll be staying upstairs," said Adele. "Need a minute to settle?"

Her father grunted and nodded. That was the extent of his greeting. They hadn't seen each other in weeks. Then again, her father had never been the most affectionate man. He was here. He'd come. That was a start. She had to give him credit.

Her father approached the barkeep and hefted his backpack. He waited expectantly, allowing the question to remain unspoken. The woman examined the walrus-shaped man, and then, seemingly approving of his silent presentation, she, too, without words, grunted and nodded toward the stairwell curling up at the back.

"First door," she said.

For Adele, it was a strange interaction. The silent gestures, the few words. Perhaps Heather was the daughter her father had never had. The cynicism, the outlook, the distrust.

Vaguely, she wondered if bringing him here perhaps wasn't the best idea after all. It took a few minutes for her father to settle. He was a clean, neat man. She knew he wasn't the sort to live out of a backpack, no matter how long he stayed in a place.

He would unpack, clean up, and then return.

And so, in the intervening minutes, she stared out the glass window, peering into the valley below, her gaze scanning the treetops, darting over the snowbound hills and rocky outcrops. After a few moments, Heather disappeared behind the bar into a back room, likely to change into her uniform for the day and address her earrings.

Her father returned a bit later, approaching the circular table and sitting down with a great huffing breath, placing his hands on his knees.

He wore a jacket, unzipped, and beneath it he had the same sweater as before.

"Well?" he said.

"Thanks for coming."

"Yes. Well, you needed my help."

Adele tried not to frown. She certainly hadn't phrased it as *needed*. Then again, she supposed she did. Her father was a bright man. But he also knew *their* past. He had access to the memories she'd somehow shut out. Again, she thought of the snowbound cliff, of her family together, laughing, crowded around the fire, drinking hot cocoa. She thought of arguments at night. Anger. What had started the arguments? Had that led to their divorce? She couldn't remember. Why couldn't she remember?

She stared at her father, the questions on her lips preparing to spring forth. Then she thought better of it. Best not to ambush him this moment. Her father would clam up. He was a man of few words. And fewer still if he was pressured.

"They were murdered," she said, "an Italian couple. Mr. and Mrs. Beneveti. Oil tycoons. Wealthy. A lot of the employees here say they were also jerks. No one really like them. Though they tipped generously."

Her father listened as she filled him in on the details. Some of the information was classified, and she could probably get into trouble for sharing it in the wrong places. Then again, with Interpol, she had a lot of leeway. She decided it was best in these situations to ask forgiveness rather than permission. For now, she needed her father with her.

"Questioned any of the employees?" her father said, once she'd finished.

"Yes. A couple. The manager didn't like that."

"Think the manager is involved?"

Adele shrugged. "He seemed angry. But I think he's mostly concerned with the resort. There's another one opening nearby. Very expensive one. Thousands of jobs. You know the sort."

Her father nodded. "I read about it in the paper. Not sure we need another one. But it is what it is. Good for the country. Good for tourism."

Practical, economical. Her father always had been.

"All right," she said. "What you think the next step should be?"

Her father studied her. He paused for a moment in consideration. Adele could hear Heather in the back room, moving about. In a low voice, her father spoke at last, tapping a large, calloused finger against the smooth glass table. "Why did you need me?" he said. "Don't you have your own partners to work with?"

Adele nodded. "A German girl. BKA. I'm not sure I can trust her."

Her father raised an eyebrow.

"No, not like that. She's not involved. But I think her orders have more political incentives than they do otherwise. I'm not sure they are interested primarily in catching the killer."

The Sergeant circled a finger over a particularly large, polished green stone beneath the glass. "Think they're right?" he said. He spoke nonchalantly, carefully, as if commenting on the weather. Adele knew he spoke like this whenever he thought he might be saying something which would offend.

At least this was an improvement. In the past, he rarely cared at all.

"I think," Adele began, carefully, "that jobs and money are important. People's livelihoods are crucial. But I'm not willing to believe you can't have both jobs and justice. A couple was murdered. Another couple is missing in France. This could go deeper than you might think."

Her father's eyes narrowed. He stroked his walrus mustache and stared at her for a moment, studying his daughter. His eyes held something indeterminable. She thought, for the faintest moment, of the look of panic he'd displayed when she'd fallen into that hot tub all those years ago. It was a strange thing to see concern on the Sergeant's face.

"Either way," Adele said, "my orders are to find the killer. I'm not working with BKA, and I'm not involved with the Italians. A lot of them are doing their own investigations. I'll leave them to it. It's why you're here. You need to blend in."

"I can pretend to be a tourist." He glanced out the window over Adele's shoulder, and sighed a soft, pleasurable sound. "I could get used to this. How much does a night's stay cost?"

Adele told him, and her father nearly coughed. He wasn't the sort to swear, and he reprimanded anyone who did, but still, he stared at her and descended into muttering about the state of the country and the wastefulness of its people. Adele wasn't entirely sure she'd agreed. Perhaps, simply because her father thought it was wrong, she wanted to see the good side of it. People needed a place to relax. People needed experiences they couldn't have elsewhere. The business, the jobs, all of it made sense.

Just then, she felt her phone buzzing. Adele quickly fished it from her pocket. She glanced at the number, and an eyebrow quirked. Robert.

She held up a finger, silencing her father mid-sentence as he continued to grumble about the cost of the resort, and she held the

66

phone to her ear. "Hello?"

Static. Then, "Adele?" It was John.

She frowned. "John? Is Robert okay?"

"I'm here," said the voice of her old mentor. "I'm fine. John didn't have your number."

Adele glared at the table, trying just as quickly to disguise her frustration. "It doesn't take long to save a number," she said.

There was an awkward pause, then John said, "I only keep two numbers in my phone. Forget about that. We found the Swiss couple."

Adele's anger faded, and she raised an eyebrow in her father's direction. She glanced toward the back door where the barkeeper had disappeared, and lowered her voice. "Alive?"

"Definitely not," Robert said, his tone grave. "Butchered. Looks like a similar attack to the one the Italians suffered."

"Did you get the files I sent?" Adele asked.

"The medical examiner? Yes. Murder."

"Also, my father's here. I invited him in on the case. Is it all right if we speak English, so he can chime in?"

Another longer, awkward pause. Robert said, in clipped English, "It's good to meet you, Mr. Sharp."

The Sergeant grunted.

John said, in French, "I didn't realize we were in the habit of bringing civilians into an investigation."

"He's not a civilian," Adele replied in English, testily. "Where did you find the Swiss couple?"

"Resort. Old abandoned buildings from the previous owners," said Robert. "It wasn't pretty. As in, it really wasn't pretty. Still makes my stomach turn thinking about it."

Adele winced sympathetically. She glanced at her father, who was rubbing the backs of his knuckles with his calloused fingers. He raised an eyebrow to her questioningly, as if looking for permission to speak.

Adele nodded once.

Her father cleared his voice, and, to her surprise, there was a bit of excited energy to him as he said, "Any leads?"

Another hesitation, but this time Robert smoothed over it by saying, "We're looking into things. We only just discovered the bodies this morning."

John added, his accent in English as heavy as Adele remembered, "Could have discovered it quicker; Robert had made me dig for three hours."

Adele could detect the annoyance in her old partner's tone. For some reason this made her smile.

"We should probably narrow it down then," her father said, either not detecting, or indifferent to, John's surliness.

"Narrow it down. How?" John asked.

The Sergeant replied, "We can't investigate everyone. Someone has to have motive here."

"Multiple murders. Maybe a serial killer?"

John muttered something Adele couldn't hear over a sudden burst of static. She said, "I sure hope not. But it was nearly two hundred miles apart. Maybe a group of killers? Moving from one resort to the other?" Adele shrugged at her father.

He carried a look on his face she couldn't quite place. She felt vulnerable all of sudden, embarrassed even. This was her job. Investigating—the one thing she did he was proud of. It felt strange to have him there for it. She glanced down at her phone, and then back up, and her father said, "Both of the victims were wealthy, yes?"

"Damn rich," said John.

Her father wrinkled his nose. "Careful with your language." Before John could retort, the Sergeant continued, "Wealthy victims, brutally killed. Feels personal. We had cases like this on the force before. The more violent, the more emotion involved. Why would they have emotion here? Would they have known the victims?"

Adele nodded with a flush of gratitude. Her father made a good point. Somehow, this felt validating in the presence of Robert and John, though they weren't actually here in person. Another burst of static, and Adele frowned, holding the phone a bit higher in case they were losing reception.

"He's not wrong," said Robert. "Maybe it was personal. Someone slighted by them? Someone with a grudge against the super wealthy?"

John snickered. "That puts you on the chopping block, doesn't it?"

"John," Adele snapped. "Don't joke about that. You better be looking after him."

"Looking after him? I just gave him a piggyback—" Before John could finish he yelped as if he'd just been pinched.

"What was that?" Adele asked.

"Nothing," John said, sounding as if he was speaking through gritted teeth. "Look, we have to go. But you're right, we need to narrow down the suspects. I think we should start with the employees."

"It's a good start," Adele's father said. The Sergeant adjusted the hem of his shirt and glanced toward the bar where Heather had emerged once more. "If anyone has a personal grudge, it might be resort employees."

Robert said, "But that would only make sense if both the couples had visited both resorts."

Adele hesitated, scratching at her chin with her free hand. "Or," she said, "one of the resort employees has worked at both places. There's a chance, however narrow though it may be. Either way, we're working with thin margins here. The couples were killed two hundred miles apart."

"Too many similarities to ignore, though," Robert came back.

"No, you're right. Both of them wealthy. Both of them involved in the oil industry. Both of them at ski resorts in the Alps."

"But separated by countries," John said. "The Italians in Germany, and the Swiss in France."

Adele frowned. "You don't think there's a political motive, do you?"

A lingering moment. "Seems strange," said Robert. "Why brutalize them like this? Why hide the bodies? A political motive would want the bodies to be found, yes? To make a statement? Someone trying to disrupt this new resort's opening today would want to cause as much uproar and fear as possible. No," he said, carefully, "I don't think this is political. But if it is, I don't see the angle, at least not yet. Let's start with the employees. I like that idea."

Adele bid her farewells and then clicked her phone and placed it back in her pocket, zipping up the pouch. She acknowledged her father with a nod.

"Friends of yours?" he asked.

"Colleagues. Back from DGSI."

Her father grunted. "Their English was hard to understand. That one with the bad attitude had a thick accent."

Adele smirked at the description of John's voice. "Definitely," she said. "His French isn't that much better either." She pushed off the table, getting to her feet. "I think we need to start moving through the different employees, and finding out who might hold a grudge against the Benevetis. And check and see if the Haneses have visited this resort also."

Her father nodded. "What do you want me to do?"

"Stay here, pose as a tourist. Alcohol has a way of loosening lips. Heather says you're welcome; she's going to keep your identity under wraps. If any employees come through, especially a boy named Joseph Meissner, see what they think of the Benevetis. See if you can pick up anything. Go with your gut."

"I always have."

Adele turned and headed for the door, leaving her father sitting in the Respite in the Cliffs, now officially part of the investigation.

She still had questions she wanted—*needed*—to ask him. She had memories she couldn't place. But they would have to wait.

CHAPTER FOURTEEN

A soft, grating sound of a dull blade against a whetstone. *The friend* caressed the hilt of the knife, tracing his fingers over the grooves. A well-used thing. A gift from his grandfather once upon a time. His grandfather was buried in these mountains.

The friend whistled beneath his breath, a small fire crackling across from him.

He glanced up, peering across the tops of the trees from his purchase on the hill. He knew these mountains like the back of his blade. The perfect lookout spot. The friend peered toward the resort in the distance, his eyes tracing the glass and the concrete structures set against the tall, imposing buildings.

Beyond, one of the mountain peaks dwarfed the buildings. The friend smiled, his eyes lingering on the shadows cast by the mountain, spreading over the entire resort.

The friend—that's what he considered himself. And that's what he was. A friend to the trees, to the mountains, to the creatures in the forest. A friend to the earth. A friend to the way things were, and should be.

But these folks, encased in their glass cocoons and stone structures, these people who even now, this very day, were spreading their fear across the mountains. Fear in the form of safety lights, of helicopters, of disturbances. Fear in the form of glass houses and stone siding.

The friend didn't need fear to survive. He was an ally of the mountains. But not all could be seen this way. Not all were as dedicated. And weakness...weakness wasn't to be punished, *no*. Not punished.

That was a weak-minded thought. The man placed his knife on the stone, got to his feet, and moved over to the nearest tree where he had built his shelter, hidden in the forest. He grabbed an axe leaning against a low branch, wiggled it a couple of times in his hand, and then swung, splitting a log clean in two on the first blow. He gripped the axe and hefted it, testing its weight. He would need it again soon.

No, the weak wouldn't be punished. They had to be culled. For the good of the herd. For the good of the mountains. For the good of the Alps. The man swung his axe again, splitting the standing partition of splintered wood.

He whistled and smiled to himself. Just then, the small pager, the only electronic he allowed himself, began to beep. The man's eyes narrowed in annoyance, but then he relaxed. The small beeping noise marred the trees and the snowy silence of the beautiful Alps. And yet it heralded a death knell. They were calling him into work.

He glanced toward the resort once more, his lips curling. He would be given a chance to cull the herd once more. A good shepherd. A friend. Serving the mountains, serving his species, and serving the future.

A servant's heart. He swung the axe one last time, and it split the final log with a dull *thwack!*

CHAPTER FIFTEEN

Adele watched her father shake the phone and wiggle it beneath his nose. He glared at Adele. "What am I supposed to do with this?"

She had been lost in thought, nursing a beer while sitting in the bar. The Respite in the Cliffs was opened, and now, in the glinting sun of late afternoon, had filled with customers.

There weren't as many people as before. Perhaps, she supposed, many of them were at the opening of the other resort. The sky outside was streaked with grays and cloudy wisps of fog under the sunlight.

Now, she nursed her beer and examined her father with a raised eyebrow.

"Is that my phone?" she asked, frowning. Adele had turned it on silent for the last hour. Sometimes this helped her think.

Her father nodded and shook it again. "I think it's a file? A downloadable video file in the system hardware."

Adele blinked. He was clearly trying, but it was hard not to smirk at his description of anything to do with technology.

"A video file," she said. "Who's it from?"

"It says Robert."

Instantly, some of Adele's good humor faded. "Robert sent a video?" She extended a hand, wiggling her fingers, and said, "Give it to me, please."

Her father shrugged after one long look at the phone, as if suggesting this wasn't over between them, then handed the device to his daughter.

Adele unlocked the phone with a finger pattern and scanned the message. Indeed, Robert had sent her a video. She scanned through the contents, and a small, dark scene played out before her.

Robert's voice, low, huffing as if out of breath, said, "Couldn't reach you. You didn't pick up." He emitted a coughing sound before continuing. "But you need to see this. We found this at the scene. It took a while, but the locals spotted it before cleaning and bagging."

Adele stared at the video, grazing it nearly to her nose so she could see where Robert had been pointing his camera.

"What is it?" her father demanded.

Adele saw blood streaks on a wooden floor, a dusty cabin. Support beams filled with rot. Mold along parts of the walls. A glass window shattered. But then, *there*, as Robert's hand became steady, she spotted two red fibers stuck beneath a nail slightly bent to a horseshoe angle in the wall.

The phone gave a brief view of the remains of the carnage they discovered. The medical examiner and his team had been through already, but Adele could still spot parts of blood and frozen chunks of flesh that had yet to be cleaned up.

She winced, and then Robert returned the phone's view frame back toward the two red fibers.

"Tell them to hold it still," her father demanded. "I can't see it."

Adele sighed. "It's not a call, it's just a video. This was taken an hour ago."

Her father crossed his arms and huffed, causing a portion of his walrus mustache to shudder. For her part, Adele studied the frame, paused the video, and examined the two fibers. Red: a pretty common theme in resort employees' uniforms in Germany. The same in France?

There was a crackling, staticky sound, and then Robert turned the phone to himself. Adele glimpsed John, his dark silhouette in the doorway behind the lead investigator. She then watched Robert as he smoothed his neatly trimmed mustache and smiled at her, displaying two missing teeth in the front of his mouth. "Hello, dear," said Robert. "John and I are cross-referencing employees right now between the two resorts. Just wanted to keep you apprised and up to date. We should have the full record to you sometime this evening. Let us know if there's any way we can help."

Adele heard John grunt, but the sound faded through the phone speakers. "Think it's about time she starts helping us?" John called out, crossly.

Robert smiled and gave a little wave, ignoring John's comment. "Take care, Adele." And then he clicked the phone shut.

"Well, at least they're cross-referencing common employees," said Adele's father. "Better than us, sitting here on our thumbs."

Adele raised an eyebrow at her dad, but didn't say anything. She wasn't sure if he was taking a shot at her investigative tactics, or if he was just expressing frustration in general. John and Robert had easier access to the DGSI resources than Adele had to BKA. Agent Marshall was once again back at the hotel, and Adele was running out of excuses to come see her father. She supposed eventually the cat would be out of the bag. For now, though, she was grateful to have her father incognito in the resort.

"Did you hear anything?" she said, quietly.

Her father examined her, rubbing one of his well-muscled forearms. "I heard a couple of rude comments about how I spend too much time in the bar," he said.

Adele quickly coughed, hiding a chuckle. "Anything related to the case? The Benevetis?"

Her father glanced toward the far corner of the bar, where a couple of young men were chatting up the same girl. They'd come in together from what Adele could recollect.

"Just some of the same. A few of the employees found the Italians obnoxious. The busboy, Joseph Meissner, had a particular grudge for Mr. Beneveti. Something involving a drink thrown in his face."

"Yeah, I heard that story. Think it was enough for him to go murderous?"

"Hard for me to know. The employees shelter their own. They're not particularly interested in befriending tourists. There's a clear division between us and them."

"Sounds like most establishments. Did you manage to find out anything else?"

Her father rubbed at the corner of his jaw and glanced toward the door as another couple entered the bar; the arrival announced with the tinkling of a small bell above the glass frame. He waited for them to pass and move out of earshot before continuing, "Sounds like some of the employees were fearful of the new resort that opened today. Thought it might cost them business, which could cost them their jobs."

Adele nodded. "So you think maybe they wanted to scare away customers?"

"Perhaps. Or perhaps someone from the other resort wanted to scare away customers from their competition."

Adele looked at her father and smiled. It seemed like a good thought, at first blush. And her father was often clever with his ideas. But he'd never made a very good investigator. Already, she could think of a couple of reasons why this theory wouldn't fit. For one, the bodies had been hidden, suggesting that whoever had killed the people hadn't wanted them found. The bodies in the French Alps had nearly rotted

75

before they'd been discovered. For another, neither of the families had any financial ties to the resort, so they would've been chosen at random. And so if a new resort were trying to muscle in on territory by scaring other customers, it wouldn't be smart to do it on opposite sides of the Alps, suggesting that the new resort was also a potential target. It would simply drive down business for everyone. It was a good thought, but not a complete one.

Adele nodded her gratitude to her father. "Well, just keep an ear open."

Her father sniffed and took a long drag of his own beer. "I don't have any good soup," he grumbled.

Adele frowned at her hands, gripping the brown glass. She looked up and cautiously said, "I was wondering if you remember the last time we went on a ski trip."

Her father didn't stiffen. He didn't breathe heavily. He didn't betray anything, except his eyes didn't blink. He was playing it casual, but something in his gaze suggested she had piqued his attention more than her questions normally did.

"Can't say I recall," he said.

"I remember vaguely. I actually think it was the last vacation we took as a family. Mom was there too."

Still not blinking. Still, his tone casual. "Oh? You'd think I would remember that. Strange. I'm sure it was lovely."

He returned to drinking his beer.

"Yeah, you'd think so," said Adele. "I seem to remember a lot of skiing, fires. We played by the hot tub." She waited, also not blinking, staring directly at her father's face.

"Oh," he said, hesitant. "Right, well, I guess you could be correct."

"Is that ringing any bells?"

"I suppose so. Yes. I remember. A small resort; nothing as nice as this. I think you were ten."

"Exactly. It was the last occasion we went out. I also remember other things. Arguments. I can't quite recall what."

"Well, now I think you're just failing to remember correctly," her father said. "Elise and I never had the most loving relationship. Sometimes we would argue. But nothing unusual. Don't let bad thoughts ruin a good memory."

Her father was now staring at his own beer, refusing to meet Adele's eyes.

76

Was he hiding something? It felt like he was hiding something. She thought to press on, but then, her mouth half open, she decided against it. There was no sense antagonizing him. Not yet. She was determined to get to the bottom of it, but for now, pressing him would only make him hostile.

Still, she felt like he was hiding something from her. But she couldn't quite recall what. Why?

Her father continued to drink his beer, and Adele joined him, allowing the silence to linger and spread between them.

For the next hour, they chatted vaguely, quietly, exchanging few words in the entire time. Talking with her father had never been as easy as talking with someone like Robert or even John. With Robert, she could sit by fire and immediately launch into a comfortable, cozy conversation. The warmth of the fire alone was tepid compared to the warmth from Robert himself. He was a safe presence, and had often made Adele feel welcome in his own home. She wondered why it was so hard for her father to model the same thing. They were of a similar age, after all. Robert dyed his hair, and had hair replacement. Her father was bald, with a bit of a paunch. But they still came from the same generation.

She tried not to let bitterness overtake her. One couldn't choose their family. But at the same time, as she watched her dad, she couldn't help but let niggling thoughts creep in her mind. Thoughts of her mother, without a husband, alone in France. Thoughts of her father, sulking back in Germany. Thoughts of little Adele forced to move to another country, to choose between her parents.

Just then, her phone began to ring. Adele glanced down and quickly picked it up. "Robert?"

"John," said the voice.

Adele sighed. "Why are you using Robert's number again?"

"Adele, we've been over this. Look, no time. There is a connection."

Adele paused, going stiff, one hand braced against the circular, smooth wooden table, the other gripping her phone steady, as if her life depended on it. She stared straight ahead, her eyes narrowed. Something in her posture, her tone, must've alerted her father, and he looked up as well, his nose a bit red, his eyes laden; from sleep or the beers, she couldn't tell. But now he looked alert all of a sudden, studying her.

77

"Connection?" she asked.

"An employee. A ski instructor. His name is Hans." John grunted, suppressing a small snort of laughter. "Actually, Hans. Can't make that shit up. But he was at our resort just a few days ago, but moved to yours this weekend."

Adele felt her fingers tingle where they touched the smooth surface of the device. "A shared instructor between the resorts?"

"Exactly. He's over there with you guys now."

"Are you on your way?"

"Still looking for clearance," said John. "All of this is still pretty political. Just wanted to hand it along to you. Hans Vosloo. Ski instructor. Look him up; he won't be hard to find."

Adele nodded to no one in particular. "All right, thanks."

Then, before John could do his usual disappearing act, she hung up first and allowed herself a small smile of smug satisfaction as she closed her phone and placed it in her pocket.

"What is it?" her father asked.

"A lead," she said. She glanced at the sky outside. It was still early enough in the afternoon for most skiers to get a few more trips before dark. Perhaps the ski instructors would still be active in a resort as high-end as this—there were only so many billable hours in a day.

She crossed the small room and approached the bar. "Do you know a ski instructor by the name of Hans Vosloo?" she asked, gaining the attention of the barkeep. Heather furrowed her brow, but then she tapped her teeth with a long fake fingernail. "Yes," she said, "he's not a regular. He shares time between resorts. He should be on the intermediate hill. It's behind the main resort on the cliff facing east."

"Thank you," said Adele. She turned to leave, but Heather reached out, snagging her sleeve, and tugging her gently. Adele glanced back, raising an eyebrow.

"Is Hans a suspect?" said Heather, staring at Adele.

"Maybe," she said. "We don't know yet. Nothing to suggest he's dangerous. Why?"

"No reason." Heather paused, and then, glancing at a couple of customers who were now looking in their direction curiously, she lowered her voice and said, "I know you've been looking at employees. I want you to know, I don't think any of them did it. No, I know you think of course I'd say that. They're family to me; a lot of them. Many of them have worked here for more than a decade. But I mean it.

78

You've been talking about Joseph, too. I know that. He's a good kid. All of the people here are hard workers. They're not killers."

Adele met Heather's gaze. "I hope it's true. But people aren't always what they first seem." And with that, Adele turned and left Respite in the Cliffs, moving down the steps with her father in tow.

"What now?" her father said as they stepped into the chilly evening air.

"You can't come with me," Adele replied, pausing on the middle steps and glancing back at the Sergeant framed against the exterior of the bar. "You're supposed to be incognito, remember."

"At least tell me where you're going."

"Intermediate slope, just beyond the main building. It might be closed, I don't know. But if it's open, we're looking for man named Hans. He could be our suspect."

Her father's eyes brightened, a quiet glee coming over him. He rubbed his hands together, and then seemed to realize he'd forgotten his gloves inside and quickly clasped them together for warmth. "You sure I can't come?"

"Sorry," Adele said, apologetically. She descended the remaining stairs and got into the small golf cart she'd parked on the side of the road. She waved to her father, moving back toward the main building. She would have to talk to Agent Marshall and call in the BKA for backup. Then they would make their move.

Adele could feel the thrill of the hunt, and she smiled as she drove her golf cart back along the snowy trails toward the main resort.

CHAPTER SIXTEEN

Adele glanced up the trail in the direction of the bar… just in case.

Just in case what? Adele knew her father was a stickler for the rules. He almost seemed to take a pleasure in following orders from anyone except his daughter. This was the source of her concern. If she told him to do anything, it was a coin flip whether he would do the opposite. Still, there was no sign of the Sergeant following them on the trail. Hopefully that meant he'd stayed put.

She adjusted her parka, glancing toward where Agent Marshall was muttering instructions to the other agents. Italian, Swiss, and German. Operators from more than three countries gathered together now, preparing to head up the snowy cliff of the intermediate trail to find Hans Vosloo.

The Italians from AISE, three of them, stood off from the German agents, murmuring to each other and shooting distrustful glances in Adele and Agent Marshall's direction. For her part, Adele stood with one foot on the protruding wooden step that led up to the base of the ski lift.

"Is he still up there?" Adele asked, meeting Marshall's gaze.

The young BKA agent turned away from the two other German investigators at her side. "As far as we can tell, yes. The shift manager says he goes until seven. Another hour."

Thick clouds were inserting themselves across the horizon, threatening black against the gray streaks of foggy sky. Adele could glimpse the top of the sun, over the mountains but hidden by the obscuring gray cover. The illumination cast the slopes in a lonely glow; the last vestiges of light, threatening to fade and leave them in darkness.

Most of the skiers had gone due to the change in weather, but thanks to the various floodlights set throughout the mountain, a couple of the trails would be open for another half hour.

Adele guessed the floodlights themselves were brighter than most football stadiums. The snow was illuminated with bright blue beams. Adele's eyes scanned the blue-lit slope, beneath the floodlights, up toward where she spotted small figures moving about on the intermediate trail.

One of them, the instructor Hans Vosloo, the killer? Possibly.

"We go up and get him or wait for him to come back?" Adele said.

Agent Marshall glanced up at one of the other Germans, an older woman with deep wrinkles in her skin. She murmured something beneath her breath, and Marshall said, "Might be best to go fetch him. If he spots us he might make a bid to escape. Better to get this started now than let the resort start coming around and having looky-loos. We're not exactly inconspicuous here."

Adele nodded in agreement. She glanced again over her shoulder in the direction of the bar and hesitated. For a moment, she thought she spotted a single figure moving up the trail heading in their direction. Her father? She tried to keep her temper in check. She couldn't be sure from this distance. The person moved with a strange waddling gait, though, suggesting perhaps the Sergeant wasn't as interested in staying put as Adele would've liked.

Still, she had a task before her that required complete focus. The Italian agents, at direction from Agent Marshall, moved toward the ski lift. The operator waited for instructions, and then, again at Agent Marshall's command, started up the lift once more. The Italians took the swinging seats ahead, and Adele got into the next row with Agent Marshall. The other German agents embarked the lift behind them.

The Italians, the Germans, and Adele all moved up the ski slope on the lift, passing beneath the bright, blazing blue stadium lights.

"Nonlethal," Agent Marshall called out. "Make sure to relay that to your agents, Michael."

One of the Italians shifted, glancing back at Marshall in annoyance, but then he nodded and rattled off something in Italian to his compatriots. Adele checked her own holster, making sure her weapon was tucked securely beneath the buttoned leather strap.

The cold blistered her skin as they moved higher up the slope at a slight, gentle pace. Certainly not the steepest of the ski trails. Adele regarded the many trees, the rough terrain, moving all the way up toward the peak pointing at the sky.

She felt a quiver of excitement, supplanted by a shiver of fear. Why fear?

She shifted and felt her legs dangle beneath her, protruding over the edge of the ski lift. A single metal bar had looped over their heads,

81

providing the only separation between her and a twenty-foot fall into the snow below.

She licked her lips, and stared up at the figures on the mountainside, trying to locate Hans. Eventually, the Italian agents dismounted, kicking off from the ski lift and jogging a couple of steps to clear the rotating seats. Adele braced herself, looping the metal bar back over head, and then, in tandem with Agent Marshall, also dismounted, jogging as well to avoid the next row of seats swiping past.

The top housing unit of the ski lift turned and rumbled, emitting the sounds of the engine working the rotating chairs. Adele dusted off her gloves from where they had frosted a bit gripping the metal bar. And then, once the group of German agents had exited the ski lift, they moved toward the skiers in quick motions.

For a moment, Adele wondered if perhaps they should have brought skis themselves.

"Hans Vosloo," Adele cried out, raising her Interpol badge. "We're looking for a Hans Vosloo—please announce yourself."

A few of the tourists glanced over in confusion. One figure in a blue jacket paused, staring out at them from beneath a shaded visor. The man's hands gripped the ski poles, his feet at an angle, preventing further progress down the mountain.

Adele pointed him out. "There," she said to Marshall.

Marshall stepped forward, also flashing credentials. "BKA," she called. "Mr. Vosloo, you're wanted for questioning in regard to—"

Before she could finish, the man in the blue jacket turned and propelled himself sharply down the hill, racing along the ski slope away from the agents. Adele cursed and saw a couple of the Italians reach for their weapons, but at a gesture from their leader, they went still.

"Dammit," Marshall said, "what now?"

Adele glanced toward the other skiers. For a moment, she thought to grab their equipment and race after the man. But then she glanced back toward the ski lift, and, with a slight flush to her cheeks, she shrugged and said, "I guess we go back down."

Inwardly, she was thinking how stupid it was. They hadn't left any agents at the bottom of the trail. Certainly they should have predicted this. Still, it wasn't normally in her job description to collar criminals on the side of a ski slope. She filed this information away for further use.

Adele didn't wait for the other agents before getting into one of the rotating ski chairs, and she tapped her fingers wildly against the metal bar as it descended slowly. She could see the blue figure darting past a couple of trees on the edge of the ski slope, playing it dangerous, but also gaining maximum speed. She watched as he skidded to a halt at the bottom of the slope, kicking up a cloud of ice and snow.

She looked over her shoulder, back to see Agent Marshall and the other agents reluctantly clambering back on the ski lift.

Adele felt another flash of embarrassment. She was glad her father wasn't here to witness this. How stupid could they be? He had run. Bolted. Did that mean he was guilty? Had they found their killer?

Adele tapped her fingers even more rapidly against the metal bar, feeling the quiet squish of her gloves against the firm safety feature. At last, the ski lift deposited her back at the bottom of the valley. Adele peeled off, jogging away from the lift, her hand already moving toward her weapon, but then she pulled up short. A scene confronted her.

Hans Vosloo, in his blue coat, lay unconscious on the ground.

Above him, rubbing his knuckles, her father stood, smiling down at the man he'd apparently punched.

"Dad," Adele said, incredulous.

Her father glanced over and smirked. "I think I caught him," he said. "Er…I mean, he slipped."

Adele glared at her father as he continued to rub his fingers. "You should wear gloves," she snapped as she hurried over toward the fallen form of Hans. She withdrew her cuffs, still glaring at her father, and secured Mr. Vosloo's hands behind his back. "You should get out of here," she said quietly, beneath her breath. "Before they start asking questions about you."

Her father seemed hesitant, as if unsure. "Are you upset?" he asked.

Adele just waved her hand, shooing him away. "Please, just go. You can't be here."

Her father frowned now and seemed to want to make more of it. Again, she was struck at how hard it was to get him to comply with the most basic of instructions. But before her father could speak, Agent Marshall called out behind them, and Adele turned, waving a hand. "I've got him," she said.

She glanced up, relieved to see her father finally stepping away and moving nonchalantly back in the direction of the trail leading away from the ski slopes.

Adele determinedly looked away from him, hoping to avoid drawing attention. She wasn't sure if any of the other agents had spotted what had transpired, but she hoped that in the flurry of snow, the embarrassment of the situation, and their desire to see the man caught, they wouldn't question their good fortune.

With the help of a couple of the Italians, Adele managed to lift Hans to his feet. The man was slowly starting to come to and muttered something beneath his breath. She ignored him and began to shove him along, moving him back toward the hotel.

"Do we have a conference room set up?" she asked, glancing at Marshall.

"I'll call ahead," said the younger agent. "It will be arranged."

Adele felt the prickle across her skin beginning to fade. Embarrassment, anger, and frustration left her in quiet gusts with each swallowed breath. They had found their man.

"Please," she heard him mutter, regaining his senses. "Please, this is all a mistake."

She pushed him along, guiding him firmly but carefully up the trail and back toward the hotel.

CHAPTER SEVENTEEN

The interrogation room was much nicer than any she'd used before. The conference room had a three-hundred-sixty-degree view of the forests and mountains around them. It was situated in the top of the tower at the edge of the eastern portion of the hotel. The protruding glass ceiling had walls of glass with no tint whatsoever as if, perhaps, they were out in the open—an illusion ruined only by the faintest smudges along the translucent surface. The table itself was designed for meetings of boardrooms and the like, and spanned the entire length of the room. The chairs were much more comfortable than anything Adele was accustomed to. Leather, stitched seamlessly.

Adele reclined in her seat, staring across the long table toward where the handcuffed man tried to find a comfortable purchase. His hands were cuffed still, but had been allowed in front as in these chairs there was no way to wrap his arms behind him.

Adele cleared her throat, staring at the man. "Your name?" she said.

Darkness had fallen now, and the thin veil of moonlight was seeping through the towering windows around them, illuminating the back of the man's head in a halo. Now that his visor had been removed and his hood thrown back, she realized he was quite handsome in a sun-kissed, overly tanned kind of way. The sort of good looks that came from just a little bit too much effort.

She studied the ski instructor.

At her side, Agent Marshall also clasped her hands, a single notepad in front of her, her pencil pressed to it with the name of the suspect at the top, and a couple of notes describing his demeanor and personality.

Adele tried not to glance at the parchment, but instead focused on the ski instructor. Her eyes glanced down to his blue jacket, which he'd requested they open due to the heating inside. He had a tight shirt, suggesting a strong chest and muscular arms.

For a moment, she wondered if she should be impressed her father had managed to knock this guy out.

"Your name?" she repeated.

The man shifted uncomfortably. "Shouldn't I have counsel?"

"You're not arrested for anything yet. We just want to talk. Your name came up—we were hoping you could clear up some questions."

"Questions, yes? I have one, perhaps. Why did you hit me?"

Adele felt a flush of embarrassment, and she pulled at the collar of her shirt. "I did not hit you. I'm afraid that was an overzealous guest at the hotel."

Hans frowned. "*Was glaubst du wer du bist?* I'm not accustomed to being hit by guests."

Adele shrugged. "As it is, he wasn't one of ours. I'm sorry that happened. But why did you run?"

Mr. Vosloo slouched, rubbing at his handcuffed wrists. "You still haven't said what you wanted with me," he said, sullenly.

Adele glanced to the conference room door and then back at Hans. "We're investigating the disappearance and murder of two couples. The Benevetis here, and the Haneses in France. Both in the Alps, both at resorts where you worked, both within the timeframe where you moved from one resort to the other."

Hans's cheeks reddened even more. He muttered a series of expletives beneath his breath, which would've made Adele's father bristle. For her part, she just stared at him, waiting. Clearly he was nervous, uncomfortable. Angry?

"*Was auch immer.* I knew this would occur," he said. "I knew it!"

He tried to jab a finger at her, but only managed to give himself a painful jerk across his wrists. Instead, he settled to pointing both his fingers in her direction. "*Polizei* always does this," he said. "You settle for the obvious thing. And you capture innocent folk."

"Innocent?" said Adele. "So you're innocent. Did you know the Hanes family? The Benevetis?"

The man sighed. "Look, *natürlich* I knew the Benevetis. I've been at this place a long time; they would sometimes receive lessons from me." His face flushed a bit more, and he cleared his throat. And, a bit too quickly, added, "Mrs. Beneveti had some private lessons not long ago."

He didn't add anything and was glancing his fingers as if hoping they wouldn't comment on this last part. Adele thought for a moment, but switched tack. "And the Hanes family, in France? You're an instructor at their resort too."

He shook his head firmly. "Never met them. I would tell you if I did. I told you I met the Benevetis. Why would I lie about the others—

Heinz?"

"Hanes." Adele crossed her arms, trying to gauge the man. He seemed honest in an oily, unctuous sort of way. "Of course, having ties to only one of the victims isn't nearly as alarming as both. But as I said, you're one of the only employees who has moved back and forth between both resorts."

At this, he jutted his chin out over the collar of his blue jacket. "Yes? That's because I'm the best instructor around. No, really. I once was on the Olympic team, you know."

Agent Marshall flipped through her small notepad, paused, then said, "He's right. He trained with them, at least."

"Damn right I trained with them. For years," he said, proudly. "A lot of clients at these places come because of me. So of course they want me to go from resort to resort. I'm a tourist trap." He smirked at this.

Adele cleared her throat. "All right, you still haven't explained why you ran."

His good looks seemed strained under the pressure. He rearranged his features, though, and smiled, trying to flash his teeth in a disarming way. "Like I said, there was just a miscommunication."

"No miscommunication," she said. "You ran. Why? Stop wasting my time."

He studied her a moment longer, then glanced at Marshall as if looking for a way out. But the young German agent was still scribbling notes.

He seemed off-put by her lack of attention. At last, he shook his head. "Look," he said. "This doesn't have to get out. It has nothing to do with their disappearance. But sometimes, *sometimes…*" he added, emphasizing the word, staring Adele straight in the eye, no lick of shame about him, "me and lonely wives in the slopes have our own sorts of therapy and instructional sessions. If you catch my drift."

"Good one," Agent Marshall chuckled. "Drift." She nodded to herself, smiling, and then continued to take notes.

Adele frowned. "You're telling me you sleep with some of the wealthy women?"

He shrugged. "Not a crime. They're lonely; I'm horny."

Adele stared at him. "Charming."

He smirked. "I never said it was. I'm just saying I knew you would jump to the wrong conclusions. Because—"

87

"Because you slept with Mrs. Beneveti," said Adele, "is that right?"

He stared at her. "You knew?"

She shook her head. "I do now. Why not just tell us that there? What did you think it accomplished by running?"

He glared at her. "I'm a man of passion."

Adele groaned but then covered it as a cough. "All right; so you're telling me you slept with the murdered wife. Did her husband know?"

He shook his head. "I'm very discreet."

"Yeah, you seem like it. All right, well, we'll check out your story. Is there anyone else I can verify with?"

He glared at her. "I'm not going to tell you who I've spent nights with."

Adele snorted. "Even if it gives you your freedom and avoids a couple of decades in prison?"

He looked at her again, his mouth half agape as he glanced at Marshall, as if looking for backup. Again, he received none as the young agent continued to scribble. He let out a sigh, which turned into a whimper toward the end. Finally, he began to list names, various clients over the years, that he'd slept with.

"I'll let you take those down," Adele said, patting Agent Marshall on the shoulder and then rising and moving toward the conference room door.

She felt a flash of disgust as she moved away. Another dead end. The man seemed sleazy, but trustworthy. Trustworthy enough to defend his own self-interest at least. He didn't seem the sort to kill two couples in brutal fashion. He'd be too busy admiring the reflection of his teeth in the metal ski lift seats.

No, Adele decided, this wasn't their man. Besides, he was wearing a blue jacket. She glanced at the phone where Robert had sent the video evidence. They'd found red fibers at the crime scene.

She shook her head and turned away, moving from the conference room and leaving Agent Marshall to collect the names of the various conquests Hans Vosloo claimed.

CHAPTER EIGHTEEN

Adele moved with slow steps out of the makeshift interrogation room. She heard the door swish behind her, moving on well-greased hinges. Everything in this resort was well maintained. Even the tiles beneath her feet glinted, as if polished this morning. Adele glared at the ground, hands bunched at her sides as she stalked up the long hall, moving toward the stairs at the far end of the corridor. She passed a side room labeled Rest Room A, and she spotted someone sitting in front of the TV.

She peered through the opaque glass, looking at the images shift across the television set. This only soured her mood further as she recognized the news. She leaned in closer and read the German scroll across the bottom of the screen.

The image displayed a tidy man in a neat suit speaking into a microphone in what looked like a press room. Adele frowned as she read the scroll. The Italians, by the sound of it, were condemning the investigation.

Even as she studied the screen, the images shifted to show a helicopter shot of the resort below. *This* resort.

"Shit," Adele muttered.

A German television host came on, announcing the attacks had been determined as murders. Adele swallowed. That couldn't be good.

A tourist appeared in another shot, a microphone practically shoved against her chin. The woman was shaking her head, adjusting some earmuffs as she spoke, a bit too loudly, into the microphone. *"They arrested him, right on the slopes. My ski instructor."*

Adele felt her cheeks redden even further. Another scene played across the news, this time of a couple of Swiss bureaucrats—according to the heading—also condemning the investigation by the looks of it. A disaster, travesty—the investigation was one giant mess.

And while no one singled her out specifically, the scroll across the bottom of the screen was impossible to ignore. Comments like *"failed investigation."* Or *"lack of investigative integrity."* Or *"overzealous detectives."*

89

"Investigative integrity, my ass," she grunted. Adele half turned, wanting to spite the television by showing it her back, but then she realized she recognized the person watching the screen. Her mood didn't improve.

She pushed open the glass door, pressing her hand against the cool opaque surface.

"Dad?" she said.

Her father turned away from the television, raising an eyebrow in her direction.

"What are you doing here?" she said, and then she tried again, realizing her tone sounded a bit harsh. "What are you doing here, Dad?"

He held a finger to his lips, and he pointed the same digit toward the screen.

Adele sighed, air leaking from her like from a punctured balloon. She approached the screen, and realized the study room in the hotel was just as luxurious as the rest of the resort. Thick carpet doused the sound of her footsteps. Her father's chair looked to be made of leather and was comfortable to the touch as her fingers grazed against the headrest. Next to the chair was another one, made of brown leather. Across from the chairs, beneath the TV, there was a fireplace. Except no fire. Her father hadn't turned it on.

Vaguely, Adele thought of Robert's study back in his mansion. He'd always had a fire in the hearth.

She glanced toward her father and then quietly moved over to the other chair. She sat down and cleared her throat. "Why did you leave the bar?" she said.

Her father shrugged. "Can't stay cooped up all day. I thought you wanted my help."

"I did. But you're supposed to be incognito. You're not supposed to come try to hunt down criminals with me."

Her father raised an eyebrow again. "So he was a criminal?"

Adele collapsed even further into her chair, half hoping it would consume her so she could disappear for at least a while.

"No," she said. "Nothing illegal, just sleazy."

"Why did he run?"

"Dad, it doesn't matter. You shouldn't have been there. You hit him. You're a civilian in this investigation."

Her father's nose wrinkled. "I'm not a civilian."

"No, but in this investigation you're as good as one. You don't have the jurisdiction."

Her father raised a hand, swatting away her words. "Bah," he said. "Look, Adele, I just wanted to make sure the investigation was done right."

Adele bristled at this, and at first she wasn't sure why. Perhaps it was something in his tone. Or perhaps just something from their past. They'd never been particularly good at working together, or communicating, or really anything. She glared at the side of his face. "What does that mean?"

Her dad didn't say anything, but waved a hand airily toward the TV, gesturing at the scroll across the bottom. Again, they were showing another clip of the Italian investigators condemning the investigation.

"You think I screwed this up?" she said.

"I think I was trying to stop a criminal from getting away. I did what I had to do."

"And I asked you to stay back at the bar."

"Right. And I ignored you."

"Dad!"

"You're welcome. We caught him, didn't we? If we'd done it your way, he would've gotten away. That was your choice. You needed me."

Adele stared at her father. "I didn't need you."

Now he rounded on her, shifting his bulk in his leather chair. He no longer glanced at the screen, but fixed his gaze on his daughter, his walrus mustache quivering as he set his lips into a firm line. "Oh? You're supposed to be a professional. A big shot. Right? And yet you have to call me in."

He shifted back, crossing his arms.

Adele stared at the side of her father's face, stunned. First, she wasn't sure what to say. She heard footsteps muffled behind them, drifting through the study room door. She glanced back and watched as Agent Marshall, along with another BKA operative, escorted Hans, no longer in handcuffs, toward the exit. Marshall caught Adele's eyes and nodded once at her, a note of sympathy on her face.

Adele looked away and said, "I don't need your help, Dad. I wanted to ask you some things. How come you don't remember our vacation?"

Her father crossed his arms again, and seemed to be pulling his body close, defensive. "I told you, I do remember it. Vaguely. We went on a lot of vacations."

"No, we didn't. We went on a few. And rarely did we go skiing."

Adele swallowed, allowing the memories to play across her mind's eye. She remembered the bunny trails, the skiing, the hot cocoa, the hot tub, the yelling, the fighting.

She shivered, and this time it was her turn to cross her arms and hug herself. "You and Mom would fight. Why? Something happened. I just don't remember."

"I told you, I don't remember that well. I remember the trip. But I can't remember everything about your childhood, Adele. I have a life too, you know."

"I didn't say you don't have a life. I just find it surprising you wouldn't remember is all."

Her dad turned on her again, his eyes fierce. He jabbed a thick finger toward his daughter. "Are you calling me a liar?"

In the past, Adele would back down when her father got like this. He was an intimidating man, a demanding man. Someone you shouldn't cross, and so she never had. But now, with criticisms of her job rolling across the screen, her father watching it, allowing it to loop, his hand near the remote… He could've turned it off the moment he saw her. Yet he'd left it on. As if he wanted her to see them. Wanted her to see the Italians, the Swiss, the hotel manager, everyone insulting *her* investigation. Was her father jealous? Was she just better?

Sometimes, she couldn't help but feel like she hated the man. If he wasn't so mule-headed, her mother wouldn't have left him. If he wasn't such a bad investigator, he would've solved her murder!

"Yes," Adele said, voicing the simplest of her thoughts. "Yes, I say you're lying. You know what I'm talking about. And yet for some reason you're not willing to discuss it. Why?"

In answer, her father turned the volume up on the TV, waving a hand once again toward the screen. "You think I'm a liar?" he said, his voice rising. "I'm a liar? Is that what they teach you at your fancy academies? That's why you're such a good investigator? You can't even determine the truth in front of your nose. You're the liar! You're lying to yourself!"

"That doesn't make any sense."

"You're the one who needed me here. You're lucky I came. Your suspect would've gotten away."

Adele stared at her father. "Dad, I'm a good investigator. I'm good at my job."

Her father pointed toward the screen again, as if revealing a key piece of evidence. "Oh?" he said, his voice rising. "Oh?"

He said it in such a patronizing way that Adele could feel her own anger burbling up. She wanted to control herself, and normally, when riled by suspects or colleagues, or even the unfortunate events with Agent Paige back in France, she'd managed to keep her calm, for the most part. She was good at long suffering. Yet, for some reason, her father's obstinacy, his arrogance, his seeming commitment to making Adele think she was bad at her job, boiled into something close to hatred. Years of living under him, under his stupid rules, under his obnoxious lack of emotional availability, his sheer lack of affection, came bubbling to the surface all at once. Fine, let him keep his secrets. Let him keep the memories of the last vacation together. The last time Adele remembered the three of them together, happy.

And yet the anger didn't stop there. It continued, and Adele, with a trembling voice, said, "I'm good at my job, but you sure as hell aren't! If you were a half decent investigator, you would've solved Mother's murder! She would still be alive if you could even keep a woman!"

CHAPTER NINETEEN

The words came out scathing hot, like acrid whips zapping forward. The moment she said it, she regretted it. She felt the tang of guilt peal sharply through her chest. But the anger swirled through her, the vestiges of hatred also twisted in her gut. She wanted to apologize immediately, but pride stopped the words. A look of hurt also transformed to anger on her father's face. She leaned back in her chair, wondering what he would say.

The Sergeant stared at her with angry, vengeful eyes. And then he turned the volume up on the TV, got stiffly to his feet, and marched to the door, leaving her alone, abandoning her in the dark of the room with only the loud, blaring screen of the nightly news for company.

"Typical," she shouted after him. "Just typical! Just walk away, like you always do. You're the one who refuses to have a heart! You're the one that doesn't even know how to talk!"

The door shut behind her father, and he continued to march away, disappearing down the long hall. Adele swallowed, and with a violent motion reached out, snagged the TV remote, and turned off the screen.

She leaned back in the leather chair, staring at the empty hearth. For a moment, the rage and anger continued to cycle through her. The guilt and embarrassment and shame also had their say. But as the emotions collided, filling her with anxiety, prickling her skin, they too began to fade, disappearing along with the sound of her father's footsteps.

Then, just loneliness.

Alone, in the dark study room, at the top of the tower of the resort. The screen was off now, but the words still splayed across her mind. Condemnations. Judgments. People who thought she had done a terrible job. People who wanted the resorts to function rather than find the killers. People who didn't care about justice nearly as much as they cared about checkbooks.

And yet, these things served only to rile Adele further. Maybe she was lying to herself. Maybe they had a point. Maybe she really was bad at this.

Adele's sighed, a long breath ending in a weak, soft sound like half a whimper. She wished she hadn't spoken to her father like that. She wish she hadn't lashed out.

But why should she care? He'd spent her entire childhood and much of her adulthood speaking to her, his only daughter, in much harsher terms. He had done it for her own good according to his philosophy. He wanted to toughen her up, to help her make something of herself.

And yet, Adele still felt the guilt. She knew it was wrong to have said it *how* she said it, but not *what*... No... the *what* she actually believed. In a way, in the darkest recesses of herself, she did. If her father had been better at his job, he would've found Elise's killer. If he'd been a better husband, she never would've left Germany to begin with.

Harsh, biting accusations. Yet, not entirely untrue. And still, none of that made Adele feel any better. She could feel tears leaking from the corners of her eyes, and angrily she reached up, brushing them away with the back of her hand. Her skin was rigid and rough from the cold.

She knew she was supposed to use moisturizer in the Alps, but had neglected to do so in the events of the last couple of days. There, in the dark, facing the lonely hearth, with no one for company except for her own accusing, vengeful thoughts, Adele felt small, cut off from the rest of the world.

She missed...

...what did she miss?

Her mother. She missed her mother. She missed home. She never had a home. Her mother had been her home. The one person she felt safe with. The one person who had made her feel like the world might be okay. Now, though—tortured to death. Gone. Stolen from the world.

Adele missed France. Not quite a home, but not so distant. Robert, closer than her father had ever been. And John, too.

John was a strange one. She wasn't sure why she cared about the man. He was gruff, obnoxious, unprofessional. All the things she'd been trained not to be.

And yet, she cared for him. She wasn't sure in what way. She wasn't sure how far it went. But she knew she cared for him. He was a prickly sort, dangerous. But it was in that danger that she found a modicum of comfort. A danger directed. A skill set utilized on her behalf. But more than that, fierce loyalty. A dogged, trustworthy loyalty. She remembered the sound of his shrill voice at the end of the

95

phone. Remembered all pretense of cool, all pretense of teasing, fading, when she'd been in a room with a serial killer. Her father had been defenseless, helpless. He'd been tied up. John had sprinted to his car, gotten in his vehicle, broken every speed record, and then shot the man through the window with perfect marksmanship.

John had shown up more than once. He'd always had her back.

She found her hand fumbling for her phone and pulling it out. She could still feel the wet residue of tears lacing the underside of her cheeks. She could feel her shoulders trembling, her voice cracking as she tried to murmur to herself, to calm herself.

She cycled through the numbers and found Agent Renee's. She paused, but then pushed through the defenses, pushed through to a point of vulnerability. She needed to talk to someone. Someone she knew had her back. Someone she knew cared about her, in his own way.

She dialed the number and waited expectantly. She could still feel the emotion swelling through her, and saw in that moment this was a very stupid idea. She was running low on sleep, and she had drunk one too many beers with her father back at Respite in the Cliffs. She was emotionally low—perhaps this wasn't the time to call someone. Then again, perhaps it was the perfect time. Perhaps it was her father who would wall himself off instead of deal with his emotions. And maybe that was the wrong solution. Maybe it had *always* been the wrong solution.

She allowed the phone to ring, tapping one of her feet against the carpeted floor, staring into the cold hearth.

A ring, two, three.

No answer.

She could feel a jet of rejection in her gut, a slice of fear, and further loneliness.

But then, a buzz, and a voice. "Adele?"

She swallowed, tried to speak, but found a blockage in her throat. She swallowed again, pushing back the emotions. "John?" she said.

John cleared his throat on the other end. "Yeah, I saw the news. How did the interrogation go?"

"It—fine. It wasn't him. He's a sleaze bag, not a killer."

"Oh. Well then, too bad."

"Any other connections?" she said, quickly. She'd been wanting to say something else, to ask John how he was doing. Just to speak to him

96

about something besides work. But at the last moment fear had culled her words, and she'd given in.

She felt a flash of shame. She was just as weak as her father.

"Nothing," John said. "We're still looking, but nothing's coming up. No other employees between the two resorts in that time frame. None."

"Well… that's not good. What about guests?"

"Harder to find that list. We're looking into it, trying to get the records. Gonna take some time. Robert wants to do things by the book." It sounded as if John had lowered the phone for a second, and a series of expletives filled the air, but then he lifted the phone again. "By the book is what he calls it. Waste of time is what I call it."

"Clever," said Adele.

A strange, awkward stretch of time between them. Adele wondered at his expression. Agent John Renee was a very handsome fellow. He had a scar across the underside of his chin, a burn mark that extended down to the top of his chest. He was tall, much taller than Adele even. She hated to admit it, but she missed him. She missed the easy comfort of his presence. The certainty of his presence. The knowledge that he wore his thoughts on his sleeve. He was a dangerous man. She likened him to a James Bond villain in her mind. She smiled again at the recollection. She thought of the times they'd walked into danger together, just the two of them, weapons at the ready. She thought of the way he'd rush through a hotel, charging into battle, without batting an eyelid. He hated the investigative process, but when shit hit the fan, there was no one better to have at her side.

"Are you," said John's voice, hesitant, "are you okay?"

Compassion. Shit. "Fine," she said, her voice cracking despite her best efforts. She felt a sudden flash of shame. Had he heard the crack? Did he think she was crying. She wasn't crying!

She reached up and brushed angrily at her eyes.

"Adele?"

"I'm fine," she repeated, a bit angrily this time.

"Right, okay."

"You knew it was me," she said.

"Come again?"

"When I called, you didn't ask who it was this time. You knew it was me."

John grumbled on the other end, but then reluctantly said, "I was

97

tired of your bitching. I saved your number, right."

For some reason, this cheered Adele's mood. She smiled. "You saved my number?"

"Don't make something out of it, American Princess. I just don't want you nagging me about it."

"You saved my number," she said.

"Yeah? Fine, I did. And you're calling me late at night. Do you miss me? I bet you miss me, don't you? It's fine, my dashing good looks and charm are rarely wasted on the feminine kind."

Adele wanted to respond with a scathing retort, but she found the words faded. She paused, and when John didn't receive the reaction he likely was looking for, he cleared his throat awkwardly. "Sorry, was just joking."

"I know," Adele said. "But you're right. I do miss you."

Another long stretch of silence. The shadows in the room didn't seem so intense all of a sudden. The blank glare of the empty TV screen was no longer so condemning. The empty fire didn't seem so cold. For a moment, with her phone pressed to her ear, Adele felt a shudder of warmth.

"Yeah, I wish I could be there," John said, quickly. There was a note of embarrassment to his tone, but not directed at her. Rather, his own sort of embarrassment that came from vulnerability. The sort that Adele often found herself fleeing.

"Yeah?" she said. "The DGSI still keeping tabs on you two?"

"Afraid so. They don't want to get involved. Looks like the news channels are picking it up anyway. Robert's been glued to the TV ever since. They're not being very nice."

"No," Adele said. "Not really."

"Yeah?" said John. "Well, fuck them. They don't care about what we're trying to do. They just care about their bottom line. They want to make a couple of extra bucks. So fuck 'em," he repeated.

"I wish it were that easy."

"Could be," said John. "But, yeah, I guess I forget. You actually care. That's a terrible thing sometimes, Adele."

She smiled softly at no one in particular. Allowing the warmth from the phone to heat her cheek. "I try," she said.

"Well, American Princess, hopefully we can see each other soon. Like I said, don't worry about them. They don't know what they're saying. They're not good people."

"Some of them might be," said Adele.

"*You* would think that, wouldn't you? Whatever. Call anytime; I have your number after all. I wouldn't want to waste the space."

"That's not how it works, John."

"Yeah, well, it could. Look—not to change subject, but have you considered the red nylon fibers? Any thoughts?"

Adele swallowed, grateful for something to focus on besides her own thoughts. She cleared her throat and brusquely replied. "Probably from a uniform, yes? Maybe a jacket? Are they being tested?"

"Yes, of course. We shall see... A uniform, you're probably right. Look, I'll catch you later, American Princess. I've got to go. Your old friend over here, Mr. By-the-book, wants to check out records from a library or something. Or maybe go through some shredded paper. Or some other outdated stupidness."

"Bye, John. Say hi to Robert for me."

"I'll try to get a word in edgewise; we'll see if I can manage. Bye, Adele."

The line cut off, and Adele lowered her phone. She stared into the empty fireplace and closed her eyes, breathing in and out. Much of the anger and shame from before had faded. A resolve settled on her. Not a strong, angry resolve. Nor was it a determination or sense of justice. It was a simple, isolated resolve coming purely from herself. A desire to see this through, for no other reason than she'd set out in the first place. No other reason than there were people who wanted to see her fail. Who would criticize her, constantly, for no good reason. She was tired of being criticized. Tired of letting others bully her into behaving how they wanted.

No. She would solve this case. And if it cost them their resort—on their heads be it. She would solve this case, and that was the end of that. Likely, the resorts were losing guests as it was. A murderer loose on the slopes? Not great for business. But despite this, Adele knew, in her heart of hearts, that she wouldn't let this one go. Even if Interpol pulled her off the case, she would solve it. She had to at this point.

There, alone, contemplating in the dark, memories came to her. She felt the slight tickle of a cold draft of winter air, likely creeping in through a window crack or from an partly open door down the hall. The sensation caused her to frown. Her father was still on her mind—and yet, in that moment, she pictured... another man? Someone her mother had been talking to? Adele twisted restlessly in her chair and pushed off with a vengeance, striding rapidly from the small, isolated room.

Another man? Couldn't be. But what if? Was that what she was remembering? A silhouette in the doorway, her mother greeting the person, her father out for the evening. Adele in the bathroom, peering through a crack in the door. Had her mother cheated?

She shook her head and put on an extra burst of speed, desperately trying to distance herself from the horrible thoughts.

CHAPTER TWENTY

Adele slept through the alarm for the first time in years. Morning greeted her with four missed calls and two text messages. All of them from Ms. Jayne. *Great,* Adele thought. Even her Interpol correspondent was getting in on the action. She ignored the texts and didn't return the calls.

If the agency wanted to pull her off the case for "mishandling it," as the Italians and the Germans seemed to insist, then so be it. For Adele's part, she would follow the clues where they led.

She marched along the crisscrossing wooden trail, moving up the steps to the stilted bar. The Respite in the Cliffs had a grayish pallor to it—the many glass windows tinged by the bulky clouds inserting themselves across the horizon.

Adele breathed through her nose, allowing two jets of steam to arc past her face and drift away, joining the horizon in a futile claim—the sun would have its way. And Adele would have hers. She marched up the steps and pushed open the glass door.

The small bell tinkled overhead.

Adele peered around the bar, spotted Heather, and waved. "Is he in?" she asked.

Heather, who was removing chairs from on top of tables, paused what she was doing to look back. "Mighty early for you to be out here," she said. "Don't you have more resorts to ruin?"

Adele bristled for a moment, but then realized Heather was smirking. "Been watching the news?" Adele asked, sheepishly.

Heather nodded, placing another chair on the floor and situating it around a glistening table with the resin stones. "Yeah, suppose I have," she said. "Pity that. Though I guess serves you right for clobbering Hans."

Adele quirked an eyebrow. "I didn't clobber anyone."

Heather chuckled now, the smirk turning into a good-natured grin. "Not the way he's putting it. Says you choked him out—six of you. Beat him to the ground."

"That's not what happened."

101

"Too bad." Heather snorted.

Adele raised her eyebrows.

Heather waved a dismissive hand. "Hans is a pig. Won't take no for an answer; thinks he's God's gift to women. You know the type. Every now and then, he needs a good smacking like a fish needs fins. Last time, a professional footballer found Hans was messing with his girlfriend. Threw our beloved ski instructor into the pool."

Heather smiled fondly at the memory, shaking her head side to side. After a moment, though, she cleared her throat and her wistful expression and glanced toward Adele. "Your friend, though? Gone. Checked out this morning. Made the bed, cleaned the mirrors—better than most guests."

"Gone?" Adele frowned.

"Yeah, you can check if you want. But he left. Said he was going home."

Adele passed a hand through her hair, exhaling through her nose again. The slight chill she'd let in when entering the bar seemed to take this moment to settle on her, prickling against her shoulders and cheeks.

"Right, well, thanks anyway," she said.

For a moment, Adele's hand strayed to her phone. Perhaps she should call him… apologize? But no… What was there to apologize for? She'd believed what she'd said. He'd never been as good an investigator as her. It wasn't a matter of arrogance—simply a matter of fact. Besides, he'd crossed the line. Hadn't he?

Adele nodded if only to convince herself and her hand lifted from her pocket once more. She turned, preparing to face the cold wind again, but as she did, she noticed something sitting on the edge of the bar. For the briefest moment she frowned.

She took a couple of steps toward the bar and felt Heather's eyes now on her, watching her movements.

"What are those?" Adele asked.

"Er, the brochures?"

Adele nodded, reaching out and picking up one of the leaflets from its glass cradle. She thumbed through it, a thoughtful expression crossing her face. She glanced back at the glass display case. There had to be more than ten different pamphlets—each with disparate pictures on the front displaying some sort of adventure or group of people smiling and seemingly having the time of their lives against a mountain backdrop.

Heather approached, her footsteps creaking on the wooden floors. "Excursions—off-resort activities the guests participate in, mostly," she said. "Not really my area. But we have a lot of extracurricular for those in the expeditionary spirit."

Adele examined the one brochure in her hand. Orange borders displayed a German title, which, translated, read *Rafting Wild! White Water Rafting—Family Fun!*

She placed the brochure back in the display case, still staring at the counter. "Would the resort know the itinerary of the Benevetis?"

Heather hummed in thought, but then said, "Only if they booked through the resort. And that would only be information available to the couple's concierge."

Adele turned now, fully. "You wouldn't know who that is, would you?"

Heather winced apologetically. "Afraid that's outside my sphere. But it shouldn't be too hard to find out. I'll ask around. Or, you know, you could just call the information desk."

Adele nodded, her thoughts still sputtering like facets of light in her mind, sparking each other and propelling her down rabbit trails of consideration.

"I think I just might do that," she said.

***

"And who, exactly, are you again?" the man said, stiff-backed and straight-nosed. He peered down his long Roman nose, eyeing Adele with the severest of displeasure.

"I'm Agent Sharp—I work with Interpol, and I'm investigating the murders of Mr. and Mrs. Beneveti. I was told you're their concierge."

The man sniffed, arms crossed. "So what if I am?"

Adele leaned with one arm against the doorframe to the man's small office. She'd managed to track down the concierge easily enough. Turned out, the information desk was more than helpful when faced with the threat of obstruction.

"I don't know if you can tell," he said, clearing his throat, "but I'm quite busy." He adjusted the glasses on the edge of his nose and turned back to his desk, clacking away on his keyboard once more as if Adele hadn't interrupted.

She gave him a moment, but when the concierge didn't turn to address her, she took this as permission to enter his office, striding across the room and plopping on the edge of his desk.

"Hey!" he exclaimed. "Careful—you'll wrinkle those forms!"

Adele's eyes widened, and she made a big show of tugging at the paper files she'd "accidentally" sat on. "Oh? Silly me, so sorry!"

She pulled the form from beneath her thigh and dropped it in the man's lap. It fluttered, and looped, and then veered off to land on the carpet.

The concierge stooped over the grab it. As he did, Adele quickly reached out and yanked out the display cord leading from his computer to the monitor. The man sat back up, then exclaimed again as he was confronted with a black screen.

"What are you doing!" he said. "Please, I really must insist—"

"Phil, hang on—look, can I call you Phil?"

"My name is Philip," the man said, crossly. He reluctantly looked away from the blank monitor to glare up at Adele, giving another sniff.

"Right, Philip the concierge. The concierge to Mr. and Mrs. Beneveti, am I right?"

"You still haven't said who told you that."

"No, I guess I haven't. Let's trade information. You start."

Philip sighed and pushed back a bit in his chair, distancing himself from where Adele sat on his desk. At least he was no longer ignoring her. "I don't know what you want," he said. "I told you, there's nothing in particular—"

"Phil," said Adele, "I know Mr. and Mrs. Beneveti were your clients. I know that if they booked something through the resort, it would go through you. Why waste my time and yours? You seem like a busy man. Lots of clients? Not commission based, I hope, though I wouldn't be surprised if end of the year bonuses reflected client satisfaction, am I right?"

The concierge's frown now creased the entirety of his face, casting it in shadow. "I don't know who you've been speaking too. But I hope you can see *why* it's important I don't divulge the personal details of my clients."

"Mhmm, right," said Adele, "I get it. Really, I do. The only thing here, though, is that a man as busy as you might not want to be stuck in your office all day. And, if I have to get a warrant, that's exactly what will happen. I may need you to catalog your files—all of them... from, let's say, the last decade."

"What? Why? How could that possibly help?"

"You never know. But it would take you the better part of a week, I imagine. A week without interacting with your clients. A week of diminishing satisfaction. I think we can both agree neither of us want that."

"No—no of course not. But I can't just tell you my clients'—"

Adele leaned in now, pressing hard, her eyes unblinking chips of granite as she glared at the man. "Your clients are dead. I'm not asking for anyone else's information—just Mr. and Mrs. Beneveti. I'm not asking for an address or a phone number, or the color of their lingerie. I'm asking what appointments they booked through the resort. It's that simple. Don't waste my time, and I won't waste yours."

The concierge muttered a bit, but then said, "I have a lot of clients. I need to check—is that all right? Or are you going to take to my computer with a five iron?"

"I don't play golf. Have at it." Adele reached out and plugged the cable back in.

The monitor brightened. With equal parts annoyed glances and irritated mutterings, the concierge clacked on his keyboard, cycling through a series of folders on his computer. Adele waited patiently, until, a few moments later, the concierge leaned back, releasing a sigh that seeped from his lips in a slow, leaking procession.

"Great," he said. "One appointment. Every year, the same one. I remember now."

"Oh? What one?"

For the briefest moment, Adele thought she glimpsed the flicker of something across the concierge's face. Was that more anger? No... something else... something closer to... embarrassment?

Now that she studied him, she realized his cheeks were tinged the faintest hue, and he'd crossed his arms again in a defensive posture. In fact, he didn't even want to look at the computer, his eyes darting from Adele, down to his hands and up again.

"Well?" she said. "What did they book?"

He coughed a bit into his hand. "You have to understand," he said, carefully, "we cater to a *very* wealthy clientele."

"Yeah, and I'm sure they tip well too. What's your point?"

He coughed again. "It's... I just want to say, it's not a *common* expedition. You actually won't find it in the brochures or even the hotel's website."

Adele leaned in now, a slight flicker to her pulse. The concierge was starting to sweat.

"Philip," she said. "What did they book?"

CHAPTER TWENTY ONE

John tossed and turned, pulling the covers up to his chin and squeezing the edge of his blanket in an effort to choke the fabric.

"*Merde!*" he muttered as he kicked out, trying to find a comfortable position. His eyes blinked owlishly in the dark of his own flat. Normally, he slept like a babe. Except when the memories came.

But that was what he took medicine for.

Speaking of which... John groped over the edge of the bed, fumbling a bit, then snagged a glass bottle with a makeshift stopper. From his own distillery; the best of medicine. He took a long pull, feeling it burn as the moonshine poured down his throat.

He sighed, conceding his defeat to the blankets, and to a restless night. He took another long sip—acid reflux be damned—and then corked the bottle, tossing it onto a pillow which had somehow found its way onto the floor.

He felt a glaze of sweat, and cursed at the ceiling once more. John's apartment was sparse. Of course, he knew where the three hidden firearms were around the small place. The ceiling fan above didn't work, but had a Glock 22 strapped with duct tape to the crooked blade. The electricity was spotty—half the time. This was fine, as John spent most of his nights at his makeshift pad in the basement of the DGSI, or on the job. Distractions, but welcome ones.

Why couldn't he sleep, then? Normally, the exhaustion of the day cashed its check right about now. He glanced at the red numbers of his alarm clock. Five AM. Far too early. Adele was the sort to wake up around now—a hellish thought, in John's estimate. Self-subjected torture.

The previous night, he'd spent a good amount of time talking to Adele. Maybe that had thrown his sleep pattern off. A man from his background required patterns, schedule, duties. They gave shape to the world and helped make sense of it all.

He huffed. Was he restless because of Adele? No—unlikely. He just hadn't had a good lay in a while. Been working late, working cases... In fact, his normal routine of trolling the bars for willing partners had faded somewhat in recent months.

John frowned. Why?

Adele?

Fuck that. He needed a lay—that was all. A good ol' time and some forget-me juice. Yeah, that sounded about right. And yet… somehow, this didn't arouse the feelings of satisfaction they used to. It didn't fill him with a sense of the hunt, of desire, of excitement. Why?

Same answer?

Stupid answer. She was just an American girl. A flighty Yankee as scared of commitment as he was. She couldn't stay two months in the same spot. Perhaps that's why she was on his mind so much…

John gripped his blankets again, threateningly. He'd ripped comforters for less in the past. His sleep was precious, blankets were replaceable.

Slowly, he began to drift off once more, pushing thoughts of Adele from his mind as the alcohol did its usual trick. And then… as sleep came to claim him—

Bzzz. Bzzz. Bzzz.

"*Merde!*" he shouted now. A pause, then a couple of thumps upstairs as his neighbor reacted to the noise.

"Sorry, Mrs. Mayna!" he called to the ceiling, wincing. Anyone else, he would have likely just shouted again. But Mrs. Mayna was a military mom—her son lived with her. Or, at least, what was left of him after three deployments. If anyone needed—no, *deserved*—sleep it was her.

He grabbed his phone where it still buzzed from on top of the alarm clock and chucked it, *hard*, across the room. It hit the dry wall, leaving a dent, then thudded to the wooden floor.

Bzzz. Bzzz.

John growled and threw his covers off, stomping over to the phone. He raised his foot, half prepared to smash the obnoxious thing, when he saw the name.

His foot lowered. Maybe she really was causing him to lose sleep.

American Princess, said his phone. With a sigh he dropped to a knee, picked up the device, and said, "How may I help your highness?"

After a moment, Adele replied, "What?" Her voice chirped on the other end with far more energy than anyone had a right to at this ungodly hour.

"Nothing," he said. "What is it? The case, or have you missed me?

108

What are you wearing, honey?"

"John, shut up. I need you to check on something."

"What... like now?"

"Yeah, at the resort."

"I'm not at the resort. I'm back at my apartment for the night."

"Umm... why?"

"Couldn't sleep," he said, with no inflection whatsoever.

"Oh... Yeah... Sorry. Is Robert at the resort?"

"He is. I can get there in a couple hours. What is it?"

"You sure?"

"Christ, Adele, spit it out."

"Okay, jeez—no need to bite my head off. Look, I was speaking with the concierge, and did some digging after to verify... Looks like he set up an excursion for the Benevetis."

John leaned against the wall, his eyes closed. With his toes, he snagged the pillow that had fallen from his bed and pulled it toward him, like a child seeking the comfort of a security blanket.

"Okay? What expedition?"

"That's the part that's insane," she said. "I—I still can't even believe it's a real thing."

John cracked an eye, staring into the dark illuminated only by the faint blue glow from his screen. "What is it?" he said, curiosity piqued.

"It's..." Adele stuttered. "Flat out ridiculous. But apparently something a lot of the high-end resorts offer. They keep it off books. Don't want the general public to know, but for the sweet tune of fifty thousand dollars..."

"What? They don't hunt humans, do they? I think I've seen that movie."

"No, not that," said Adele. "It's ridiculous not evil. But I need you to check if the Swiss couple booked a similar expedition. Some of these groups use outside companies for the more exclusive stuff. I want to see if there's a connection."

"Okay... what am I looking for?" John passed a hand over his face, rubbing some of the sleep from his eyes.

"Have a notepad?"

John paused, allowing enough time for her to think he'd retrieved one, but sat still, motionless. "All right, go ahead," he said. "What am I looking for?"

"The company the Benevetis booked with is called Prestige

109

Entertainment. They take clients along a lot of the resorts in the Alps. The resorts all get a cut for exclusivity."

"All right, Prestige Entertainment. You want me to see if the Swiss booked anything?"

"Yeah. Check as soon as possible."

"Adele, it's five a.m. And don't give me that bullshit about justice not sleeping or whatever. Justice might not sleep, but John does. And if he doesn't, he gets cranky and dropkicks justice across the room."

"Right, fine." It seemed as if Adele might have lowered her phone for a moment, and he heard a muffled voice mutter, "And *I'm* the princess."

"What was that?"

"Nothing," she said quickly, her voice discernible again.

"What exactly does this company offer? High-end prostitutes? Fur sweaters knitted from kittens?"

"No. It's not like that. Basically, from what the concierge tells me, the super wealthy pay the price, then are flown by helicopter to the top of an Alpine peak and served champagne and a gourmet dessert made with ice shaved right off the peak."

John blinked. "That…"

"Yeah, I know."

"Sounds *awesome*," he concluded.

Adele muttered something again, but then, louder, said, "One way to look at it. But they keep it secret. Especially with the degrading conditions of the Alps. It's not readily advertised, so you might have some trouble finding out if the Swiss booked anything."

"I'll check," said John. "I'll get back to you in the morning."

"All right, take care, John. Sorry for interrupting your sle—"

He hung up, turned off his phone, slipped it into the pillowcase, and tossed it across the room before stomping over to his bed and collapsing. Adele had been excited; it had sounded urgent.

But a couple more hours couldn't hurt anything.

***

"Sleep well?" said Robert cheerfully, standing at the bottom of the hotel steps. The tall Frenchman looked like he'd been beaten with pillows.

John growled as he adjusted his sunglasses and approached the

110

shorter man. "Fine," he muttered. "Get my text?"

"Was the taxi ride back comfortable?"

John glowered. "Since when are you so interested in my comfort? Drop it. Two hours in a taxi that smelled of leaf. It was great. Now about Adele's errand?"

Robert rocked on his heels, his hands at his side in a genteel posture. "Yes. I scheduled an appointment with the concierge. You said Adele already spoke to the one at the Wolfsschluct Resort?"

"Sounded like it. He wasn't particularly helpful. Think our guy will be different?"

Robert shrugged delicately and turned on his heel, gesturing for John to follow. "I'm afraid I don't know," he said. "Whatever the case, he's willing to meet with me."

"You? Or us?"

Robert smiled over his shoulder. "I'm sure you're welcome. But, ah, my private connections are proving useful on this case."

John's glower deepened and he followed after the smaller man up the hotel steps to meet with the French concierge.

They reached the office. "Ah, yes, hello—I do believe we have an appointment." Robert poked his head through the open doorway to peer down the hall. In Robert's estimate, the room was built like a private chapel, with stained glass windows overhead. Instead of a podium for prayer, though, there was a single desk with a man seated behind. The man looked up, smiling instantly.

He was round with dimpled cheeks and a good-natured grin which was already out in full force. The smile became somewhat brittle as it flashed from Robert to John, and he took in the two hoodies and stained pants.

"Yes, of course, yes, Mr. Henry?"

Robert nodded and approached the desk, taking a seat and gesturing John should do the same opposite the concierge. "One and the same. I hope I catch you at a good time."

"Of course, of course," said the man, nodding so hard his cheeks wobbled. "How might I serve you?"

Robert tapped a finger on the desk and said, "We're wondering about clients of yours. Mr. and Mrs. Hanes."

The man's smile not only became brittle, but fractured now. "Oh?" he said, raising an eyebrow. "And... Mr. Henry, why are you asking?"

"Hmm," said Robert, steepling his fingers. "Perhaps I wasn't so upfront on the phone. We're not actually looking to partake in an excursion. Rather, we're interested in investigating one. See, my colleague and I work for DGSI."

John and Robert, in near perfect uniformity, drew their badges and flourished their credentials. And with a similar flourish, they pocketed them once more before the concierge could take a beat. John and Robert didn't look to each other, but kept their eyes fixed on the hotel employee.

"I assure you," he said, laughing nervously, his smile entirely fixed at this point, "we are all up to date. Our tax files are readily available. There are no, ah, shenanigans on our part—I guarantee it."

"Look," John said, "we're interested in the Haneses' whereabouts. Not yours. Nor your small little racket here."

"Racket? I assure you, we're properly accredited."

"Pardon my sins while you're at it?" John muttered, glancing around at the stained glass. "This place gives me the creeps. Regardless, we're specifically interested if the Hanes couple interacted with a Prestige Entertainment."

The man stared at them now, unblinking.

Robert waited, listening, as John pressed. "A nice little excursion for the average bloke's annual salary, you can visit the top of the Alps and eat gelatin or some such nonsense. I don't rightly remember."

"I don't know of anything like that," the concierge said, hurriedly.

John's eyes narrowed. Robert leaned in, placing a soothing hand on the tall agent's leg. "You're certain? No connection at all? What about the company he mentioned?"

"Prestige Entertainment? I've heard of them. We don't work with them. And, as I'm sure you're aware, all our listed activities are available in the visitor brochures. Certainly no... helicopter trips for gelatin."

"Never said anything about a helicopter," John pointed out.

"I inferred," the concierge snapped, his eyes dull chips of granite. "I'm afraid if there's nothing else, I'm a bit busy."

Robert smiled politely. "But you said when I asked earlier you had plenty of time."

"Things change," he retorted. "Good day."

Robert sighed. "Are you certain you can't help? Two lives were lost."

"I'm certain," he snapped. "Jobs are also being lost. And the longer this foolishness goes on, the fewer clients and customers there are. People have to eat and feed their families you know?"

"Feed them gelatin," John muttered.

"I think you mean gelato," the man retorted.

Robert, though, knew defeat when he saw it. He raised his hands and got up from his seat, turning to leave. John, though, didn't move. Robert glanced back and watched as the larger man leaned across the table. He gripped the concierge's tie and gave it a little tug.

"Little crooked," he said. "There you go, I straightened it out for you."

The man squeaked in the face of the scar-faced agent. "Thank you."

"Any time." John smirked. "If you change your mind, give us a call. You have his info." Then John shoved off his chair and began stalking out of the room without a backwards glance.

Before they'd left earshot, John—loud enough for not only the concierge to hear, but anyone within a few hundred feet—said, "Bastard is lying through his Colgate teeth. I'd stake my job on it."

"There, there," Robert said, patting John on the arm.

"I don't like liars, Agent Henry. I truly don't."

Robert nodded, still patting John and leading him out of the concierge's parlor and through the hotel. "Perhaps they booked it separately, outside the resort."

"Yeah, maybe," John sniffed. "Whatever, I need a breath."

Robert paused, lowering his hand and jogging now to keep up with the tall agent. For a moment, he thought he should mention his hunch. He'd been mulling it over for the last few nights now, and was starting to see a pattern. But no—perhaps too premature. Not yet... Soon, though. Very soon. What happened next would confirm everything. Robert nodded to himself, smoothed his mustache, and strode with delicate ease after the angered Frenchman.

CHAPTER TWENTY TWO

Mr. Griezmann inhaled the new air. Air filled with possibilities, beginnings. He smiled, surveying the newest addition to the Alps. A resort with the sleekest technology, cutting-edge architecture, the most highly trained staff. He examined the many white and blue buildings above the tree line. He reached up and rubbed at a crick in his neck.

It had opened yesterday, and Mr. Griezmann had been one of the first guests through its front doors. First. It mattered. It always had, regardless of what others might say.

Even the beds were delightful; normally, this early in the morning, he'd be feeling it all up and down his right side. For now, at the very least, the expected pain was localized.

He sighed. Just another one of the small indignities that came with age. He leaned against the metal railing of the outlook in the trees, examining the ski trails beyond. Already, a dozen or so folk were making their way up the slope on the ski lift and then gliding down. The instructors would be out soon, too.

He tapped his binoculars against the metal bar, wincing again at the crick in his neck. Despite his years, the man had been an avid skier. At least, until the accident last year.

Pain. Broken bone during a ski accident of all things. His ankle had never fully healed. Now, arthritis had set in, and if he was too active, or—ironically—too passive, agony would suggest itself in his body. It never seemed to particularly mind *where* it struck. A broken ankle, and now he woke with neck pains. No rhyme or reason as far as he could see; just more humiliation. An outsider, looking in.

Bird watching took his mind off the accident. A bit. Especially *bird* watching. He examined a couple of the skiers, looking to see if the silver fox from the tango class the night before might have made it to the lift. No luck.

He rotated the binoculars toward the nearest chalet. His own chalet was hidden in a grove beneath an outcropping shelf of rock. Sometimes people left windows open. Especially at night.

Bird watching. A very distracting sport. The man smiled again, binoculars pressed to his face. Then he heard a crack.

The man would have whirled around if it didn't pain him so much. Instead, he rotated with quick shuffling steps, his head facing forward, his neck unmoving. He turned completely and frowned. Normally, no one visited the lookout spots until later in the day when the tours came around. Then again, it was hard to completely track the habits of the hotel customers in a new resort. The chalet folk liked their rest.

He glanced around the trail, his eyes skipping over the tastefully arranged stone markers and dipping past the snowy ground. The tiles themselves were heated for a mile radius all the way around the resort. Another feature—another little glory of technology. Say one thing for the younger generations, they're innovative.

The man nodded and began to turn again. Another crack. He frowned and shuffled once more.

"Hello?" he called in German, scanning the rows of trees lining the tiled trail. "Hello?" he repeated.

No answer. But a flourish. A scarf? Someone standing in the trees. He was sure he could see them.

"Hello?"

Had a bird come close? The man wouldn't deny the company. He took a couple of steps closer to the trees, peering out now. He glanced up and down the trail. Empty. No one else around. He paused for a moment, but then stepped off the trail, peering toward the scarf waving in the wind. "Can I help you?" he asked, his voice hoarse.

Then, a flurry of movement. Fast—far too fast. A person in a red jacket, rushing him.

Mr. Griezmann tried to step back but slipped on the snow; he should have stayed on the trail. But too late. He fell to the ground and felt a shock of pain where he landed, immobilizing him all up and down his side. He would be feeling it for days, weeks even. He cursed, uttering a series of obscenities that did very little to release his pent up agony and despair.

He tried to rise, but no matter how he moved, his injury made itself known, twisting his body in pain. He felt tears from the sheer agony seep down the trails of his cheeks. "Help!" he called in the direction of the scarf.

But the blur of movement was on him a second later. He reached up a hand, hopeful, seeking help.

Then he spotted the hatchet. "Wait," he said, swallowing. "No…

No!"

The hatchet glinted in the first few rays of sunshine parsing through the trees. And then it swung in a silver arc like a trout over water. The bird watcher cried out in a strangled voice. And the hatchet continued its work long after the man's suffering cries and whimpers faded to sickening silence.

CHAPTER TWENTY THREE

"Why the long face?" Agent Marshall queried, glancing up from her computer. The two agents sat once more in the conference room they'd used for the interrogation. But now, the ski instructor was gone, and a bad mood had taken his place, settling on the otherwise idyllic setting in the mountains.

Adele glared at her own computer. "I'm fine," she said, shortly. She read the address a second time, searched it, and her glare only deepened.

"What is it?" Marshall said, insistent now.

Adele swallowed her pride and looked across at the young German agent with the close-cropped hair. "It's just... This company I was looking into: Prestige Entertainment. Their given address on their website just leads to a post office the town over."

"What is this company—first I'm hearing of it."

If there was a note of reproach to her tone, she disguised it well.

"I did some digging," Adele said, abruptly. "Couldn't sleep. But whatever it is, it's clearly a dead end. I'm gonna have to spend days trying to get a warrant to figure out if these guys have an actual office or if they fly out of a local airfield. And even if I get a warrant, there's no telling they have the information I need." She paused, glancing across the desk. "Besides, the warrant itself might be difficult to get given all the commentary on the investigation."

Agent Marshall didn't reply at first but abruptly smoothed the front of her shirt. All of this, Adele suspected, was to give her time to gather her thoughts.

"If they're flying, then they have a permit. And there are few airfields nearby, but only two of them cater to helicopters that have contracts with the resorts."

Adele stared.

"I also have been doing some digging," Agent Marshall said with a smile. "I want to find out who committed these crimes just as much as you."

Adele looked over the top of her laptop lid and felt a flash of guilt.

She'd underestimated Marshall. Perhaps even thought poorly of her, suspecting the woman of being there just to keep Adele's hands tied.

"So there are only two airfields where they might fly helicopters out of?"

Marshall smiled. "Yes. They have bays there for storage and repairs. There are helicopter pads around the resorts, but these two hubs are where this company of yours will be operating from."

"Does that help us?"

Agent Marshall nodded. "It should. Give me a second."

Adele waited. Her laptop made a quiet clicking sound as she drummed against it, waiting for Marshall to look up again.

A couple of minutes passed, and then the younger agent snapped her fingers. "Prestige Entertainment?" she asked.

Adele felt her mouth dry, and she nodded once. "That's right."

"They're operating out of the Three Lake Airport. It's only twenty minutes from here. Their office," she added, raising an eyebrow, "is in the airport itself. They have some buildings behind the hangars it looks like."

Adele stared. "You're sure? That information is available?"

Agent Marshall rotated her computer, displaying an old, defunct, out of date website. At the bottom of the screen, there were various names and mastheads with company logos. But beneath them, there were also addresses.

"In case you want to file a complaint," she said. "Looks like Prestige Entertainment has been operating out of this place for nearly a decade."

"Good job," Adele said. "How long do you think it would take get a warrant?"

At this, Marshall winced. "A while. My guess, if I'm being perfectly honest with you... they'll delay any of your requests in dockets, and then kick it completely. Hide it beneath a pile of paperwork." Agent Marshall shrugged apologetically.

"It's not your fault. Fine. Well, I'm going. Are you coming?"

Agent Marshall hesitated again. She sighed. "My orders are to help solve the case, but also to report back to my supervisors. All our movements." She paused. "I won't disobey my orders. But I can't report if I don't *know* our movements." She waited, allowing Adele to fill in the blanks.

"I understand. Thank you," Adele said. She turned away from the younger agent and hurried out of the room, down the corridor, practically jogging with her jacket looped over one arm.

The Three Lakes Airport. It couldn't be hard to find. Prestige Entertainment had taken the Benevetis to one of the mountain peaks. Likely, the Swiss family had been treated to a similar expedition. They had to have been. It was the only lead left.

With a slight skip in her step, Adele circled the main atrium of the hotel below and hurried out the front. A golf cart wouldn't do this time. She would have to grab the car from where they'd parked in the overnight structure behind the resort. This would take time. Time she wasn't sure she had.

CHAPTER TWENTY FOUR

Adele tapped her fingers against the closed door. After all the time around expense and luxury, it was a bit jarring to find herself in a stuffy office building behind a loud airport. The Three Lakes Airport was larger than she'd first anticipated. She knocked again on the glass. Peeling gold letters, at least a decade old themselves, read, *Prestige Inc.*...

"Hello?" she called out, knocking on the glass a third time.

In the distance, she could hear the buzz of helicopter blades against the sky, and the whir of small biplane engines. All of this competed in volume against the ancient heating system which was running now, spitting drafts of warmth throughout the corridor—far too hot in parts but then tapering off and leaving it too cold in others.

"Hello?" Adele called again.

She heard a series of footsteps, a quiet muttered conversation, and then a click of a door being unlocked. A second later, the old office door swung in.

Adele found herself facing a woman with a pleasant haircut and a face that would've been pretty if not for the two scars along the inside of her jaw.

"Hello?" the woman said politely. To Adele's surprise, she spoke English without an accent.

"My name is Agent Sharp," Adele said, flashing her credentials. "I need to speak with the owners of Prestige Entertainment."

"Who is it, Margaret?" a voice called from inside, also in English.

Adele looked past the woman with the scars and spotted an old man, hobbling out from behind a desk, wearing a sweater with soup stains. For a moment, she felt a flash of discomfort, thinking of her own father.

"It's fine, Uncle," said the woman named Margaret. "An agent."

"A customer?" the man asked, his voice rasping.

"No," the woman said, loud this time. "An agent."

A third face popped into view from one of the back rooms. This belonged to a young man, handsome. He had large muscles, a thick

120

neck, and a shaved head. Immediately, Adele's attention directed toward him, logging him as a threat.

"That's Jeffrey," said Margaret, noticing Adele's attention. "One of our charter pilots. He's on call."

Adele nodded. "Do you have more than one pilot?"

Margaret pressed her fingers together, still standing in the doorway, not quite stepping back, nor allowing Adele further entrance into the room. "Do you have a warrant?"

"Why is an agent here?" the old man asked.

Instead of ignoring her uncle, Margaret turned back, and patiently—not with an air of patience, but actually patiently—she explained, "I'm not sure, Uncle. I'll let you know in a second."

With the same polite, patient expression, she returned her attention to Adele.

"I can get a warrant," Adele lied.

Margaret bobbed her head. "We're a small family business. Catering to a very few, choice clientele."

"Oh, I bet. I know the sorts of clients you serve."

Margaret smiled. "Uncle had a lot of connections from back in his business days."

Adele glanced toward the old man in the soup-stained sweater. "Another rich oil guy?"

"Close. Lawyer," and Margaret, with a good-natured laugh. "He made a lot of connections, though with the sorts you describe. Pleasant folk. At least, some of them. Humans are humans."

"I don't disagree. But I'm looking into a murder. Two, actually. You can't tell me if you have more than one pilot?"

"We have a few pilots, actually," and Margaret.

"This is Prestige Entertainment?" Adele peered past the woman. Inside, the office looked just as dusty and old as the door had. She wouldn't have been surprised to see typewriters instead of computers. She glanced at the name on the door again, just to make sure she had the right place.

"Yes, that's us. We keep things discreet. When clients come, we don't meet them here, obviously."

"All right," said Adele. "So you have a few pilots in your employ?"

"A few, and some tour guides, and some other entertainers."

Adele raised an eyebrow. "What sorts of entertainers?"

"I'm afraid, Agent Sharp, you might need that warrant." Margaret didn't start to shut the door, but she didn't open it fully either. It was clear she wanted Adele to leave.

But Adele couldn't. Agent Marshall had made it clear that obtaining a warrant might be impossible. Which meant Adele had to press her luck. "Look," she said, patiently, "I'm trying to do my job here. People's lives are on the line. Your clients, at least two of them, were murdered. Do you understand?"

Margaret, who seemed to have been bracing one of her hands against the door, relaxed a bit, allowing the door to swing. "Murdered? Not those two they found up at the resort?"

"One and the same. I can't help but notice that your airport is only an hour helicopter flight from the French resort too."

"More like two hours," said Margaret. "But we do serve quite a few of the resorts. Why?"

"Because another couple, the Haneses, were also murdered."

At this, Margaret pushed the door open fully. "The Haneses? So you must be with him."

"Him?" Adele asked.

"It isn't often we have two agents investigating us on the same day." Margaret sighed. "Perhaps it's best if you come in."

Still confused, Adele stepped further into the office. A second later, the muscular man at the back stepped aside, allowing a fourth figure to enter the room.

"Helicopter looks fine," this new person said in English tinged with a heavy French accent. "But I'm still going to need to see those records."

This person was taller than everyone else in the room. He was handsome, and had scars up the underside of his chin and down along his chest. Adele stared. "John?" she said.

Agent Renee pulled up. He gave a small little wave. "Adele, Fancy seeing you here." He smirked.

She tried not to betray her surprise, keeping her expression as neutral as possible. "What are you doing here?"

Margaret glanced between the two of them. "Do you know each other?"

Margaret's uncle leaned in, straining to hear, but wincing as if he were finding it difficult. The air heating vents started up again, churning and howling with rusted fans.

"Helicopter," said John. "I pressed the concierge a little bit more.

122

He mentioned this place might have more answers; told me where it was." He shrugged. "Robert wasn't there at the time. Figured I'd keep this solo."

"Yeah, same, I guess."

For a strange moment, Adele stared across at John. He stared back. She wasn't sure what she wanted to say, yet this was certainly not the time. Already, their prolonged eye contact was bordering on unprofessional, if not indecency.

She'd missed him. She knew that immediately. A weight seemed to have lifted from her shoulders, if not completely, then enough to suggest maybe he'd shouldered some of the burden. For the first time in a long time, she felt like she had backup she could actually count on. Perhaps she'd been harsh to Agent Marshall, but it wasn't the same. She had a history with John. She knew she could trust him.

"So the Hanes family chartered out of here?" she said.

John nodded. "Yup. Both families are connected. They're being a little stingy on the files. Sounds like they have three charters out already today." John nodded toward the muscled pilot that Margaret had indicated earlier.

Margaret shot a scathing look toward the man, but he just shrugged, dipped his head, then moved back to the door John had emerged from, which Adele guessed led to the hangar.

"Hang on," Adele said. "There are three charters already out? Did one of those pilots take the Benevetis and the Haneses?"

John jerked a thumb toward Margaret. "That's what I was asking. She keeps going on about a warrant."

Adele turned her full attention to Margaret once more, though she was loath to look away from John. Still, she had a job to do. "You do realize we're talking about a serial murderer here, right?"

Margaret shifted uncomfortably. "I know. But our private information is important. Our clients are very wealthy. They require confidentiality."

"You think they might also require safety?" Adele insisted. "What do you think will happen if word gets out that four of your clients were murdered in the last couple of weeks? Think that will be good for business?"

John whistled in a mock sincerity. "Don't test her, she will do it. She'll sing it from the rooftops. That crazy investigator they're going about on the news, the one who screwed everything up?" He nodded and pointed toward Adele. "That's her."

Adele had been ignoring the news as much as possible. By the sounds of things they were still going after her. No matter.

"I understand your concerns," said Margaret with a sigh. "But I can't just betray our clients' trust."

"Honorable," said John. "Well, no matter. We'll just notify the resorts, the managers, the press, that there's a killer, and they're tied to Prestige Entertainment. Won't be a big deal. I respect that you want to keep your customers' privacy. And I'll help you keep their safety too. Just let them know that taking a flight with you guys might end in their gruesome death."

John actually flipped open his phone and made as if to begin dialing numbers. Adele guessed he probably didn't have any number saved, but at the same time, his bluff seemed to work.

"No," Margaret said quickly, "hang on. Just a moment. Look, let me check. There's a chance that there was no one in common anyway. We have a lot of charters, and a lot of flights. You'd be surprised at the number of people who want to take advantage of our services."

"We're in no rush," said Adele. "Check what you have to."

Muttering to herself, Margaret moved across to a series of paper files fastened to clipboards. The woman deftly sifted through the clipboards, scanning the papers as if for some sort of marking at the top.

"Hanes and Beneveti," she said, "is that right?"

Adele nodded.

Margaret tucked her tongue inside her cheek and one of the scars looped around the bulge, giving Adele something to look at, but then she quickly glanced away in embarrassment as Margaret looked up. "Well," she said, hesitantly, "they actually did have a contact point. The pilot. He took both of them."

Adele felt her heart skip a beat. "The pilot's name?"

"Brian Wolfe," she said. "He's worked for us for three years now. A reliable employee. No complaints that we've heard. Except, well…"

She trailed off.

"Brian?" said her uncle, still leaning in to hear the conversation. He cackled. "That tree hugger? Talk your ear off about the environment if you let him." Her uncle continued to cackle and waved his hand dismissively as he turned back to a desk, and slowly, with a groan, eased himself into a chair.

Margaret winced apologetically, but nodded. "Brian is quite concerned with the environment," she said. "It's a passion of his. But he's never let it interfere with his work before."

John grunted. "You don't see the irony?" he asked.

"Of what?"

"You hire a tree hugger up in those helicopters, flying rich people to disturb the mountain peaks. Shaving ice to make desserts, drinking champagne. Helicopter setting down on cracked snow. Think Mr. Wolfe might have an issue with that?"

Margaret shook her head. "No, I don't believe he would. He's a reasonable man."

"Is he's out today?" said Adele.

Margaret glanced back at the paper clipboards, sifting through them again, then puffed a breath. "In fact, he's on a trip right now, yes."

Adele stared at John, and they both regarded the woman. "Where to?"

She seemed hesitant again, glancing toward her uncle, then at the two agents. "I really can't—"

"Look," said John. "This was the same pilot who took four murdered people on trips with your company. At this point, you should be less worried about losing clients, and more worried about spending prison time for aiding and abetting."

Margaret stiffened and gripped the clipboards with whitening fingers. She stood still, having a long look in John's direction.

Adele knew this was a bluff, but she didn't interrupt. They needed that information. Besides, John was probably right. If this pilot was the one killing the rich couples, there was no doubt that whoever he was with now could be in danger.

"Look, I can show you the coordinates. If that helps."

"Perfect," said Adele. "We need those right now."

John came in closer and peered at the extended clipboard. "Adele, what are you thinking?"

"I'm thinking," Adele said, "that the helicopter you came on was what—government?"

John nodded

"Did it come with a pilot?"

John smirked. "You're looking at him."

Adele supposed this shouldn't surprise her. John had a lot of uses, usually involving his military. "All right. Perfect. Well, do you still

125

have access to that chopper?"

"Yep. Two hangars down."

"Perfect. Down for a little trip?"

John's eyes flashed as he retrieved the paper printout of coordinates from Margaret, and his lips curled into a wolfish grin. "Would be my pleasure," he said, starting for the back door.

CHAPTER TWENTY FIVE

"Hold on, John, are you sure we're supposed to be this close to the trees?"

Adele spoke into the receiver of her headset and glanced at Agent Renee, who had settled in the pilot seat like a hand in a glove. Again, Adele wondered what exactly he had done when working for the French military.

She heard a crackle, then a static-filled voice in her own headset. "This is half the fun," he said. John's lips moved in tandem with the words, but the audio came from Adele's headphones. Much of it was lost to the loud staccato of the chopper blades against the wind.

The higher they went up, grazing the trees, following the slopes toward the nearest peak, the more Adele felt her nerves twisting in her stomach.

"Tell me again," she said, making conversation, if only to suppress the anxiety swirling in her gut. "Why is Robert not here?"

Because," John said, his hands on the helicopter's controls, his eyes fixed through the windshield, "he made me dig holes for three hours."

"What?" Adele turned, staring at John, but then just as quickly whirled back around and yelled, "Watch out!"

John just chuckled, though, and flicked the controls; the helicopter lifted, avoiding the large fir sprouting from the ground in front of them. "The coordinates are programmed," he said, "we should be there in ten minutes."

Adele nodded. Apparently, the helicopter had picked up the tourists from one of the Bavarian resorts, brought them back to the hanger, had them sign some paperwork, then set out to the nearest peak for their rendezvous with luxury.

She stared ahead, toward the soaring mountaintop ahead of her. Her eyes traced the grays and blues of rock, moving along the scattering of detritus and trees. The snowbound cliffs and jagged edges were smoothed by the white powder. Her eyes grazed the top of the mountains, where fog swirled and low clouds gathered. She wondered, vaguely, if perhaps they would be too late. What if the killer struck

127

before they could reach the couple? What if the pilot had brought them there to murder them?

"John, hurry," she said.

"First you tell me to take it slow, then you tell me to hurry," said John. "Make up your mind, woman."

Normally, Adele would've been offended by the implications of that sentence, but she was too busy staring out the windshield, watching the terrain pass by rapidly beneath them, and the mountain loomed larger as they approached.

***

John tried to hide his smile, but inwardly he was a giddy schoolboy. Adele's nerves only fueled him further. He knew he didn't have to fly this close to the trees, but her anxiety was enough to encourage him. It perhaps wasn't the nicest thing, but Adele was normally cool under pressure, and it gave him no small amount of joy to see her squirm in the seat next to him. Besides, she looked really good while doing it, all long legs and toned curves.

"John!" Adele cried.

John lazily tapped the controls, pretending he had not seen the jutting shelf of rock suddenly emerging ahead of them.

Of course, they were never in any real danger. He'd flown in much harsher conditions in desert storms with sand all around them, and no controls or gauges to help him navigate. He'd flown for years. This, in comparison, was like a walk in the park. Of course, when Adele had asked earlier, he'd mentioned he'd only been on a couple of flights. Better to keep her on the edge of her seat. It was more fun that way.

John scanned the controls, narrowing in on the GPS system and following it toward the coordinates that Margaret had provided. They loped out of the tree line and moved toward the sky, hovering near the clouds, beneath the lowest hanging fog. They were aligned with the peak now, and ahead, John spotted another helicopter, landed, blades still.

"See that?" He pointed with a gloved hand through the windshield. Adele reached out and pushed at his hand, trying to shove it back toward the controls. "That's our guy," John said, his voice crackling through the headset.

"Should we take it slow?" Adele asked. "Come up unexpected?"

128

She and John shared a look, and then they both shook their heads at once. "Doubt it," said John. "They could be in danger."

Adele just nodded and pointed as well.

He resisted the urge to reach out and shove her hand in retaliation. Instead, he flew the helicopter in. The closer they got to the target, the less he goofed around. He focused, his hands gripping the controls, making sure to move in at a slow enough pace to account for the lack of a helipad. Of course, Prestige Entertainment had been doing this trip enough that they had more than one spot cleared for landing. He chose a spot within shouting distance of the other helicopter, and brought his bird in for landing.

Below him, he spotted three figures beneath an erected tent made of fabulous colors. An older couple, leaning back in sun chairs. And a third person—approaching them from behind. John frowned, but lost sight as they descended. Slowly, he brought their helicopter down, landing on the mountain.

John didn't have time to enjoy the view of the cliffs below them, the other mountains around them, the distant signs of the city, sprawling like a small rectangle against the horizon. The fog swirled and snow turned up in white powder, kicking off the ground. As the helicopter blades whirred, the vehicle touched down with a slight bump, and Adele cursed, louder and more fervently than he'd ever heard her do before.

Trying to get a good look at the three figures, John turned off the blades, allowing them to shudder to a stop. Once they were situated, he adjusted the instruments, shut down the engines, and then kicked open the helicopter door, before dropping out into the snow. His hand was on his weapon before his feet even hit the ground. Some things just came naturally.

"Brian Wolfe?" he called out, his voice booming. His words echoed across the open space, sounding tinny and desperate in the still air. The acoustics up here were strange. He tried again. "Brian Wolfe, identify yourself!"

He spotted the old couple, blinking beneath their tarp, and then his eyes settled on the third figure he'd seen. A man. Holding a knife—approaching the old couple from behind, where they couldn't see him.

John cursed and his weapon whipped up. He bolted forward, shouting, "Put the knife down! Put it down—now!"

Adele raced after him, her footsteps crunching in the snow.

129

The man with the knife pulled up sharply, his eyes wide. The older couple sat up, jarred from their reverie.

For a moment, everyone looked around in confusion.

"John," Adele said, quickly. "Look, John… It's not him—it's not."

There was another shout, and the door to the second helicopter swung open. Another man emerged, frowning out at them. "Who are you?" called this second pilot.

The man with the knife behind the old couple paused, seemingly stunned. The two older folk were glancing back at him, seemingly unperturbed by the blade, and asking questions which John couldn't make out.

Besides the knife, the figure was holding a silver tray. On the tray rested a ladle coated in syrupy contents in a glass bowl. The knife, on closer inspection, John realized wasn't serrated, so much as pointed—like a pick.

Next to the ladle on the silver tray, John spotted two small containers of shaved ice. His eyes flicked to the small tool again—less of a weapon than an instrument on closer inspection. An ice pick? Some sort of utensil?

John's eyes flicked toward the man holding the tray and the pick. He felt even more sheepish now.

The cook? A butler or some shit? Like something out of one of those British television shows.

Across from them, beneath the small erected tent, the two older figures sat up in their sun chairs, with a small wooden table between them. The table was not made of any wood John recognized. It was far too dark, chocolate even, and looked to be handcrafted.

He stared, but continued to approach and heard the crunch of Adele's footsteps next to him.

"*Wer bist du?*" called an irritated voice in German. The man; he sat beneath the umbrella, a small glass in his hand, which he had half tilted, suspended over his chest, neither straightening nor tilting further.

Alcohol in stasis, the worst type, John thought. In French, he replied, "My name is Agent Renee, with DGSI. This is Agent Sharp," he barked, in as authoritative a voice as the acoustics of the open area would allow. "I'm here to speak with Brian Wolfe."

The third man beneath the tent, who had lowered the ice pick in favor of a silver pitcher, paused; he set the pitcher on the wooden table and frowned.

"I'm Brian," called the voice from the second helicopter. The men dropped from the pilot's seat now, approaching the confused group beneath the multicolored tent.

Adele stepped forward, and in German said, "Do you speak German?"

Brian nodded, still approaching. "French, German," he said, still with a bit of an accent, "doesn't matter. What's the meaning of this? You said DGSI?"

"Yes," said Adele. "We need to speak with you about the disappearances of Mr. and Mrs. Beneveti, and Mr. and Mrs. Hanes."

At this, the old couple in their sun chairs perked up, staring wide-eyed. Adele held out a hand, in what John assumed she meant as a calming gesture. But the old couple, with many grunts and heaves, finally managed to push out of the chairs and stood to their feet beneath the tent, huddling together. The champagne lay forgotten, resting on the dark, wooden table.

The woman hugged the side of her husband. They both wore matching red and pink overcoats and mittens. She asked a question, but John couldn't understand the words in German.

The man was shaking his head and jabbered something to Mr. Wolfe.

The pilot, in slow, careful French—for John's benefit no doubt—said, "We were told this was perfectly legal. *Perfectly* legal."

"We're not here because of this… excursion," said Adele. "We have some questions for you."

The butler, holding the silver pitcher, just looked confused.

Hesitantly, Brian approached the agents, hands where they could see them. "Fine," he said, "I'm happy to help. I remember the Benevetis. I took them up on a trip a week ago."

"Yes, and you also know they were found murdered only a few days ago?" Adele asked.

Mr. Wolfe just nodded. John couldn't tell if he looked grieved or worried at this announcement.

"And the Hanes couple," John said, "do you remember them? They disappeared a week before the Benevetis. We found them too—similar state."

Mr. Wolfe shrugged. "I'm afraid not. Could you give me some details? I do a lot of these trips. This is my third one today."

John whistled, trying not to do the math involved. $50,000 per trip,

131

multiple pilots, a few trips per day. He could only imagine the amount of money that small, dingy office was pulling in. Margaret and her uncle weren't everything they seemed.

"Look," said Adele, "would you mind coming with us?"

Brian Wolfe sighed. "Well, I have to fly them back down, would that be okay?"

Adele shared a look with John. "Actually, he can fly them down, and you can come with me."

John waited, expecting Brian to resist, to avoid, to run away. But he had no signs of a guilty man. He just looked defeated, and shrugged. More than anything, he seemed confused.

"Fine," he said. "We need to pack up, if that's okay."

John shook his head, and said, "No time. We'll send someone back for it. You need to come with us."

"John," Adele said, hesitantly.

"Come on, Mr. Wolfe, don't make this difficult," John insisted. He reached out a large hand, clapping the smaller man on the shoulder.

"John," Adele said, more insistently now. He looked over at her and raised an eyebrow. "He's not our man," Adele said, her words emphasized by a swallow.

John stared at her. "You can't possibly know that. We haven't even interrogated him."

"Not your man?" said Mr. Wolfe. "Hang on, I'm not a suspect, am I?"

John stared at him. "You're not dense, are you? Of course you're a suspect. You're the only connecting point between the two victims."

"*John*," Adele said, elongating his name to try to gain his attention again. She was staring at her phone now. John frowned again and looked over. "What?"

"It's not him," she said.

"How can you be sure?" he demanded.

"Because," Adele said, holding up her phone, "another body was found. Fresh. Couldn't have been killed more than two hours ago."

John stared at her. "Two hours?"

Adele nodded toward Mr. Wolfe. "Guess who that rules out?"

"The same MO?" John asked.

Adele sighed, scanning her phone again. "Robert just texted. Sorry," she said to Mr. Wolfe. "*Das tut mir leid!*" she repeated to the wealthy couple who were still huddled beneath the tent.

132

The man said something while shaking a fist. John, simply by the posture, guessed he was threatening to sue them. Typical.

John moved after Adele. "You're sure you don't want to question him at least?" he murmured as the snow crunched beneath their boots.

Adele kept her shoulders hunched against the wind, head down, not looking back to the strange spectacle on the alpine peak. "Does he look like a man ready to bolt?" she murmured.

John glanced back toward Mr. Wolfe, who, as before, just looked confused. "I guess not. But he was our only contact point."

"Yeah, well, we have another body."

John frowned. "Just one?"

"I'll give you the details on the way back. We need to get to that new resort." Adele promptly picked up the pace, muttering to herself as she maneuvered back along the mountaintop toward their helicopter.

John seemed caught, unsure what to do. It seemed so abrupt. He glanced at Mr. Wolfe then back at Adele.

"Stay in town," John said, jabbing a finger toward the pilot.

He raised his hands. "I live here. I own a house. I'm not going anywhere."

"Yeah?" said John. Then, because he had nothing better to add, he said, "You better not."

That would show him. His cheeks flushed with something close to embarrassment, John turned and hurried back toward the helicopter, grateful once he was back in the cabin, hidden from view. He could feel eyes burning through the glass, staring at them.

"Why didn't you check with Robert sooner?" he demanded.

Adele glared at him. "I did, just now. Why didn't you fly like a sane person?"

John turned the engines back on and waited for the whipping blades to build up speed once more. "Another body," he said. "How's that for an alibi?"

Adele glanced across John to where Mr. Wolfe was seemingly apologizing to the elderly couple, gesticulating wildly. "Pretty damn good one. If you ask me," she said.

"It could still be him," said John. "Maybe he has a partner?"

"Yeah, maybe. But the same MO and everything. Multiple pieces."

"Well," said John.

"Yeah," said Adele. "*Well*. Just get us back to the resort. Let's see if we can find anything new."

"You know what I like most about square one?" John said, grumbling as he fiddled with the instruments, preparing for their journey back.

"Pray tell," she said.

"It's just so familiar."

CHAPTER TWENTY SIX

Adele approached the crime scene nervously, trying to conceal the knots twisting in her stomach. She felt John brush against her, his two layered sweatshirts soft against her forearm. She glanced down and noticed his hand rigid as it swung stiffly at his side, his fingers twitching every time they passed his holster.

"Easy there," she said.

John ignored her, his eyes fixed on the investigators ahead of them. "Not good, Adele," he said, growling. "Another corpse. That's on us." He looked at her hard, his eyes wide. "You get that, right? This body dropped on *our* watch."

Adele set her teeth. "I don't like it any more than you," she replied, trying to suppress the sudden surge of guilt in her belly.

John just muttered in frustration and stalked ahead of her toward the scene.

Already a red and yellow caution tape line had been set up, keeping people back. Beyond, on one of the lower peaks, she spotted the new resort. Winding gray paths along the snowbound cliffs brought vehicles up to it. The buildings were constructed of modern materials and, in Adele's estimation, looked more like an airport than a vacation stop. And yet, from what she'd heard, the level of technology rivaled any of the other tourist attractions in the Alps. They boasted the latest endeavors in entertainment, with rooms equipped with virtual reality tours, and home theaters in every chalet or hotel. She spotted some buildings with staggered glass and white walls that made her think of a science fiction novel.

Parts of the buildings blended against the snowy backdrop, displaying only the blue windows as if they were hovering in the air, suspended in nothing. Spectacle aside, though, this new resort had only opened a couple of days ago. A murder on the second day would hardly be good for business.

"Looks like the rats have come for cheese," John murmured quietly.

Adele frowned and followed Agent Renee's attention. He was staring at a single van parked beyond the caution tape line on the gray road. A man with a large video camera was standing in front of a white-paneled van. In front of him, a woman with very neatly cut hair and a beaming smile was grinning into the lens while intermittently describing the scene behind her.

Adele heard: "...another murder in the Alps! Investigators continue to scramble, unable to apprehend the culprit..."

John grunted. "What's she saying?"

Adele glanced over and quickly translated the German. The tall agent's frown only deepened, and went quiet. Adele had seen him like this before; John didn't take it well when innocents were harmed on cases he worked. She felt the same surge of guilt in her gut. Another body. On their watch. She felt a lance of frustration shoot through her chest, and her eyes narrowed. They needed a clue—*something. Anything.*

Adele patted John on the back of the hand, which had flicked by his holstered weapon again.

She approached a couple of uniformed officers, and they lifted the caution tape once she flashed her credentials. Agent Beatrice Marshall was standing over in one corner of the crime scene, discussing something quietly with a man and a woman, both in suits. Adele guessed they were probably higher-ups from the BKA.

A couple of Italian agents were there, as well as a Swiss investigator she recognized from back at her resort. All of them seem to have sequestered into corners, and, to the best of their ability, seemed to be ignoring each other as they moved about the crime scene. All of them delicate, careful not to step on anything, but at the same time, Adele couldn't help but remember the phrase Ms. Jayne and Agent Grant had used back in San Francisco. *Too many cooks would spoil the broth.* Adele would be stunned if she found anything new that wasn't already trampled over. And the stakes kept getting higher. Others would die... She had to stop it—*had* to.

Still, she looked at the crime scene. The body hadn't been moved. The road, of course, was blocked by police cars, and the remains were covered in a thin, plastic material for preservation, and, Adele assumed, some modicum of decency.

She glanced at the white paneled van. They were beyond the caution tape, but still far too close. How had they caught wind of the murder so quickly? Had they been tipped off? Maybe they had arrived before the police. In which case, why were they allowed to film?

136

She supposed right now those in charge of the resorts would be doing damage control. Alienating the media, at this point, would likely cost them. The cat was out of the bag. The murders were public knowledge. Suppressing it would only look bad. Still, Adele knew in moments like these, they would need a scapegoat. She had an inkling of suspicion, which came in the form of a tingle across the back of her spine, that she know who would end up beneath the sacrificial knife.

Still, she kept her head down and her shoulders hunched as she moved across the snowy ground, looking one way and the other, her gaze sweeping like a searchlight. She tried not to focus too much on the many dismembered pieces of what had once been an old man, covered by tarp. She tried not to look at the spray of blood, at least not at first. She didn't want to miss the forest for the trees. She was looking for something else. Footprints. Something out of place.

But nothing… nothing of note—nothing *new*. Nothing unexpected. She could feel her frustration mounting. John was also off, glaring at the body—standing ominously still. The darkness in his eyes communicated a level of anger and guilt she couldn't place.

She paused for a moment, looking out across the slightly wooded area. Beyond the sparse scattering of trees, she noted a wooden platform with a railing. It overlooked a larger, denser portion of the forest, and also had a glimpse of the ski resort beyond. She smiled in the direction of the slopes, the expression coming unbidden to her lips. And just as quickly she frowned. Another source of emotion, not quite familiar, coursed through her. She shook her head, trying to distance herself from any thoughts that didn't have to do with the case. Her father, her memories, would have to wait.

"Bad business," John said quietly in French.

Adele glanced over at him. She nodded sympathetically. "He didn't have a chance."

"See anything?" John asked—there was a weight behind those words. An expectancy.

"Give me a second," said Adele.

She moved through the crime scene, trying not to brush into anyone else, or disturb their patterns either. She focused, careful, doing her best to study the ground, to study the trees. To look for anything.

She saw snow, blood, body parts. The killer had used his axe again. Or some similar weapon. She paused. Just below the caution tape on the very edge, she spotted a glint.

137

Adele hurried over and dropped to a knee, brushing aside some snow. It look like a footprint had pushed the item into the ice. She pulled forth a crushed pair of binoculars. One of the glass frames had been shattered. Part of it was bent, and the cord, which would have wrapped around someone's neck, was ripped.

She examined it for a second, looking it over, and then placed it gently on top of the snow where she'd found it. She gestured at John and pointed. With a long, loping gate, he took three strides across this crime scene toward her. "What's that?" he said.

"Binoculars," she said. "Might've been the killer's."

John looked and shrugged. "Maybe. Could've been the victim's? Could've been someone else's entirely."

"Maybe. But if it was the killer's, it could tell us he's been watching them from a distance."

She and John both shared a long look, seemingly settling on the futility of those words at the same time. The realization at how far they were from solving this weighed on Adele like a heap of bricks. With a sigh, she stood up, gesturing at the evidence team who worked for the Germans, and pointed toward the binoculars so they would bag it.

As one of the lab techs hurried over, plastic bag unraveling, gloves already affixed, she moved past them, approaching Beatrice Marshall.

The young German agent smiled at John as he approached. He smirked back, like a lion with sight of a gazelle. Marshall, though, didn't look away. She rubbed a hand through her short-cropped hair and said, in German. "Your friend is here again—pleasure to see him."

"Likewise," she said, quickly. Then, before John could interject, she said, "What do we know about the victim?"

Marshall pulled out the same notebook she'd been using when they'd interrogated the ski instructor the day before.

She cleared her throat and thumbed through the notebook until she found the relevant page. The two people in suits were now in conversation behind Marshall, occasionally shooting glances toward her and Adele. Their frowns deepened as they spotted John with his two hoodies and sweatpants.

"Well," said Marshall, mustering up some energy and pressing on, "We know his name was Damon Griezmann."

"Griezmann?" said Adele.

"What's she saying?" John asked in French.

Adele shushed him quietly, patting him on the arm like a mother

138

trying to console an unruly child in the supermarket. "Do you know anything else about him?"

Marshall nodded. *"Ja.* He was here with his girlfriend. Quite a bit younger than he was," she said. Her eyes slid to John for a moment, then back to Adele.

Adele nodded. "Was she killed too?"

"Actually," Marshall said, "it was just one body this time."

Adele glanced back to the remains. She fought the sudden urge to puke and her eyes darted toward the media team, who were filming the crime scene from a distance. She noticed two of the uniformed officers blocking the corpse from view. At least they had some sense of decorum.

"All right," said Adele, "what do you think that means? Did the killer deviate from his MO?"

Marshall shrugged. "I can't be sure. But Mr. Griezmann and his girlfriend arrived at the resort a couple days ago."

Adele's brow wrinkled. "When it opened? I thought only a select few were allowed in the day of the ribbon cutting."

"True. But I spoke to one of the managers. It sounds like some of the ground-level donors were given access a day early. Mr. Griezmann helped fund the project."

Adele whistled softly. "So, another wealthy patron? That part of the MO stayed the same."

Marshall shrugged one shoulder. "Some sort of day trader. An investor too, which, given his connection to the resort, makes some sense."

Adele nodded, studying the younger agent. "Anything else?"

"Nothing relevant. If you'd like, you can speak with Ms. Sophie."

"His girlfriend?"

"She's over there."

Adele turned, and, on the opposite side of the road, she spotted a black-windowed SUV. Two officers were standing by open doors which shielded the crime scene from view. In the shadow of the doors, Adele glimpsed a young woman with a gray blanket thrown over her shoulders, her hair disheveled. She refused look toward the crime scene, and seemed to be crying.

Adele frowned. "Why did they bring her here?"

"We didn't," Marshall said, somewhat tight-lipped. "She came on her own. We tried to keep her back, but she was starting to make a scene. Besides, someone needs to interview her anyway."

Adele sighed, passing a hand over her eyes.

"What's she saying?" John asked in French. "Adele, is she talking about me?"

Adele snorted. "Yes, John. All we're doing is talking about you. Because, of course, nothing else would matter to us at this moment." Then she stomped away, moving under the crime scene tape toward the squad car where Ms. Sophie waited, her shoulders still trembling beneath the gray blanket.

Adele raised a hand toward the officers with her. They glanced in her direction, but seemed to look *past* Adele, likely acknowledging Agent Marshall, and then—at a gesture from the BKA investigator—they stepped a bit back, bidding a quiet farewell to the grieving girlfriend and moving around the car to give privacy. The doors were still open to the SUV, providing a shield from the media, and from the crime scene.

Adele approached the young woman. As she did, she realized the vehicle was parked on a precarious section of the precipice. Just next to it, there was a platform of wood and the rail she'd spotted before. The ski slopes beyond were even closer now. The platform seemed to be some sort of lookout. This, she suspected, explained the binoculars.

Adele had never been a huge fan of heights, so she stayed a couple of paces beyond the SUV, grateful for the sheer weight of the vehicle between her and the tumble beyond.

Still, she had a job to do.

"Ms. Sophie?" Adele asked.

The woman was still trembling, a hot steaming cup of something in her hands, the gray blanket over her shoulders. She looked like someone who had nearly drowned. Or, perhaps more likely, as if she'd been interrupted mid-shower. Her disheveled hair, Adele noticed, was wet in places. Soap bubbles crusted on the side of her forehead, as if she'd forgotten to rinse her hair.

Adele tried to remain polite, professional, refusing to stare or bring any discomfort to the woman.

"Who are you?" Ms. Sophie said.

"My name is Agent Sharp," Adele replied, gently. "I'm working this case with Interpol. I'm very sorry for your loss."

The woman's face scrunched up. Adele decided she had to be extremely pretty beneath the soap and disheveled hair. She couldn't have been much older than thirty. And the victim, in his sixties, had likely enticed her with more than just his personality.

Still, that wouldn't undermine her grief.

"Are you all right?" Adele said, hesitating.

The woman began to cry. Her nose wrinkled, and tears slipped from her cheeks. She quickly reached up, brushing them away with the edge of the gray blanket. She coughed and shook her head. "I'm sorry," she said. "It's just so much."

Adele nodded sympathetically. "Yes, I understand."

John was standing behind her, and Adele could feel his presence like some sort of eclipse looming over her. He was quiet, though. She was grateful for this.

"Your boyfriend," she said, "Mr. Griezmann, he was with you this morning?"

"Fiancé."

"Excuse me?"

She coughed, her nose wrinkling again, as if a new round of sobs would emerge, but she managed to suppress it, and said, "My fiancé, not boyfriend. He proposed to me last week." Her voice was strained, stretched, a slight warble to the very edges, but she managed to keep it together.

"I'm very, very sorry," Adele said. "If there's something I could do to help, I would. And I think, though it won't bring him back, I'd like to catch who was responsible. Is there anything you can tell me about this morning that might help? When did you last see him?"

She hiccupped and took a sip from the steaming beverage in her hand, allowing the mist from the cup to waft over her face and drift past her shoulders, rising into the sky. "I," she said, trembling, "I don't know. Nothing comes to mind. It was the same every day this vacation. He liked to watch birds," she said. "He would take binoculars with him."

Adele felt a slight twist in her stomach, but kept her expression impassive, polite, listening.

"He didn't let me come with him on those excursions. Said he liked the privacy. Which is fine, because I'm not a morning person anyway. Sometimes, he would make breakfast, leave it out for me. Other times, he would refrigerate it, but leave a note so that I knew he had prepared it."

She sobbed again and passed a hand fluttering beneath her chin as if fanning herself. "He was a very kind man. A generous man."

Adele noticed the woman's earrings, both of them clearly diamonds. A thin circlet of a necklace, also studded with valuable gemstones, circled the woman's throat. She tried to suppress her more cynical thoughts. It was a bit of a cliché. A wealthy man dating someone half his age who was twice as good-looking. It was hard not to assume the motives of both parties involved. And yet, as an investigator, it was important for Adele to keep an open mind.

"So he likes to go bird watching—at what time was this?"

"Early," she said. "Very early. I don't know exactly."

"Before ten?"

The woman nodded.

"Nine?"

"I don't know."

Adele held up a hand. "No worries. I don't mean to press. Is there anything else you can tell me? That platform overlooks the ski slopes; is it possible he was using the binoculars to watch visitors ski? Was he a fan of the sport?"

"Actually, funnily enough, yes, he was. But not anymore."

Adele wrinkled her nose. "What do you mean?"

"I mean he used to ski a lot. But about a year and a half ago, he broke his ankle. It was horrible. A very bad injury. They operated on it. But he's been in pain ever since."

Adele felt a strange chill at these words. It started as goose pimples across the back of her neck, but then seemed to flush down her arms and along toward her fingertips. A strange, ominous sensation, but she couldn't quite place its source. "All right," she said. "Can you tell me what the injury was? He wasn't attacked or anything, was he?"

"No. Just some stupid skiing collision. I think he put the skis on wrong or something. I don't know exactly. All I know is he couldn't ski after that. And he's been living with a lot of pain. A lot. Sometimes he takes pills to help with the pain, but he doesn't like medication."

Adele nodded. "I'm very sorry to hear that."

"Yes, well," she said, her voice trembling, "I guess he isn't in pain anymore." And then she broke off into another burst of sobs.

The woman glanced toward the edge of the SUV door as if her eyes were seeking the crime scene for some sort of solace. Adele knew it wouldn't be wise for her to see the contents of the scene, and so she stepped a bit in front of the door, cutting off the view.

"So he went out bird watching on his own, leaving you in your chalet?"

The woman nodded.

"And this was a pretty regular routine for him?"

"He's been doing it every day this week," she said.

"All right, well; thank you for your time."

John was still standing next Adele, his arms crossed. Adele looked over at him, noticing the confused expression on his face. Though he could speak and understand English pretty well, the French agent had never picked up German. She would have to summarize for him on the way back to their vehicle. Still, they were indeed at square one. Again. The killer was out there, biding his time before striking again, but they were nowhere nearer to catching him.

Adele tried to hide her frustration, if anything, for Ms. Sophie's benefit. There was no sense in the grieving woman seeing Adele perturbed.

Still, as she turned away, she noted a glint in the trees, and then spotted the cameramen quickly approaching, having taken a mountain path. She glanced toward the white-paneled van on the other side of the crime scene, realizing the crew had followed her around. The female news anchor was with them, too, with her very neat hair and blinding smile. The smile was in full display as they approached the parked police car near the precipice.

Adele would have retreated if not for the sheer drop-off behind them, and instead, gritting her teeth, faced the media crew. "You can't be here," she said, sternly.

The woman gestured at her cameraman; his video camera blinked with a red light, completely ignoring Adele. "Were you the wife of the murdered man?" she called out, pointing toward Ms. Sophie.

Adele stepped forward. "You can't be here," she said again, forcefully.

For the first time, the woman with the smile acknowledged Adele. She sniffed. "I have permission to be here. Private resort. They want the story told as honestly as possible. I'm not disturbing the crime scene." That was said in a rehearsed, rapid way, as if her words were a weapon unsheathed; she then turned again toward the woman. "What's your name? Why was your husband killed?"

"Leave her alone," Adele said. "You're obstructing an investigation."

143

The cameraman behind the woman licked his lips nervously, and seemed to want to edge back. But the woman stared fearlessly at Adele. "I see you don't know who I am. But *you*, I know," she said.

She gestured at the camera, which now leveled on Adele, the red light blinking, glaring out at her. Adele felt a pickle up her spine again, and she felt an urge to turn and flee. But she suppressed it, glaring into the cameras and at the woman.

"You're the investigator who's been looking into the murders in the Alps, is that right?" the woman said.

Adele growled again. "You need to leave. This is an open investigation, and the crime scene boundary extends beyond this."

"The crime scene boundary is over there," the woman said, nodding toward the caution tape. "No one else has had a problem with us being here."

Adele still wasn't sure why this was, but if she had to guess, she would have supposed some political agenda. The resort owners, the wealthy donors, the many agencies likely knew the media would only make things worse if they were suppressed. But still, allowing them to harass victims, to film a dead body, to trample around a crime scene was as unprofessional as it got. Still, Adele suspected—as before—the higher-ups weren't so interested in solving the crime as much as they were concerned with image management. They needed the media on their side, so they could get support for the resort. Adele hated everything about it.

"You need to back off," she said.

The woman, though, gestured nearly imperceptibly with one of her hands behind her back, and her cameraman stepped forward, his lens glinting in the faint light above. Adele stepped back, keeping a distance between her and the ogling video recorder.

"Is it true you are no closer to solving the case than when you started?" asked the reporter. She kept her tone professional, seemingly objective, but Adele detected a malicious glint in her eye.

"Is it true there have been more than five murders? That you had another attack at a resort not fifty miles from here? Is it true you arrested and beat an innocent man? A ski instructor? Is it your habit to arrest innocent people and assault them?" rattled off the reporter as if reading from a teleprompter.

Adele could feel her blood boiling, but she knew that if she reacted it would only hurt the investigation further. So she turned to walk away.

She heard the crunch of snow as the cameraman and the woman followed.

"Hello, do you have any comment? Is it true you have nothing further on the case? That you're no closer to solving it? Is one of your own involved? Do you make a habit of assaulting civilians? Why do you think you're above the law?" the reporter asked.

At that, Adele heard a grunt, then a quiet yelp. She glanced back and stared in stunned silence.

John Renee had plucked the camera from the operator, and was now holding it in his hand. The cameraman was trying to scramble toward the tall agent, to grab back the device. The news anchor swiveled and stared. Her demeanor changed, if only imperceptibly, as she seemed to realize there was no lens on her at that moment. Some of the professional façade faded to be replaced by an angry snarl. "Give that back!" she said. "This is assault; I will press charges!"

John stared at the woman, and Adele could see the frustration over the course of the day bubbling up and simmering behind his eyes.

"John," Adele said, "careful. Don't do anything stupid."

John winked at the news reporter, and then tossed the camera over the sheer cliff. The long extension of cable attached to the cameraman's headphones snapped like elastic, yanking the headphones from the operator's head. John whistled as the device plummeted far, far below into the precipice.

The cameraman yelled in horror and swiped helplessly at the air. "How dare you!" Adele felt her stomach sink.

"Whoops," said John.

"Oh no, John," Adele muttered, beneath her breath.

The cameraman was leaning on the railing, pointing through the trees, trying to locate the expensive recording equipment. The news anchor was shouting at John, but also fishing her phone out of her pocket, desperately, with fingers trembling with rage, trying to dial a number.

For his part, John ignored all of them and approached the car door with the woman in the gray blanket. He said something quietly to her, but it was clear she couldn't understand his accent. Then, gently, he gestured toward the front seat and raised an eyebrow.

Still trembling, she shook her head. John nodded as if an understanding, and then jerked his head toward the other side of the path, in the direction of the chalets. The woman looked him in the eyes, and then, quietly, she allowed him to guide her away from the scene, down the trail.

John didn't touch her, but he stood protectively between her and the rest of them, guiding her along the trail in the direction of the chalets. He moved away from the crime scene, away from the irate camera crewman, and away from a stunned Adele.

Adele didn't even want to think what the nightly news would play on repeat now. *Rogue agent attacks cameramen. Interpol correspondent continues to botch the operation.* The headlines were clear enough in her mind.

One thing was for sure, she needed to get John out of here before this became a bigger deal. She watched the tall agent escort the grieving woman away from the scene and away from her dead fiancé.

CHAPTER TWENTY SEVEN

"What did they say?" Adele asked, staring at her partner.

John shrugged, massaging the bridge of his nose. "Nothing. Said there'd be a review of my conduct. It's nothing."

Adele looked at him hard. "They're not pulling you off the case?"

John raised an eyebrow at her. "You would miss me if they did that."

"Not sure I'd miss the smart ass comments," she said.

The two of them sat in the third victim's chalet. Miss Sophie was upstairs, and Adele could hear the shower running as she rinsed out the soap from her hair. John had escorted her back, and Adele had followed. She'd asked if they would be willing to stay.

The chalet was large, luxurious, comfortable. Adele had wanted to refuse, but she'd seen the state of the woman. The trembling, the fear. She'd asked them to stay, to look out for her. Adele and John had needed a place to regroup anyway. So Adele had agreed, reluctantly, to keep an eye out for the next few hours, to give the woman upstairs a chance to recoup her senses, to calm down.

Also, it gave John and Adele a place to hide out while the media went into a frenzy. Adele was already getting notifications on her phone, but she had turned them off an hour ago. Now, they sat in the confines of the cozy living room of the chalet. The entire west wall was just glass, displaying picturesque scenery of the resort and mountains around them.

Still, Adele couldn't believe John had thrown the camera off the cliff. Well, perhaps that wasn't right. She *could* believe it. In fact, if she'd had her wits about her, she would've predicted it.

"They're going to review you back at the DGSI?" she said.

John snorted. "I've done worse, and they've given me a slap on the wrist. Besides, that cameraman was an asshole."

"True, but you can't just throw their possessions *off a cliff*."

He frowned at her. "Whatever, American Princess. Let's move on. We're laying low, just like you wanted. What next?"

Adele sighed through her nose, trying to readjust. John's decisions were his decisions. In a small, quiet, deeply hidden part of her, she was grateful he had reacted as he did. Some people were the sort to secretly resent the media, but feel their hands were tied. That's how Adele felt. But John was a man of action… rash, stupid action.

"Fine," she said. "Who do you think it could be? All of the victims were wealthy. But not all of them were couples. All of them were at resorts, but they were different resorts separated by a couple hundred miles. The only employee connection we found was a dead end."

"Corporate assassination?" John asked. He quirked an eyebrow. "They all had money. From what we know, Mr. Griezmann," he lowered his voice, and his eyes darted toward the staircase leading upstairs, "had money in this resort itself."

"It's possible. But he also retired. He used to make money day trading, but why would that piss anyone off? And even if it had, he doesn't have his fingers in any pie really. He has a company do the investing for him."

John sighed. "You think there's a personal connection we're missing?"

Adele and John regarded each other across the small coffee table in the shape of a tree stump. John had his hands clasped behind his head, and had taken off his shoes, placing his feet on the edge of the couch. Adele sat primly, carefully, her feet on the floor, one leg crossed daintily over the other, her eyes narrowed in thought.

"It would take too long to delve further into their histories," said John. "Besides, they were wealthy. As in super wealthy. No one hides skeletons better in their closets."

Adele snorted, but didn't disagree. "Seems like the killer is escalating," she said. "The murders are becoming more rapid, just as violent as before. I don't think we have time before he hits again."

John rubbed his jaw, brushing at the stubble and frowning in thought. "Well, we can ask your old mentor to see if he can find any more leads," said John. "Besides, the parameters are wider now."

Adele frowned. "How so?"

"We thought the only victims were at the two resorts. But this new one adds a new parameter to the possible connections. It might turn something up we didn't think of at first."

Adele shrugged one shoulder. "It's worth a shot. I'll give him a call."

"Read that name to me again," Adele said, sharply.

She and John were still at the new resort. They had relocated to a small café, a mile's walk from the residential part of the resort. She and John were staring across a strangely shaped white table. Again, Adele was reminded of a science fiction book. There were so many white lights and marble counters and black-and-white walls around them. There were other tourists here too, but the lull of the customers' conversation was quiet, hushed.

John was staring at his phone and read the name Robert had come up with back at the DGSI.

"Joseph Meissner," John repeated. He frowned. "Why? Has that name come up for you?"

Adele blinked. She couldn't believe it. She hadn't followed up with Joseph. But it had been the same person, the valet, who the Benevetis had a falling out with.

"Explain to me again how we missed him the first time," asked Adele

"Because," said John, "he doesn't *work* where my couple were murdered. But he has family in the French mountains. His grandmother actually. He stays with her during the summers but will visit every couple of weekends as well."

John continued to scroll through the information Robert had sent them. Adele tapped her fingers against the cold marble of the table between them. She could smell the faint odor of greasy food and alcohol. "He has a family member where the Swiss victims were killed?" she asked.

John nodded. "And he works at the Bavarian resort. The one where the Benevetis were killed."

Adele's expression grew troubled. "Yeah, his name came up. He had a falling out with them. Something about bringing the wrong drink to her room. Mrs. Beneveti tried to have him fired. By the sound of things they cut back his hours."

John nodded, stroking his chin. "Well, it looks like he made up for those hours. And guess what else: he now works *here*. Part time, but he's a valet."

Adele could feel her stomach twist. "So Joseph Meissner has family where the Swiss couple were killed, worked where the Benevetis were killed, and was recently employed here, where Mr. Griezmann was murdered. And we know, at least in one case, he had a severe falling out with the victims."

She shook her head. A nineteen-year-old could kill someone just as easily as anyone else. She'd been blind.

John scraped a thumb sharply along the underside of his jaw. "We need to find exactly where he's working. We could check with any of the valet services."

Adele paused. "It's not a bad idea, but actually, I have another one."

John angled an eyebrow as Adele fished her phone from her pocket, dialed a number, and raised it to her ear. She waited for the buzz, and then a quiet voice answered. "Respite in the Cliffs, how may I help you?"

"Heather?" Adele replied.

A lengthy silence. And then, "Who is this?"

"It's Agent Sharp. Adele. I have a question for you."

Adele heard the barkeep swallow on the other end. "I held my end of the bargain," Heather said. "I hope you're holding yours."

Adele winced, but said, "I'm doing my best to keep the employees out of it. But I have to be honest, we're looking at Joseph; do you know where he is?"

John was staring at her across the table, his eyebrows high on his forehead. Adele kept her voice low, trying to avoid attention from the tourists around her. Her nose wrinkled a bit at the smells and the odors of the fast food. She tried to glance out the windows toward glimpses of the trails and ski slopes beyond.

"I can't say I know where he is," said Heather, quietly.

"What do you mean? You *can't* or you don't know?"

"I mean, that he was actually supposed to show up for work tonight, but didn't."

Adele felt her pulse quicken as she stared across the table at John. He seemed to notice a shift in her demeanor, and watched her carefully. "Do you have any idea where he might be?" she asked.

"Joseph's a good kid, hear me? But..." A hesitant swallow. "Joseph wasn't in trouble with the Benevetis just for bringing the wrong drink. He has sticky fingers."

"Come again?"

"Mr. Beneveti found him going through his wife's purse. That's when he threw the drink on him. That's when they complained, and

150

tried to get him fired. Of course, the resort was starved for personnel. They cut back Joseph's hours, though. He lost a big chunk of time. He had a week where he wasn't even working."

"Joseph was stealing from your customers?"

For a moment, Adele thought she'd lost the connection. But then she heard a clink of glasses, a grunt from someone, likely a client calling for Heather's attention.

"Look, I have to go."

Before Adele could say anything else, she heard the dial tone.

"Well?" John asked. "What was that about?"

Adele pushed away from the table and grabbed John by the arm, tugging him toward the door. "Joseph Meissner—I think he's our guy."

"And where is he?"

Adele paused, blinking owlishly as if trying to piece it all together. "I think… He didn't show up for work… And he was caught stealing from the first victims—the Benevetis… I think…" Adele exhaled softly. "It's just a hunch… but people like Joseph don't change their stripes."

"Where, Adele?"

"I think he's going to rob Ms. Sophie's chalet."

John stared at Adele, and then the two of them hurried out the door, breaking into a jog. They were only a mile from the residential area of the resort. But a mile without a vehicle would take time. Quietly, with huffing breaths, Adele and John jogged, hurrying up the heated tile trails, moving through the darkening resort beneath a bleak sky as they raced back toward the chalet of Mr. Griezmann and Ms. Sophie.

CHAPTER TWENTY EIGHT

A faint orange light glinted from the window on the second floor. John nodded toward it. "Ms. Sophie," he said, quietly.

Adele nodded just as quietly.

They were on the porch, listening. Their hands on their weapons, eyes peeled.

"See any sign of forced entry?" Adele asked, her voice barely a whisper.

John scanned the sliding glass door and shook his head. His gaze flicked back up toward the orange glow from the window above. "Ms. Sophie?" he called, his deep voice booming.

No reply.

"Think she went to sleep?" Adele asked.

John glanced at the dipping sun in the late afternoon sky. "Too early, don't you think?"

"She's been through a lot."

John raised his voice again. "Ms. Sophie!" His voice echoed with concern. Adele couldn't shake the look of guilt and fury he'd had in his eyes at the discovery of the fifth victim. *On our watch.* He'd kept repeating that phrase. Adele wouldn't let the suspect get away this time, though.

If this valet, this Joseph Meissner, was as much of an opportunist as everyone seemed to think, he would be here."

"Are you sure that—"

Before John could finish his sentence, Adele thought she heard a sound of scuffling in the darkness. She held out a hand, quickly pressing it against John's chest across the patio furniture. They both waited in the dark, staring through the sliding glass door.

"He's in the bloody house," John said, suddenly. The tall agent stepped forward, pressing his eyes against the glass, and then cursed.

"What?" Adele implored.

But John ignored her and broke into a jog, racing around the side of the house toward a basement window. "A-ha!" he crowed.

Adele spotted a smashed window, small blue pieces of glass

152

scattered across a concrete divider. The ground-level window had a thick white sweater thrown over the glass, and the opening was wide enough for a small person to enter.

Another sound, this one from behind.

Adele whirled around, gun in her hand now. Two glinting eyes appeared between trees. A raccoon. Adele relaxed a bit.

"Come on," she said, quietly. "He's in there."

John nodded, put a finger to his lips.

More shuffling from inside, and then a black bag was tossed through the window.

Adele and John both stared. The bag sat on top of the pieces of crumbled glass. Then a pale hand extended through the window as well.

Adele heard soft muttering, a few curses in German, and then a face began to appear. The moment the face spotted the two of them staring down, it screamed, pushed off, and tried to bolt. But John was quicker. The big Frenchman roared, grabbed the person by the still extended arm, and dragged them, bodily, with muscles heaving, through the open window.

"Gah!" the person screamed in German. "Help! Stop! The glass— damn it!"

Adele pressed against the wooden structure of the chalet, beneath the blue glass terrace above, and kicked out, shoving the person to the side with fewer shards of scattered glass. Most of the glass had fallen into the room below, but some of the larger, jagged pieces were on the ground, suggesting this perhaps wasn't the home invader's first trip.

The person was still squawking and waving his arms desperately.

"Hold still!" John demanded in French. "Stop it!"

But the person kicked and there was a loud clatter as a garbage can toppled over. There, gasping on the ground, still gripped by John's oppressive grasp, was a slight, thin, wiry youth. Now that the garbage can had toppled, Adele had a better view of the trails behind the chalet. A stone's throw away, behind the house, on a park trail, Adele spotted a rusted out jalopy with the headlights off, but by the sound of things, the engine was still rumbling.

The wiry, thin person pushed to a sitting position, trying to reclaim their wrist—but John refused to let go. The youth kept cursing to themselves in German. He paused, though, noticing Adele and John staring at him.

For a moment, he stiffened, blinking in the dark. Adele noticed his dash of dirty yellow hair.

He had a slight stubble, but not like John's, rather more like the peach fuzz of a youth trying to grow his first beard. He had some acne marks up and down the side of his face, and in one hand, he held a hammer, and the other gripped the small bag that had preceded him through the window.

"That's him," John said, snarling. "What did you do to Ms. Sophie? Here to finish her off? You bastard!" John shook him, hard, and the boy protested in pain.

Recognizing him from the pictures, Adele called out in German, "Joseph Meissner, stop struggling—now!"

Despite the weapons rising to attention, the boy got one look at them, and tried to reach his feet and sprint away. But John snarled like a wounded bear and yanked the boy back to the ground. "Sit!" he roared.

"Get off me!" Joseph shouted in German. "Help! Rape! Fire!"

"Shut up," John said in French. "I'm DGSI."

"It's a French maniac!" Joseph screamed in German. "Help!"

John shook the boy. "Stop it," he snapped. "Speak French."

Adele remembered Joseph had a grandmother near the French Alps. Sheepishly, the young, wiry boy stopped moving; he sat gasping with John still half on his chest, a knee holding him down.

"Hey, hey, wait," he said, "I was just here to collect the garbage and—"

"Shut up," John said. He grabbed Joseph's hand and ripped something from it before dangling it in front of the boy's nose. "You don't think I know a bump key when I see one? The hammer too? You were on a break-in. *Thief.* What did you do to Ms. Sophie!"

"It's not what you think," said the boy, shaking his head wildly from side to side.

Adele came over, her handcuffs ready. With John's help, she cuffed the boy and then sat him up, pushing him against the chalet's wooden wall. John stared down at him.

"I've been wanting to talk to you for a while," Adele said, coldly. "Why did you bolt?"

"Why do you think?" Joseph Smith snapped and spat off to the side. "A rhinoceros just tackled me. If you really are law enforcement, I will sue!"

154

He had a sullen, petulant way about him, which immediately made Adele dislike him. At the same time, she remembered her promise to Heather. To do right by the employees. And so, she stifled any retort, and in an even tone, in the darkness surrounded by the orange glow from the chalets, she said, "We're not here to hurt you. We need to know a couple of things. John," said Adele, "would you mind checking his car?"

"I'm going to check on Ms. Sophie first," John growled. "Then I'll check the car. Do you have him?" He prodded the boy with his foot.

Adele nodded and watched as John broke into a jog, around the house again, back toward the front of the chalet. Adele heard loud knocking of a fist against glass. More knocking, then, the creak of stairs, and the sound of movement from within the chalet.

Someone was still alive within the house. Ms. Sophie? Most likely. Adele felt a flush of relief, and released a breath she hadn't realized she'd been holding. "You are Joseph Meissner?" she said.

"What of it?" the valet retorted.

"You probably know why you're here, then," she said.

He jabbed his chin at her and shook his head. "It's nothing," he said. "Like I said, I was just going to go through some trash. Rich people around here always throw out interesting things. There's no crime against it."

"Actually, there is. Not just trespassing, but theft. You're not allowed to go through people's trash cans on private property. But besides that, you weren't here for trash, were you?"

Adele stood across from the suspect; the afternoon faded to evening, leaving them beneath dark skies with the glow from the chalets behind them, and a crackling fire from one of the neighbors' homes.

"I don't know what you're on about," said Joseph.

"You had a falling out with the Benevetis. In fact, some of your coworkers seem to think you had something against the wealthy. I spoke with some other employees at Respite in the Cliffs. By the sounds of things, you didn't particularly like the clients."

Joseph snorted. "Rich fat cats, so what? No one likes them."

Adele nodded, putting her hands in her pockets and staring at the handcuffed boy. He wasn't quite looking at her, but seemed to look askance every which way, as if trying to plot an escape through the trees.

155

"Look, I'm trying to help you. Heather put in a good word for you, more than once. But I need to know where you were six days ago."

For the first time, he looked straight at her, blinking. "Six days ago? Nowhere. My hours were cut short; didn't Heather tell you that? Seems like she liked talking a lot."

Adele frowned but covered and said, "That was part of your hour shortage after the Benevetis? I heard you were caught rooting through some of their stuff? In fact, we looked you up. You had a few incidences of petty theft before your time at the resorts. Is that right?"

He snorted. "It was nothing. Just shoplifting for fun."

"Yes, fun. But with the Benevetis it wasn't so fun, was it? Your hours were cut; you spent an entire week without working."

Joseph Meissner fidgeted his shoulders almost as if he were trying to cross his arms, but then winced as if he realized his hands were still cuffed. He grunted and said, "Look, I don't have anything to say. Six days ago I wasn't working. I was with some friends; we were lighting up behind an old abandoned supermarket. Hell, I can show you the cigarette butts if you want. Why?"

Adele stared at him. "Friends? What were their names?"

"I don't remember," he retorted.

"So you don't have an alibi."

He blinked. "Why would I need an alibi?"

"Because, Joseph," she said, "Mr. and Mrs. Hanes, I'm sure you're aware, were murdered six days ago. A day after that, the Benevetis were found, also killed." He stared at her now, as if seeing a ghost. "I looked into it," said Adele. "You weren't working when they went missing either."

"I," he stammered, "I-I didn't hurt them. I didn't like them. Why would I kill them? I'm not insane!"

Adele nodded. "And yet here you are," she said. "Trying to rob another murdered *fat cat*—as you put it. You had motive, opportunity, and association."

Each word landed like a hammer blow. And now, some of the petulance and resentment seemed to fade from Joseph's face. He was shaking his head wildly, side to side. "Please," he said. "You've got it all wrong. I didn't kill anybody."

"I'd like to believe that," said Adele.

"Look," he said. "I was approached by that fat man who works for you. I told him. So I was late here; I wanted to get here an hour ago."

156

He cursed a couple of times, shaking his head. "But I would've if fatty hadn't detained me."

Adele frowned. She thought of the other agents working the case, but couldn't determine anyone who fit that description. "Someone spoke to you? About what?"

He waved his hand dismissively. "The same crazy shit. Killings and murders. I had nothing to do with it."

"And yet you're here. At a murdered man's house to rob it."

"I wasn't—"

"If you say anything about going through the trash again, I'll slap you silly."

"Fine, look, I like to borrow things. Sometimes. For long periods of time, maybe forget to give it back. Whatever. So sue me."

"That's for the civil courts," Adele said, curtly. "My job is to put people in prison for their crimes."

He paled at this, and even in the dark she could tell the blood was leaving his cheeks. He shook his head again. "You don't understand. I'm not a murderer. I might have a bit of an issue with taking things that don't belong to me, fine. Not that I'm admitting anything, mind... But I didn't kill *anybody*!"

She stared at him, unconvinced.

"Just asked the fat man," he said, desperately. "He believed me."

Adele still wasn't sure what he was talking about. "Who is this person? You said he questioned you an hour ago?"

"Yeah. He's been at the resort for a couple of days now. Big fella, walrus mustache, never smiles."

Adele stared. Of course, now she recognized the description well enough. Part of her resented it, but another part of her was stunned. Was her father still in the Alps? He'd left, hadn't he?

She hadn't thought he would stay. When she left Heather's, she thought he'd gone home. But what if he'd stayed in the Alps investigating on his own? She gritted her teeth. This was exactly the sort of thing he would do.

She tried to hide the emotion, and, in as careful a voice as possible said, "Where was he?"

"Staying at one of the hotels. Half off, cheap ass place. For people like us; one thing this resort is doing well. It's expensive, but is not meant to just be for the bigwigs. You know?"

Adele sighed. "Look, Joseph, I want to believe you. But you don't

157

have an alibi for either of the murders, and right now, we caught you rooting around the house of a man that just died this morning. I need you to give me a reason."

He stared helplessly at her, shaking his head. For her part, Adele stared back, trying her best to make up her mind. At just that moment, though, John came around the corner, holding something.

"What's that?" Adele asked.

"Ms. Sophie is fine," John said, growling. "Surprised to see me. She took a sedative to try to get some rest."

Adele's sense of relief heightened and she nodded gratefully.

Joseph tried to turn in his chair, but couldn't rotate completely, and had to wait for John to approach the table. Wordlessly, John tossed the item he was holding onto the patio furniture.

Adele stared; Joseph stammered, "Okay, so what? That's my work coat."

It was the uniform for the new resort. And on the sleeve, a German flag was stitched into the fabric. A flag that was slightly torn. Specifically, a flag that was slightly torn with some of the red fibers jutting out in haphazard patterns.

"See that?" John said.

"I see it," said Adele, feeling a pit in her stomach. She wasn't sure what she would tell Heather. "Joseph Meissner," she said, still staring at the rip on the sleeve, "I'm afraid you're going to have to come with us."

The look of shock and horror on his face matched some of Adele's own. Partly, shocked her father was still in the Alps. Partly that they had discovered a coat with missing fibers. The same red thread they had found back at the murder scene of the Swiss couple. They couldn't ignore it. Not now. Adele had given her word to Heather she would do right by the employees. But she'd also given her word to catch the culprit.

"Joseph Meissner, you're under arrest," Adele said, lifting a breath to the sky.

CHAPTER TWENTY NINE

Ms. Jayne's voice came crisp and clear over the phone. Adele blinked, surveying the screen and watching the video shape of the Interpol correspondent nod her head in a precise way before saying, "You have done well, Adele. Things looked rough at the start, but with the apprehension of Mr. Meissner, resort operations have a chance to go back to normal."

Adele nodded, holding her phone so the camera would catch her portrait. She wasn't sure what to say. She thought of the media, and the resorts' efforts to use them as a tool for their narrative. She thought of John, and the review he would face back in France for conduct unbecoming. She thought of what Joseph had told her last night—her father was still in the Alps, investigating on his own.

But most of all, she thought of the suspect himself.

Joseph Meissner—nineteen years old. A petty thief. He'd lied on his applications to the resorts more than once. He had connections to all five victims, be it by location, or simply interaction. Zero alibi.

Zero.

Adele winced. For some reason, this bothered her. Why?

Because even the stupidest criminals had *some* alibi. Why didn't Joseph? The killer had managed to stalk and murder five victims. So why was Joseph entirely devoid of a story? No friends to lie for him. No coincidental interactions with others at the time of the murders. No plane tickets or train tickets or sightings down in the city...

Even the dumbest criminals had *some* backup plan to excuse their actions. It was all they thought about. But Joseph Meissner had *none*. As if... As if he hadn't thought he'd need one.

Adele winced again at the cycling thoughts; she nodded to Ms. Jayne in farewell, then clicked the phone shut.

She passed a hand through her medium-length blonde hair and breathed a soft sigh where she sat at the cafe's table, witnessing people come and go through the glass. The resort—new though it was—still had attracted a decent amount of traffic, especially now that the news was announcing the *Slope Slayer* was in custody.

159

She wrinkled her nose, but then the expression faded as her gaze landed on a single person waddling along the trail, hands jammed in his pockets. His quivering, walrus mustache seemed rigid, as if breath particles had frozen along the edges in the cold.

Adele had been waiting. Joseph had said he'd been confronted by a man fitting his description while he'd been working. Adele had waited patiently for the last few hours, watching the main road from the cheapest hotel in the resort.

And now, there he was. Just as Joseph had suggested.

Adele pushed away from the table and moved with rapid motions toward the door, jamming an elbow into the push bar and stepping out into the cold. "Hey!" she shouted.

A few of the tourists glanced over, but then looked away again. Her father, though, stiffened as if he'd heard a gunshot.

The Sergeant paused, then rotated ever so slowly, his dark eyes seeking her face across the pathway between the cafes and restaurants.

For a moment, they both just stared at each other, their eyes reflecting the memories of the harsh words exchanged, of the equal parts injury and shame. They held the look, and then, with a sigh, the Sergeant began to approach, hands jammed in his coat pockets, eyes fixed on her. He was wearing another hat now, this one blue and gray, displaying the insignia of the German police.

"Hello," he said mildly, nodding as he came within reach.

"You're still here," she said, carefully.

"Yep."

Adele glanced over her shoulder and stepped aside as a couple of pedestrians moved past toward one of the cafes. She felt the chill settling on her and rubbed her hands together through the gloves. She adjusted her hood, pulling it further over her ears. "Thought you'd left."

He tugged on one end of his frosted mustache. "Left Bavaria, but not the Alps," he said. "It's a free country."

"Why?"

He hesitated, and again met her eyes, staring at her. The look, his actions, spoke heaps more than he'd ever communicated with his daughter before. He scratched at the side of his chin during the awkward pause, gathering his words. "Investigating," he said, quietly. "Getting to the bottom of it all."

In that moment, Adele realized: her words had struck a chord. She

160

watched him a moment longer. Her words from the other night had stung—had been harsh. But perhaps her father had sensed a grain of truth. He'd never been a man to back down from a challenge, especially if honor was involved. Adele had insulted his ability to investigate—so he'd stayed to prove her wrong.

She passed a hand wearily through her hair, wrinkling her nose as she realized she'd forgotten to shampoo it in all the excitement. She hadn't been on one of her early morning runs in a while either. She sighed. She'd never considered the influence she might have on her father. Seeing him here... seeing him react to what she'd said... It felt odd. Unusual. She didn't like it.

"About all that," Adele said, slowly, "I want you to know..."

Her father waited for a split second, but then seemed to decide he didn't want to hear whatever she settled on, and quickly interrupted. "Look," he said, "I found a lead."

Adele blinked. "Oh?"

"Yes," he said, sounding mighty pleased. "Was talking around one of the gyms with some of the older folk. There's a fellow here from the French resort—the one where the Swiss were killed. He left after that—didn't feel safe. Anyway, he said he'd spoken with the Haneses the night before it all happened. Fellow was shook, of course."

Adele noticed her father wasn't quite meeting her gaze. The two of them stood quietly, their feet at shoulder width. Both seemed to take turns glancing at the other, and a sort of awkward atmosphere hung between them.

"So this fellow you were talking to," said Adele. "He knew the Haneses too?"

Her father nodded, glanced at her, then looked away again, scratching the underside of his chin. He reached up and tugged at the bill of his baseball cap. "It might not be anything," he said. He sniffed and continued, "But he said the Hanes family were involved in a skiing accident. The year prior. They've been to the resort a couple of times."

"A skiing accident?"

"Nothing broken. Barely a sprain, actually, by what he said. But enough to call paramedics in."

Adele paused. She felt a flicker in her pulse. A quiet change in tempo. She wouldn't allow herself to get too excited. Not yet. And yet, somehow, she found herself leaning almost imperceptibly forward, her eyes fixed on her father. "Paramedics? But in the Alps, they probably

161

don't call the normal healthcare, do they?"

Her father tapped his nose and pointed at her. And for the first time, they held eye contact for longer than a few seconds.

"But I don't think that's relevant," she said. "I mean," she quickly added, at the sudden furrowing of her father's brow, "it's good work. Definitely something I hadn't considered. But what's the connection?" Even as she said it, though, she trailed off. She remembered what Ms. Sophie had said about her fiancé, the latest victim. About his love for skiing, and about the injury he'd suffered the previous year.

"What?" her father demanded. He shifted a bit, his feet tapping against the heated tiles of the technologically advanced resort pathway.

Another group of tourists moved from a café, past a restaurant, up a spiraling staircase toward a viewing platform with an impressive glass and steel observatory at the top.

"Nothing," Adele said, "well, *something*. The latest victim…I'm not sure I should be telling you this, but the latest victim also had a skiing accident."

"You're sure?"

"Pretty sure."

"Well, we need to look into it then, yes? I mean, you do. Obviously I'm not a part of this."

Adele cleared her throat uncomfortably. Her father was right, in a way. He wasn't a part of it. She wasn't sure if she wanted to bring him back in. Not after the way things ended. Then again, he was the one who brought the lead.

"Honestly, if you want to come with me, fine. It's not going to be a pleasant meeting anyway."

Her father raised a bushy eyebrow.

"If what you're saying is right," she said, "the Haneses were involved in an accident in France. Here, in Germany, Mr. Griezmann experienced an accident as well, and I'll have to find out which resort. But that also means the Benevetis are the ones we need to look into. See if they had a connection."

"Why the long face?"

"Means I'm probably going to have to speak with the manager." Adele felt even colder all of a sudden, and pulled her jacket tight around her, shoving her hands deep in her pockets and glaring grumpily past her father now. "He wasn't too pleased last time he found me snooping. And with the way things have gone recently," she said, "not sure he's going to be super pleased with seeing me now."

"He'll treat you respectfully," her father said.

Adele smiled. "I'd like to hope so."

"No," said the Sergeant. "He *will* treat you respectfully."

Then her father turned and began marching in the direction of the parking lot where she'd parked her government issue. For a moment, she just stared after him, but then, with a small smile twisting the corners of her lips, she moved after her father. The idea of confronting the manager about the Benevetis didn't sit well at all. But perhaps her father had accidentally stumbled on the next lead. The only remaining lead.

***

The drive with her father back to the Bavarian resort was an undertaking in tentative silence. Neither Adele nor her father made much of an effort to speak. But at the same time, it was nothing in comparison to the silence that fell over the room when Adele pushed open the expensive wooden door and stepped onto the Turkish rug of the office for Mr. Adderman, the manager of the Bavarian resort.

For a moment, Adele paused, clearing her throat and staring out across the long office space.

Her eyes darted across a couple of bookshelves with decorative covers that seemed more for show than reading. Her eyes glazed over a small minibar in the back of the room, and an oak table, with an ashtray for cigar butts.

A large desk sat beneath what looked like a sparse chandelier in the ceiling. And behind the oversized desk sat Mr. Adderman.

The small, red-faced man looked up from a computer and stared across the room at Adele.

She recognized him from their interaction in Respite in the Cliffs. At the time, he'd been yelling at her. Now, his confusion was quickly being replaced by another surge of anger as he stared.

"You?" he said.

Adele nodded in greeting

"I'm sorry, Mr. Adderman!" called the voice of the assistant manager from the hallway. The woman had led them to the manager's office, but had also informed them he was indisposed. Adele hadn't cared.

163

The manager got to his feet, as if to look over Adele's shoulder, but she quickly reached out, grabbed the handle, and closed the door shut behind her as her father also stepped into the room.

"What do you want?" the resort manager demanded. "As if you haven't done enough already!"

"Please," Adele interrupted, "I'm here for some information, to help put this investigation to bed. You'd like that, wouldn't you?"

The manager looked like he was about to bust a gasket. His cheeks continued to redden, and his eyes were bulging again as they had back in the bar when he'd first confronted her.

"See," she said, quickly, cutting him off before he could speak again. "I'm not talking to your employees. This time, I'm coming straight to you. That's what you wanted, wasn't it?"

The manager drew a long breath, as if trying to calm his nerves. "What I want," he said, growling, "is for you to get out of here and stop meddling. You don't even understand what you're costing this place."

Adele clicked her tongue. "I did not murder those five victims. I'm here to help prevent any more deaths. Don't blame me for the killer's doings."

For a moment, she thought he might throw the ashtray at her. He stepped around the table, though and passed his desk, glaring and shaking his head so wildly, his round cheeks trembled. "You need to get out of here," he snapped. "You don't have a warrant. No, don't pretend. If you did, you would've led with it. Get out."

He approached Adele, finger raised, jabbing toward her. He only got within a couple of feet, though, before Adele's father sidled forward, stepping between his daughter and the charging resort manager.

For a moment, Adele bristled, annoyed. She didn't need the Sergeant fighting her battles for her. But then she saw the look on the manager's face.

He pulled up short, staring, his jaw half unhinged. "And who are you?" he demanded.

"You'll speak kindly to Adele, understand?" her father said, his voice a low growl.

Adele felt a slight tremble up the back of her spine. She had heard her father speak in this tone before. It never boded well.

The manager, for his part, spluttered and took a step back, as if unsure. He glared at Adele's father. "Get out, both of you!"

164

But her father crossed his arms. "No," he said. "You want this to end? You want your business to go back to how it was as usual? You should listen to her," he said, jabbing a thumb over his shoulder.

"It's all right," Adele said, quietly, but her father ignored her.

"She's one of the best damn investigators they have. But idiots like you keep getting in the way, preventing her from doing her job. You want this to be drawn out, months on end, given over to the locals? You want to know how I know they'll take their sweet time about it? Because I'm one of them. Once this goes to the locals, it'll be shunted around from office to office. Homicide won't want it. No one's gonna want it. This is a tainted case. They might even have to shut down your resort. In fact, I'll tell you right now, I know a few that will push for it. The unions won't like it, but some of the environmentalists, they have a big sway downtown nowadays. Not sure if you heard."

The manager tried to speak, but Adele's father held out a finger and made a shushing sound, so precise and stern that the smaller man fell quiet, staring up at Adele's father.

"But she," he jerked another thumb toward his daughter, "has worked with DGSI, the FBI, and now is on an assigned taskforce with Interpol. Understand? She has ties with BKA, and any other intelligence agency you might think of. And all of that in her thirties. She's one of the best you've ever seen. And you're too stupid to get your head out of your ass, and help her solve this case so you can get things back to normal."

Adele stared at the back of her father's head, stunned. For one, she had never heard him swear before. For another, she had never heard him talk about her like that.

She swallowed, feeling a lump in her throat all of a sudden. Just as quickly she cleared her throat and it was gone. The manager, though, on the receiving end of this tirade, had a different reaction. At first, he looked like he wanted to shout for security. But then he seemed to see something in Mr. Sharp's face he didn't like. The Sergeant loomed over the smaller man, not backing down.

The manager glanced between the two of them, then huffed a breath, not quite in defeat, but an impatient, compliant sound, suggesting he would at least hear them. "What do you need? Make it quick."

It was only then that Adele's father stepped aside, glancing back at her and raising his eyebrow, one side of his face tilted away from the

165

manager and quirked in a half smile.

Adele suppressed her own grin and said, in an even tone, "We're looking for records on skiing accidents at your resort."

"The paramedics deal with—" the manager began.

"Yes, they would have records. But you would too. A place this high-end? There's no way you don't. Liability would be your worst nightmare."

The manager shook his head. "Okay, what specifically? It's not like I personally go through records."

"No, but you have the number of the guy who does. All I need to know is if the Benevetis also had a skiing accident recently."

"And then you leave?"

Adele crossed a finger over her heart in mock sincerity.

"Fine, stay there; don't touch anything." With the same annoyed energy as before, he moved back to his desk.

Adele waited, patient but excited.

He yammered on the phone for a bit, more eye rolling and huffing breaths, more reddened cheeks, suggesting if he wasn't more careful, he'd be dealing with cardiac issues more frequently than BKA agents.

At last, though, he looked up and stared across the oak table. "I'll have you know, it was only a very *minor* incident," he said.

Adele perked up, refusing the urge to look at her father in giddy, schoolgirl excitement. "Wait, so there was an accident?"

The manager passed a hand over his sweaty face. "The Benevetis were repeat visitors to our establishment. Trusted visitors. They had their own chalet. A couple years ago, yes, they were in a small accident that required ski paramedics. It's a shared resource all the resorts use. It's outside my influence," he quickly added." If there's some complaint—"

"No complaint. Just investigating. So these are like EMTs or firefighters?" Adele said. "They're a shared resource between the resorts, you say? How many resorts?"

He looked annoyed again, and began to gesture toward the door. But Adele's father growled slightly, and Mr. Adderman seemed to catch himself and said, "About a two-hundred-mile radius or so. I don't know exactly. They cover a lot of resorts. They're not tied to any particular country's jurisdiction. They just operate in the mountains. Is that all you need? You said you would leave."

"Last question, then I promise I'm gone," said Adele.

"What?"

"These mountain paramedics, where, *exactly,* can I find them?"

CHAPTER THIRTY

"*Nein.* No records," said the man behind the desk. He didn't look even look up. His Coke bottle glasses amplified his eyes to comical proportions. Except there was anything but a smile on Adele's lips as she stared at the dispatcher.

Adele felt her father shift next to her. "Check again! *Bitte!*" she insisted. Adele felt like she could scream. They were standing in the ski paramedic depot which the Bavarian resort relied on. This same paramedic depot had various outposts throughout the Alps. Adele wasn't too sure of the mechanisms. She'd never had run-ins with ski paramedics before. Now, she hoped she never would have to again.

The office building was a gray stone structure that at first she'd taken for an electrical tower in the distance. A mesh wire gate surrounded the thing, and inside, it was nearly as cold as it had been outside. The man, for his part, had been wearing earmuffs when they'd first arrived. Getting his attention had been an endeavor in patience.

"How can there be no records?" Adele demanded. "Surely you have to have something on file? You service the three resorts I've mentioned, yes?"

The man sighed and look up at her. There was no one else in the office. It was a lonely, colorless setting.

The man nodded. "We service resorts in a couple-hundred-mile radius," he said, proudly, his chest puffing out a bit. The man had a whiskery face, but a very patchy beard. He had longish hair tied back in a ponytail, and a bandanna wrapped around his neck.

The man reached up and adjusted his glasses for the first time, causing his eyes to look even wider and more googly behind the frames. "I mean," he said, "we don't keep track of minor injuries. I just work in the office. I don't actually go out on the expeditions. But the rescue teams, like I said, we service hundreds of miles all up and down the slopes. Most of the resorts have contracts with us. We couldn't possibly keep track of everything. Minor injuries are logged for the purposes of payment, but nothing else is kept."

Adele pointed at him. "So you're saying you do have *something* on the Benevetis?"

He shrugged. "Two years ago; hiking accident. But that's it—none of the records are filled in."

Adele wanted to scream. "And the Haneses?"

He nodded. "Also in the system. And, before you ask, yes, Mr. Griezmann, he's also here. His was a nasty ski accident, though."

Adele felt like pulling hair. "*Who* went?"

"We send teams of four in cases like this; when they're serious."

"So you have four names?"

He nodded once and rattled them off without hesitation. "Jacob Marks, Stephanie Gretz, Jeremy Asbury, and Corey Bjerg."

She gritted her teeth. Four names was too many. Nothing about the MO suggested the killer worked with someone. One of those names had to be involved, though, didn't they? But how could they narrow it down?

"And the paramedics who went for the Benevetis and the Haneses, they would have been on their own, yes? Since it wasn't as serious."

The office worker nodded. "Possibly. For the more mild injuries, we only send one or two rescue workers. But, like I said, we don't have that record. All we know is the name of the injured party, and a couple more descriptions of the issue. We don't have records of who went to treat whom."

Adele bit her lip. "But you do for Mr. Griezmann!"

"Yes. Because his was serious. But not for the others." He crossed his arms. But then, after a second, he snapped his fingers. "Hang on," he said, pushing up from his chair and moving across the cold, concrete room. He reached a floor to ceiling file cabinet, then muttered beneath his breath.

"What is it?" Adele demanded.

"Hang on!" he said, still rooting around. At last, though, he snapped his fingers and crowed, "A-ha!"

He pulled a paper file from the top drawer and wiggled it beneath his nose. He rounded on them and strode over to Adele, smiling as he did.

"What is that?" she said, staring.

"Overtime forms," he replied. "Have to file manually—all the employees do. And this," he wiggled the form again, "was from the man who went after the Benevetis, nearly two years ago. It isn't in our files, but if he's claiming overtime, chances are, he took the call."

169

Adele stared. "You're saying whoever filed for overtime was the same person who helped the Benevetis?"

"Yes."

"Well?" she demanded. "Who was it?"

He pushed the file toward her, and Adele opened it, scanning the information. Only a few relevant details stood out. The date, indeed, was from more than eighteen months ago, on another excursion the Benevetis had taken in the mountains. The required pay was on a line below that. And then, below that, there was a printed name.

"What were those four names again?" Adele demanded, glancing toward the dispatcher. "The ones who helped Mr. Griezmann after his ski accident."

Without missing a beat, the operator rattled off, "Jacob Marks, Stephanie Gretz, Jeremy Asbury, and Corey Bjerg."

Adele stared at the paper overtime form. At the bottom of the page, printed, next to a signature, were two simple words—only two. A tenuous connection. Nothing certain… She was reaching for straws and she knew it… But a connection all the same.

Adele's heart skipped a beat. She lowered the file, handing it back to the paramedic dispatch with a shaking hand.

"Well?" her father asked.

The paramedic stared at her as well.

Adele cleared her throat, and with a daunting sense of urgency, she said, "Corey Bjerg. Where is he, *right now*?"

The dispatcher blinked a couple of times, but then returned to his computer, clacking away. After a moment, he looked up. For the first time, a hint of an emotion crossed his countenance, and he cleared his throat. "He's out on a rescue mission right now, actually. I can tell him to call you when he gets back…"

But Adele was already shaking her head. "No, that's not going to do. Where is he? We need to get to him, *this* instant."

"I'm not sure I can—"

"Tell me where he is right now or I'll have you arrested for aiding a murderer," she shouted.

The operator winced, but then, in an even tone, seemingly deciding on the spot, he said, "I can text you the coordinates to the number you contacted me with, if you'd like. But that's the best I can do. I can't tell you where Mr. Bjerg is, since he's en route, but I can tell you where the wounded party is located. It's a twenty-kilometer hike from here. You don't have skis, do you?"

"I'm afraid not."

"Adele," her father said. Adele glanced back at her dad. "Your friend—the loud French one—he can fly us, yes?"

Adele nodded quickly, already dialing John's number. She turned now, starting out of the dispatch center with quick, hurried steps.

"Text me the coordinates, *now!*" Adele shouted over her shoulder. And then, with her father in tow, they raced back to the parked car. Already, Adele had her phone to her ear, but could hear the buzz of failed reception. "Dammit," she snarled. "Dad, try your phone. Mine's getting spotty reception."

As they both got into the front seats of the government loaner, Adele flashed John's phone number on her screen toward her dad as he typed it in.

She felt her phone vibrate in her hand and checked to see that the dispatcher had sent the coordinates for the victim. Twenty kilometers through rough terrain and treacherous mountain passes. It would take some time for Corey Bjerg, the paramedic, to reach the fallen victim. But would they be able to catch up in time? By helicopter it would be easier to reach the destination, but much, much harder to land.

With trembling hands, she turned the key in the ignition and heard her father muttering next to her. "Yes, is this Agent Renee?" her father demanded. "I'm Adele's father. Yes, really. No, that's hardly appropriate. Look—we need you to meet us at the hangar. Same as before. Yes *now!*"

Adele glanced sidelong at her father, her cheeks flushed. "Tell him to hurry," she said, quietly. Then, louder, adrenaline sparking, she shouted, "Tell him to hurry!"

Her father relayed the message as Adele veered down the mountain path, heading back toward the Three Lakes Airfield.

Corey Bjerg. He'd been there for the Benevetis. He was there when Mr. Griezmann was treated. The one contact point they had. Someone who knew how to find weakened, endangered folk to target. The murderer? Perhaps. But if that was the case, he was nearing another wounded lamb, like a wolf on a hunt. The snow around them was starting to pick up, and the skies above lumbered with gray clouds.

CHAPTER THIRTY ONE

Adele twisted her hands together in her lap, her pulse racing, the sound lost in the dull thrum of the helicopter blades whirring overhead. She stared out the window at the forests below, her eyes tracking the many trees and precipices. The wild of the Alps was different from the domesticated resorts.

No trails, for one. No clearings among the trees except for harsh falls and long slopes laden with ancient snow. Occasionally, she spotted the gray-brown blur of some creature moving in the terrain below, but then John maneuvered them past, leaving the spectacle behind. Adele also kept an eye out for snowmobiles or skiers—no sign.

"They went deep," she said, quietly, speaking into the microphone of her headset.

Her father sat in the passenger seat behind her, staring out the side window of the helicopter. John was once again at the controls, but this time seemed to be playing it safe—flying at an acceptable distance from the tree line and maneuvering over the forests without getting too close.

The tall French agent had been uncharacteristically quiet for most the trip, ever since they'd met at the Three Lakes hangar. Adele had seen it before in him; like an animal zeroing in on its prey, its senses heightened for the hunt. John's hands were steady on the controls, unyielding, and his eyes stared out of the front of the chopper, tracking the forests.

"No clean landing near the coordinates," he said after a bit. "You're sure those are right?" He didn't look over, his gaze still fixed on the terrain.

"Dispatch gave them," she said. "They're right. The injured party is down there."

"What were they doing out here?"

"No clue. Can you get us in close?"

John circled the chopper, moving around the lowest peak, his eyes fixed on the terrain below. "Give me a second—looking for logger's outpost or a cross-country trail. Whoever the injured party is, they got

172

here somehow."

"Hiker maybe?" Adele asked.

John just shook his head, still fixated on the task at hand. At last, he circled once more then muttered something sharply and adjusted their heading. "Ahead," he said. "Rocky outcrop. In the trees—see?"

Adele's eyes narrowed, and she placed a hand against one of the headphones, holding it in place as if somehow her hearing were connected to sight. "No, what?"

"The tree blind," he said. "See it? Illegal—those," he said. "Poachers, or hunters. Not supposed to be on public land. Means the area around it is sturdy, though."

At last, Adele spotted what John had noticed so quickly; a wooden scaffold of sorts buried in the branches of a low fir, like some sort of tree house. John was indicating the rocky outcrop beneath the tree. Not very large. Not large at all—but just large enough for the helicopter to land, clear of the forest.

"Are you sure?" Adele began, but John had already set them into a descent, heading toward the outcrop.

She clenched her teeth, her hands wringing tightly in her lap as she stared, unblinking at the bank of trees. The coordinates, according to the GPS, were just beyond the ridge of the peak.

"Can't get us any closer?" she asked. She didn't relish the thought of the hike to the actual accident site.

"No suitable landing," John retorted. "There will be ski trails— gotta be. Hang on."

And with that, he set to, his hands a blur over the controls as he adjusted the vehicle for descent. Adele nearly cried out as they drew within spitting distance of the tall row of fir trees. Large branches, thicker than the chopper blades, extended dangerously close as if to ensnare them mid-air. She blew air sharply as John wedged the chopper just beneath the branches, like manipulating a Tetris piece, and then lowered them gently.

"The edge, the edge!" the Sergeant called out.

John cursed, checked a mirror, and then readjusted. The smooth descent was interrupted by a jarring jolt and Adele felt her stomach in her throat. But then, a split-second later, they landed with a clatter, crunching into the snow-strewn rocky outcrop beneath the illegal blind.

For a moment, they all paused, breathing heavily, staring straight ahead. Adele yanked the headphones off, listening. For a vague, spine-chilling moment, she thought she heard the sound of cracking—ice? Stone?

But then the noise settled, the chopper blades droned to a quiet wump-wump and then died completely as John cut the engine.

The three of them sat for a moment, gratefully breathing and quieting their racing hearts. Then John cleared his throat and said. "See—easy."

"Yeah," Adele replied. "Easy."

She didn't have time to contemplate her mortality—nor did she have time to berate John for the risky landing. A killer was on the loose in these slopes, and a victim was in his sights. They had to move.

"Do you both have the coordinates?" she asked.

John nodded. "Have to stabilize, make sure everything is in order first."

"No time!" Adele said. "We have to go now!"

John shook his head, turning to look at her for the first time in a good ten minutes. "We will, but not yet. I have to return the bird in one piece—understand? I'm already on thin ice. I need another set of eyes to help me clear the branches."

"I can't stay—I'm going."

"I can help," piped up Adele's father's voice. "If only for a few minutes. I can help—we'll come after you."

Adele glanced back, nodding in gratitude at her dad. Then she swung open the helicopter door and dropped onto the snow. For a moment, she half expected the rocky outcrop to collapse, but it held firm and she moved quickly beneath the blind in the trees. If hunters used this place, then trails would have to lead to it. She checked her phone, eyeing the GPS, and set out, vapors of breath shooting past her face as she moved purposefully away from the ridge and toward the direction of the injured skier.

Had Mr. Bjerg already reached the victim? Was she too late?

Adele lowered her head, and without looking back, she hurried forward, breaking into a jog across the flat terrain and ducking under the first row of tree branches.

***

"You're moving slowly!" the Sergeant snapped in English, glaring at the helicopter pilot. His daughter had given his name as John Renee.

174

A Frenchman of all things. He could feel his mustache quivering on his lip and the cold nipping at his wrists and cheeks, making itself known across every inch of exposed skin.

"Agh! Calm yourself," replied the man in a heavy accent. "You wish for us to have no way back? What if there is an injured party on that mountain? We would watch them bleed out—yes? No. We need this bird sky-bound."

The tall agent was doing the once-around, circling the helicopter and checking the edge. The front lip of the windshield extended precariously over the precipice, but at last, Agent Renee winced and said, "How much space do I have back there?"

The Sergeant glanced toward the trees, then his eyes flicked to the branches. "Only a few inches," he said. "Not much."

John grunted. "I'll clear some of the branches. Need you to keep an eye."

The Sergeant, though, was glancing nervously toward where his daughter had disappeared, shaking his head. He helped John onto the back of the helicopter, hefting the man up by gripping the tall agent under the arm and heaving. For his part, John—with a long knife in hand—began tearing at some of the smaller tree branches extending dangerously close to the helicopter blades.

"Too long," the Sergeant kept muttering. "Taking too long!"

John glanced down, blinking aside a spattering of leaves and small twigs. He said, "I'm fine now—I have an eye for it. Just tell me which branch is closest—can't see from this angle."

The Sergeant pointed at the offending object and watched as John set to with his knife. Shavings of bark and bits of leaves fell, raining down on the agent's upturned face.

"Mr. Renee," said the Sergeant. "You need to hurry. Adele is—"

"Go—go, it's fine," John said. "I have it from here. Go after her!"

He needed no second invitation. He left the tall Frenchman clearing their takeoff spot and without a second glance back hurried toward the small trail beneath the hunter's blind. Adele's tracks were clear in the fresh snow, but the snow wasn't too deep—suggesting that the trail was kept clear by hunters. The Sergeant didn't have GPS, but he could follow Adele's footprints clear enough. His daughter was heading to face a killer all on her own—she needed all the help she could get.

He set his jaw, his hands clenched at his sides, swinging wildly. He fixed his eyes ahead and moved quickly, one step at a time through the

175

desolate terrain. After a minute, following his daughter's tracks, he was already huffing for breath. He spent a good amount of time in the weight room, but often neglected cardio—something Adele was excellent at.

Still, he was a man of will. He pushed through the exhaustion, or, more accurately, embraced it, accepting the pain as truth, but continued on regardless. One foot in front of the other, the cold nipping at him while he sweated underneath his three layers.

"Come on," he muttered to himself, "come on." He uttered the words in a quiet chant, allowing the cadence to propel him up a particularly steep portion of trail. He could still see Adele's footprints ahead, but no sign of his daughter through the trees, or the makeshift trail bordering the snowbound cliffs.

For a moment, near the low boughs of a distance copse, he spotted movement. The Sergeant's eyes narrowed, but before he could focus— he failed to keep track of the path—a shout! His foot fell through the snow. He yelped and tried to right himself, but cried out again in pain— his voice echoing in the cliffs—as his ankle buckled beneath him.

"Dammit!" he shouted.

Snarling, he yanked his leg from the snow, where he'd accidentally ventured off the path. He tested his ankle and winced. His knee, also, an old injury from work, seemed to be acting up. He wanted to curse again, but this time managed to contain the expletive. No sense in betraying his character for pain. Pain wasn't worth it.

Muttering crossly to himself, suppressing his frustration and anger, he doggedly began moving up the trail again, limping now, his eyes fixed on his daughter's tracks. For the first time, he felt a chill up his spine that had nothing to do with the cold. He glanced around, examining the hills, the rows of trees and snow-burdened rocks. A loneliness, a solitude descended on him. He glanced back—no sigh of Agent Renee. Ahead, no indication of his daughter. Limping, out of breath, in pain, he maneuvered alone up the mountain.

CHAPTER THIRTY TWO

Two things the friend knew. One, a secret—his grandfather's secret. He kept it to himself. The second, though, he'd learned from his grandfather: kindness came in many forms. Was it kind to allow the life of a mewling kitten, starving, stray, dying? Was it kindness to see the injured doe stumbling, blood spilling onto virgin ground, while one looked on in compassion?

Compassion alone was dross.

And yet, it was compassion—or a friend of it—that curdled his lips into a simpering smile.

Compassion that compelled his words.

"Are you feeling all right? Tell me if this hurts."

The woman below him on the stretcher nodded weakly, her face pale and tinged with gray from the premonition of frostbite. The friend knelt in the snow, rolling his neck and peering up at the dark clouds above. He smiled in the face of the lumbering sky; the crown of the Alps.

Snow around them, wet. Some seeping through the layers of his waterproof clothing, despite the lining. The victim—the injured party—the wounded doe beneath him, strapped to the stretcher, where he'd placed her.

He glanced over across the cross-country ski trail. Nearly twenty kilometers from the nearest resort. The woman had traveled far. Impressive. But now...

He examined the elbow, placed in the makeshift splint and eased against the side of plastic. A lame duck. A mewling kitten. An injured doe.

He smiled down at her—the grin of a wolf, the leer of a crocodile. He adjusted his hood, keeping his face warm, but directing his attention to the woman's bundled form beneath the blankets and straps of the stretcher.

She spoke, her voice weak, probing the chill air—a tentative murmur.

"It's all going to be okay," he replied in a soothing tone. He reached out, his hand hovering over her for a moment, then he touched her, his fingers stroking the knuckles of her injured arm.

The woman winced and protested weakly, but lack of water, sunstroke, and pain stopped her words. He stroked her hand a bit harder in what would be perceived as a comforting gesture misplaced.

Really, a test. A test of will. Of response.

The woman squirmed, trying to distance herself from him. But she was strapped in place—going nowhere. A failed test.

His countenance darkened and his eyes narrowed. He licked his lips now, eyeing the woman on the stretcher. His eyes flicked to the snowmobile. Twenty kilometers was a great distance. No one would hear the screams; she wouldn't scream, not in this state.

His eyes shifted down to the workman's sheath on the back of the snowmobile. A first-aid kit, some bandages, and also... the length of a wooden handle. His axe.

The woman squirmed some more beneath him. She was young—thirties, perhaps. She might recover. She might yet be strong. Then again...

The man felt a churning in his gut, just above his navel. He felt prickles across his skin and a sudden thirst, a hunger. He focused on his breathing.

Not yet... the friend thought to himself.

Not yet... no... not yet...

He wasn't a fool. To be a fool would be weakness. And then the man was committed. The friend knew the cost of weakness and he would exact it in increments, even upon himself if necessary. The scars along the backs of his legs were proof of this. He was a man of will.

And so, he ignored the urge in his stomach now traveling to his chest. He marched to the side of the snowmobile, hitching the stretcher to the back, careful to secure the plastic edges of the sled in place. The woman's skis lay discarded, a crumpled heap by the tree she'd crashed into. Her phone, in the friend's pocket. She was helpless. Defenseless.

The man made a quiet sound, close to a purr, and he sat astride the snowmobile; he began to turn, preparing to leave.

"My husband..." came the mewling voice of the little lamb.

The friend frowned and glanced back. "Excuse me?" he asked, his tone still gentle, concerned.

"My husband—he was skiing too!" she said, her voice rising now, panicked. Some of the weakness fell from her, and with it, the man's

178

arousal diminished. No—perhaps not so weak. Perhaps she would recover. An unsuitable gift to these mountains. He wouldn't sully them with strong blood.

"Your husband is out here?" the man asked.

The woman nodded weakly, her head shifting in the blankets pulled tight to her neck. "He'll be looking for me. We… got separated." She gasped, her small form heaving from the effort, and pain flashed across her face. The man looked quickly away, as if avoiding the sight of indecency.

"He'll be fine," the friend said. "He'll follow the trail out. You slipped down a ravine. It could take him hours to find the path to us."

"Please…" she mewled.

But he ignored her now. The woman's husband might very well be out on these slopes. But if he'd been cross-country skiing with his wife and lost sight of her, then there was little to do. He would find her back at the resort.

The friend prepared to leave again, slowly, the snowmobile growling beneath him as he took the careful trail back in the direction of the resort, heading down the mountain once more. The woman's groans and moans were lost in the sound of a churning engine. The snow, slick around them, gave rise to rapid speed, but the friend kept the pace slower than usual. Slow enough to give him time to recover his senses. To remember the chore.

Not now. Not yet.

Still, an appetite had come upon him. A strong one… Was it starting to get out of hand? An appetite unsatisfied was natural. An appetite insatiable was unnatural—weakness.

Just then, the man spotted a flicker of movement through the trees. He pulled up, cutting the engine and gliding to the side of the trail, peering down the slope. On one of the lower paths, he spotted a man. A waddling fellow, with a drooping moustache beneath an upturned hood.

The man was limping, huffing breaths in painful spurts, his eyes glued to the trail, neither looking left nor right. Limping. Limping.

Gentle, gentle doe.

The friend cleared his throat, his appetite rising once more. The woman—the injured skier—they could tie him to. They'd sent him for her.

But this fellow? The husband? No—too old. Far too old. Then again…

179

Did it matter? He wasn't looking. He was out of breath, he was clearly injured, in pain.

"Where are you going?" came the weakened voice, now audible again in the still air.

"Hush," he replied, gently, slipping from the saddle and reaching toward his work belt.

"What is it?"

"Nothing. Quiet, darling. I'll be right back."

The appetite had come strong, and like all wolves, the man needed to feast. He felt the soft swish of his axe as he drew it from the holster and hefted it in his hand. Then, ignoring the snowmobile, his eyes leaving the doe strapped to his sled, he began stalking down the trail, his gaze fixated on the limping man.

Gentle, gentle doe. Hear the wolf howl?

The friend smiled to himself; he could hear his grandfather's laughter now, echoing in the mountains. Their mountains. The herd must be culled. The good shepherd always shears his sheep.

CHAPTER THIRTY THREE

Adele's GPS was beeping now, but as she surveyed the last known location of the accident victim, she spotted nothing. No one. She wrapped her arms around her coat, drawing the cushy warmth closer, her eyes darting through the trails. The ski trail had been an arduous one, parts encumbered with old snow. Yet, she'd spotted tracks eventually.

Skis and a snowmobile.

But now, no sign of anyone. She studied the snow again; disheveled. For a moment, in the distance, she thought she heard the sound of an engine. John starting the chopper again? The snowmobile?

She breathed heavily once more, focusing on the task at hand. For a brief moment, tendrils of cold probed at her spine and made their way up.

"Hello?" she called out, whirling around.

No one. Just the cold, lonely mountains and the abandoned forests.

She felt an outsider in the Alps, all of a sudden, as if she were trespassing. She was a long way from San Francisco, that was for certain.

"Hello?" she repeated.

Again, no answer, save the faintest echoes of her own voice pealing back to her from the cliffs in the distance. The peaks of snow and rock burdened with clusters of stunted trees provided both shelter and ominous features to the landscape. The air up here was cold, but also thin, and Adele—despite her athletic condition—found it difficult to draw breath. Her cheeks were stinging from frozen sweat and her heart pulsed in her chest.

She spotted something beneath a tree and moved quickly over.

Abandoned skis. Someone had been here, at least. She glanced at the GPS; this was the exact location. So where was the victim? Had they been taken back to the resort? Had Mr. Bjerg already been this way? Perhaps he wasn't the killer after all. No bloody carnage, no scene of violence.

And yet, Adele could still feel the prickle along her back.

181

Then, the sound of a crunch.

Adele twisted sharply, peering through the trees. She spotted someone—not her father, not John—a man in a red coat, moving slowly through the forest. Something clutched in his hand. Her heart hammered, and she stared. Was he armed? Was that a rifle in his grip? No... too thin. What then?

She crouched low, still peering through the trees as the figure approached. The figure was muttering to himself, shaking his head from side to side. His features were indiscernible beneath all the layers.

The paramedics in the mountains also wore red. Was this Mr. Bjerg?

He hadn't spotted her yet. Adele remained low, allowing the thin copse of trees to disguise her as the man moved up the path. She could feel her breath, seemingly stuck in her throat. Adele inched forward, one hand pressing against the rigid shape of the tree limb in front of her. The rough texture of the bark could just barely be felt through her thick gloves. Her other hand moved toward her hip, but then hesitated. The paramedic hadn't been approaching quietly. Clearly he thought he was alone.

Adele moved forward, ever so cautiously, her eyes fixed on the man.

She could hear him muttering still. She just barely, through the tree branches, spotted whatever he was carrying in his hand. He also had something strapped to his back.

Adele waited until he neared her, approaching with crunching footsteps. His shadow cast across her hiding spot, intermingling with the thin branches and extending toward her like the probing fingers of dark fog.

She heard the crunch of a stick, meaning he'd reached the copse of trees. She heard the moderate breath, and glimpsed whatever he was still holding, clearly long. A weapon?

With a shout, she flung herself forward, tackling the man around the waist and sending both of them to the trail in a heap of limbs and disheveled snow.

"Ack!" the man screamed. "Help! Attack!"

The man was strong, and kicked and bucked his hips, dislodging her and sending her flying. A second later, Adele realized her mistake. The man had been holding ski poles. Those were skis strapped to his back, not a weapon. Groggily, Adele pushed to her feet, her movements slow, encumbered by the many layers she wore.

Across from her, the man in the red coat moved a bit slower. He rocked on his hips, as if trying to get momentum, and also pushed up. He glared at her, staring from beneath a furrowed brow.

She didn't recognize him, and, judging by the fear across his face, he didn't recognize her.

"Who are you?" Adele said, gasping, one finger pointing sharply at the man.

"Who are you?" he retorted.

"My name is Agent Sharp," she said. "I'm with Interpol. Are you Corey Bjerg?"

"What? No, my name is Stefan. I was here with my wife. Are you part of the rescue team? I haven't found her! I can't reach anyone!"

Adele stared at him and felt her heart skip a beat. She whirled around, glancing up the trail along the snow, and shook her head. "You need to get out of here," she said. "Now. Your wife is fine, I'm sure she's being well taken care of. But you can't be here right now."

"You know where she is?"

Adele didn't know, but she could guess. The paramedic had already reached her. She was either dead somewhere, or back at the resort. Either way, he couldn't be up here. And while he did have a red jacket, there was no insignia suggesting he was involved with the paramedics. He didn't have the look.

"I'm serious, get out of here. Your best bet is to check back at the resort."

"Did someone come through? Is that why you're here?"

Adele sighed. "The paramedics were sent. They've already been here. Your wife should be fine. Just head back to the resort and we'll sort this all out, okay?"

The man stared at her, a ghost of a frown across his face. He looked worried, nauseous, but also scared. Hesitantly, he moved back toward the trail, gathering his ski equipment that had fallen from where she tackled him. He shot a couple of grudging looks in her direction, but finally managed to set himself on the trail once more, affixing the skis and setting off quicker than he'd arrived. Heading back to the resort.

For her part, Adele looked around and swallowed. No sign of the paramedic. No sign of his victim. She glanced back along the trail. Where was her father? Where was John?

The burden of being alone in the mountains descended on her once more, and she pulled her coat tight again, gathering it around her for comfort and warmth.

***

The friend thought he heard voices coming up the trail from the plateau above. The ski trail would curl around the mountain, circling it. Whoever was up there would take some time to reach him. No matter. Had dispatch sent in another paramedic?

He frowned at the thought, but suppressed it. It offended him to think he wasn't trusted fully with the job. How incompetent did they think he was?

Still, he hefted his axe and returned to the task at hand.

The poor, limping, bumbling doe was trudging through the snow. He'd veered off the path by accident; little did he know in five hundred paces, he'd fall off the side of the mountain. Plummet to his death.

The friend hurried, also following through the snow-laden undergrowth, tracking the limping footsteps of the old man.

He gripped the handle of his weapon. Three times, he'd quenched its thirst. Three times, he'd allowed the mountain its culling. Well, once before. The first secret.

But he tried not to think about it. No—all must be culled. Even those the friend loved. Weakness was a disease, and it would spread.

Ahead, he could hear the huffing breath of his prey. The old man limped, then slipped, then limped some more. His eyes were still fixed ahead, no sign that he'd noticed his stalker.

The old man with the mustache was continually muttering, waving a hand beneath the brown branches above, as if scrambling for some purchase, some guard rail. But in the forests, in the mountains, in the Alps, there were no safety rails, no locks and keys, no concrete walls of feigned protection.

The older man doubled over now, still groaning and rubbing at his knee. He leaned against a tree, one hand braced to hold himself upright. The snow was now up to his knees. He was far from the trail, and continued further still.

In that lull, the friend made up ground, moving along behind the bent over doe. Approaching quietly as he'd been taught.

His shadow extended toward the limping fellow. The old man stiffened, but didn't turn. His hand still clutched his knee, his body still

184

bent, begging to be broken, to be purged from these slopes.

The friend was now in reach. He hefted his axe, his eyes wide, unblinking in his skull as he stared down at the wounded kitty, the injured doe, the helpless creature.

He raised his weapon, and then…

A sound. Imperceptible to anyone else, but the friend had grown up in these mountains. He whirled around and flung his axe, *hard*. Precision, training took over.

A tall man shouted in pain, crying out. The axe had caught his upraised hand, knocking a gun loose and, by the looks of things, severing a knuckle. Panicked, for a brief moment, the friend stared. This new man was tall, agile, a scar across the underside of his chin. This new man clutched his bleeding hand, cursing and spluttering.

How had the friend not seen him? How had he been tricked? In a split second, the brief moment of contemplation allowed him, he realized: when the old man had veered off the road, he must have communicated something to the other. Perhaps they'd spotted each other. Perhaps they'd spotted him.

Not such a helpless doe after all, perhaps. The friend spun around, taking two quick steps back.

The old man was in the middle of lunging, but ended up eating snow, landing in the ice where the friend had been standing a moment before. The friend didn't wait, didn't hesitate. Instincts kicked in now.

He lashed out with a heavily booted foot. He felt the satisfaction of the top of his foot colliding with the old man's jaw. The fellow tumbled to the ground, releasing a sound like a toppled tree. But the friend couldn't stop, and had to move again. He was unarmed. He spotted the tall, lanky fellow who he'd hit with the axe scrambling in the snow, desperately searching for his firearm.

The friend had no need for such weapons, though. He'd thrown his blade perfectly. He severed a finger, disarmed the attacker, but also, in the same throw, buried the axe in the nearest tree.

The tall man was still looking for his gun as the friend circled, lunging with long strides through the snow. He snared his axe from where it had hit the tree.

Only two paces away, the tall man pulled up, his weapon recovered, and he flung himself back to distance himself from the man.

A flicker of fear. The tall man was trained. He knew what he was doing.

185

But he'd never faced someone like the friend before.

The friend surged toward the tall man, closing the distance. At the same time, he flung himself to the left, placing himself between the old man behind him and the tall man. Perhaps compassion would cost them. And, in that moment, the tall man hesitated. He had a split second, where he had distanced himself enough to get off a shot. He could have taken the friend down. But the friend knew he feared hitting his accomplice. And he stayed his trigger finger.

With a snarl, the friend surged, swiping with his axe and slamming it into the man's hand again, with the flat of the blade this time.

It wouldn't cut him, but it would crush.

The gun was knocked loose again, this time sent soaring into the trees, disappearing in the snow.

The tall man surged back again, moving fast. But the friend was smart. He'd seen the weakness.

"Careful!" he shouted with glee. Of course, he was simply looking for the man's attention.

The tall man afforded him a brief glance, and the friend raced back in the direction of the injured fellow, his blade raised.

The tall man cursed, and instead of pursuing his weapon, now raced after him as well, rushing to the aid of his friend.

Compassion. Weakness. It would cost them both their lives. The herd had to be culled. A good thing. The man was used to taking two lives at a time anyway.

CHAPTER THIRTY FOUR

Adele heard the sound of conflict only a few minutes after leaving the man she tackled.

The sound arose from below, on the plateau beneath her. She searched for the trail again, desperately, looking, and then racing down along the snow-bound ski path with reckless abandon. She knew this was a good way to slip, to fall, to accidentally stumble over the edge, but the ski trail would have to be trusted. Others were in danger.

She heard grunts, painful shouts, yelling. She thought she heard a gunshot, but then no more.

"John?" she shouted. "Dad?"

But she didn't have the breath for anything else. She pushed herself even harder, sprinting breakneck down the mountain, along the trail, and racing in the direction of the sounds of conflict.

She spotted the struggling men from a distance. And for a moment, her stomach lurched.

A man in a red coat, with the hood thrown back, was swinging an axe at her father. John managed to grab his arm from behind, but received a vicious kick to the groin for his efforts. John collapsed like a sack of flour, toppling into the snow, and the axe spun around, swinging down at the Frenchman now.

The Sergeant, though, weakened, gasping, flung out a hand, snaring the attacker by the boot and pulling *hard*. The man howled and slipped. He kicked out once, twice, vicious attacks both colliding with her father's jaw.

Adele spotted the Sergeant's eyes roll into the back of his head, unconscious. John, for his part, was clearly wounded. His one hand was clutched inside his sweatshirt, blood spilling down the front of his second hoodie. He was trembling and gasping and trying to rise again, but the man in the red jacket was on him in an instant.

This time, the axe wouldn't miss.

Adele reacted fast, hand darting to her hip, gun drawn, two quick shots. In the air.

No hope of hitting him without risking her father or John, but this

187

way, the man hesitated and looked up, snarling.

He had a thick, brown beard and wild, curly dark hair framing deep-set eyes. He glared up the trail at her and John used the opportunity to scramble away, kicking and rolling on his back.

The man laughed and wagged his axe in John's direction. "No, little lamb. Stay with me today!" he crowed. "Don't you hear the mountains?" He screamed now, raising his voice and tilting his head back; he loosed a wild, bloodcurdling howl followed by another laugh. "Can you hear them whimper, whisper? Can you hear them crow— row-row!" He laughed again and wiggled his axe once more, pointing it toward Adele.

For a brief second, he stood, chest puffed, seemingly impervious, indifferent to the weapon raised in her hand. And, in that moment, Adele hesitated, staring. The man had an air of invincibility. He stood in the snow, snowflakes speckling his beard, his head thrown back, chin jutting forth in pride. Two men lay injured or unconscious at his feet. Both of them barely moving. John was still trying to crawl away, but the axe-wielding attacker noticed this and made a tutting sound. "I don't think so," he whispered, his voice carrying across the open terrain, but then being brushed away by the whimpering wind.

"Don't!" Adele shouted. Her gun was pointed at him now, but he seemed to come to his senses and dropped low, cowering behind John's crawling form.

"You don't understand!" he shouted back. "It is what the mountains wish! Don't oppose the circle—life has its say! Don't you hear it? Can't you hear it, little lamb? Listen to the slopes? Heed the breeze? Notice the inclination of the trees. They laugh, they cackle—we burn and pillage and rape, and yet they will have the final say! They will! They will!"

Adele was no longer paying attention. She continued along the trail, approaching now, having reached the curling switchback and the lower plateau. She stepped off the trail, following the churning footsteps the men had left in the disheveled snow.

Carefully, she stalked forward, and the man with the axe maintained his crouch, circling slightly, keeping John's fallen form between him and Adele. He peered over the tall Frenchman's gasping chest and bloodied hand, his eyes bright and wide like a prairie dog peeking over a hill. And yet there was a malicious glint in the man's eyes that seemed foreign in this landscape—that for all this speak of nature and mountains seemed strangely and uniquely *human.*

Adele kept her weapon raised. She knew the moment she lowered her gun, the attacker would use his axe. John was still trying to crawl away in the snow, gasping in pain, leaving droplets of blood from his injured hand.

"Who are you? Corey Bjerg?" she said. "Is that you?"

The man's face creased in a smile and he winked. "It was my grandfather's name, you know? He's in these mountains. It's a secret. A quiet secret. A whispered secret. Don't you hear the breeze? Don't you?" He seemed angry now and his eyes pulsed, widening in their sockets in madness as he stared at her.

"Mr. Bjerg, you're wanted for questioning in regards to the murders of the Benevetis, the Haneses, and Mr. Griezmann." Adele felt they were long past the point of technicalities, but she needed to keep him talking, to figure out what to do next.

She continued to move cautiously forward. But whenever she stepped to the side, he moved, still keeping John's fallen form between them.

"Dad?" she called out. "Dad are you all right?"

No answer.

"John?"

A grunt, a groan, but no words.

Her pulse quickened. "Mr. Bjerg, I need you to back away. Drop the axe and put your hands where I can see them."

This seemed to irritate the man. He frowned and gripped his axe, raising it. He prodded at John with the edge of the blade, eliciting another groan from the Frenchman.

"I will if you will," he said, chuckling softly. Then the smile died, but his eyes remained fixed on her. "I will if you will. As the mountains intended. You toss yours, I toss mine. Strength to strength, yes? And I won't cut your weakened lambs. I won't cut or cull. Strength to strength, yes?"

Adele swallowed. She didn't understand half of it. But the way he was indicating toward her gun, and the way he dragged the axe across John's back, gently now, threatening, not gouging yet, she knew there was little choice.

She raised her hand and ejected the clip, tossing it to the side, watching them fall into the snow. "There!" she called. "I did it. Now you."

189

"Your gun too!" he snarled. "I'm no lamb!"

Adele nodded. "At the same time, yes?"

He fidgeted, still gripping his axe. Adele approached, one bullet still chambered. One shot. Her hand trembling. John would know what to do. John wouldn't hesitate, would he? She hated guns—her least favorite part of the job.

And yet, now, she was more than grateful she had one. To discard it would mean death. He couldn't be trusted, she knew that.

Then, to her astonishment, he tossed the axe. It arched, spinning through the air and landing in the snow, handle protruding, right at the edge of a drop-off. Her father still lay unconscious in the ice. John still struggled to rise. But the man winked at her, and tilted his head toward the axe. "Yes?" he said. "I obeyed. Now you."

Adele felt a cold chill. Abandoning her gun would be stupid. She raised and fired.

But at the last instant, her instincts, her training, were betrayed by a surge of guilt. She couldn't kill him—even unarmed, could she?

She hesitated. A costly mistake.

The man ducked and her bullet went wide, slamming splinters from a tree behind him, near the precipice and near his axe.

"A-ha!" he crowed, as if presenting some evidence.

And then he spun and sprinted toward the axe. Adele, completely spent on bullets, thought twice, but then sprinted after him, determined to beat him to the axe. Unarmed, they would all die now. She'd missed. She'd missed the shot. Now, the axe would end them unless she reached it first.

But the man was closer to it than her. She sprinted through the snow, kicking ice and powdered white, gasping as she raced. The paramedic also rushed forward, his red jacket flickering against the gray and white outline of the mountains.

Adele was ten paces away, five, three. The man dove for the axe, snared it, shouting triumphantly as he rolled to his feet, raising the weapon.

A split second to decide. A split second. Her father behind her, unconscious. John injured, unable to help.

If she allowed him at them, he'd kill them as sure as anything.

She didn't stop. Instead, Adele lowered her head and barreled straight into the man, catching him in the sternum. Her head throbbed—pain burst through her skull. At the same time, the man let out a sickly gasp of surprise and shock. And together, the two of them tumbled off the precipice edge.

Adele lost track. Spinning, falling, head over heels. Tumbling, down, down. Fear, terror. Frost, freezing. She couldn't scream, couldn't even remember how to breathe as she plummeted...

And then.

Whoompf.

She landed in snow, hard. Virgin, untouched ice and frost. Her body plummeted straight through, deep, carried by the impact. For a moment, she lay there, certain her spine had been crushed. But her thoughts still whirled—pain still flickered through her. She tried to move, but found herself encumbered. Adele blinked blearily, and realized she'd landed on her back, face up. She was *deep* in snow. Buried alive.

Around her, the walls of frost that hadn't caught her mass still extended toward the sky. Walls of snow, a cocoon of ice. She felt sheltered for a flickering moment.

Then terror seeped in like the melting ice around her. Adele conserved her breath. Desperately, she remembered her training. She turned and spat, watching the way the saliva dribbled. Down was below. Good. That meant up was *that way.*

She began shoveling, rapidly—probably too rapidly. But it didn't matter. She needed to get *out! Out!*

She crawled and kicked, packing the snow beneath her, pushing it down, shoveling it below her, desperately dragging herself from the pit of ice.

And then...

Her head burst toward sunlight.

She blinked, gasping, desperately, greedily gulping in soothing air, allowing it to fill her lungs, ignorant and indifferent to the sting of ice. Her cheeks were frozen—she couldn't feel them. Her face was stinging. Then, ahead of her, she spotted him.

Corey Bjerg hadn't been so lucky.

She stared... he'd landed on a portion of hardened earth. The snow had been repelled by the slick slope of the fir trees extended up. One such tree had snapped, from wind or weather, she didn't know. The protruding branch, though, had caught Mr. Bjerg.

The paramedic's red jacket had reddened further. He was staring at the sky, impaled on the sharp branch, gasping and wiggling like a caught trout.

Adele stared and then, carefully, moved through the snow—extending her body, more swimming than walking until she reached the packed earth around the grove and pulled herself up to the trees.

"Mr. Bjerg," she said, cautiously. "Mr. Bjerg, can you hear me?"

He continued to move and twitch, the jutting tree branch pushed through his chest. Blood spilled down his jacket. Spittle flecked his beard. His wide, maddened eyes fixed on her below, like a scarecrow witnessing a trespasser in his field. Still, somehow, he clutched his axe in one hand.

"Who—who are you?" he gasped, his chest rising and falling in rapid succession.

She stared up at him in pity, in disgust, in anger. She shook her head. "Mr. Bjerg, we'll get you down, okay? Stop struggling. John!" she shouted, angling her head back, but keeping her eyes on the suspect. "John—call paramedics! John!"

She heard a faint cry of response and turned back to Mr. Bjerg.

But the man was still moving, still shaking his head. He coughed, and his whole body shook with spasms of pain.

"The mountains are clear," he said, his eyes fixed on her. Spittle now trickled along his jaw and seemed to frost on his lower lip. "I… I am the lamb."

She stared at him. "Mr. Bjerg, please, wait one moment. We'll get you help. Just lower the axe, all right? Put it down."

But instead, he stared at her, still suspended above, still impaled and, with a trembling hand, he lifted the axe.

"To cull is to be a good shepherd," he said, quietly, his eyes fluttering.

And before Adele could shout, before she could say anything, he reached up and dragged the axe sharply across his exposed neck. She resisted the urge to look away, too startled, to shocked to react.

Blood now spilled from a deep cut in his neck. His fluttering eyes closed, and his gasping breath faded. In one last, desperate attempt, he seemed to speak, but the words were lost to the quiet moan from the wind in the Alps.

Adele stood beneath the corpse, staring up at him. Then she spat off to the side, muttering, "What a waste." And turned, trudging back toward the sound of John's voice, now calling out for her.

192

CHAPTER THIRTY FIVE

This paramedic outpost was a bit more comforting than the last one had been. Four of the seven beds were occupied. John and her father flanked her, resting on either side. The fourth bed, by a red privacy curtain, was occupied by a woman who'd been found strapped to a sled on Mr. Bjerg's snowmobile.

All four of them would recover—mostly.

John's trigger finger was half severed now. The piece of flesh lost in the snow. Her father had bandages along his face, and a couple of paramedics—also in the same uniform Mr. Bjerg had worn—were treating him, and murmuring quiet questions as they tended to his wounds.

Adele sat propped up, two cushions at her back, and she stared at the dappled ceiling, breathing in and out, slowly, cautiously.

Case closed, she thought to herself. A flicker of a smile crossed her lips but then she winced. Even smiling was painful. Her whole body felt like one giant bruise. Nothing broken, it seemed—but close enough.

Adele's phone rested on the simple white tray table between her and John. She'd turned it off. No texts, no calls, no news notifications. Just silence for the moment.

The paramedics continued to treat the Sergeant, patient despite his annoyance and short temper. He kept waving a hand and pushing them away from his face, and they persisted, gently trying to adjust his bandages and murmuring things like, "Mr. Sharp, if you're not careful, you'll redo the fracture." And also, "Sir, no—I am qualified to do this, yes. Please, just sit still."

Adele tried not to smirk, but for once, she was glad not to be on the receiving end of her father's ire.

She turned, her back to her dad now, and faced John. The tall agent was staring at his injured hand, frowning. For the first time since arriving in the Alps, he now wore a jacket—a bright, orange, puffy thing that made him look a bit like a nectarine. A handsome, scarred, weathered nectarine at that.

"What are you smirking at?" he said, crossly.

Adele shook her head. "Nothing. It's nothing."

He waved his injured hand at her, revealing the half-missing trigger finger wrapped in white gauze. "I know you're laughing at something, but I can't quite put my finger on what." He flashed a grin and smirked.

Adele groaned and shook her head. "Terrible, John. Just terrible."

He shrugged. "I've known brothers who've had worse. I'll recover. Have to use my left hand now, though."

"Can't imagine the friendly fire involved with that endeavor."

John stared into his lap, seemingly lost in thought for a moment, and Adele thought she might have crossed a line. But when he looked up, she was surprised to see his eyes misty. He cleared his throat and said, "Thanks for being there."

"Yeah, well," she replied, just as quietly, "you saved my dad. You've saved me more than once. Makes us even, right?"

He chuckled. "By my score, you've got one up on me. But never let it be said that John Renee wouldn't take an advantage when it was given."

Adele felt the smile spread in warmth, across her cheeks, down her chest, and to her stomach—a fire in her belly. She continued to smile, no longer speaking, just listening quiet. John's eyes closed eventually, and he slowly drifted off to sleep.

Adele peered through the large windows across from the beds, beyond the red privacy curtain. She glimpsed the white and blue structures of the new resort.

For an hour, she sat, thinking nothing, wanting nothing. The emptiness was more welcome than sunshine—more welcome than air. Just… quiet. Peace.

John started snoring and the paramedics eventually abandoned her father with mild cussing and grumbling—which he reprimanded as they retreated. Adele continued to stare out the glass window at the resort in the distance, sighing softly as she did. A quiet frown crossed her countenance.

"Do you want to return?" said a voice.

Adele glanced over and found her father watching her, standing now, his face still bandaged, but his bed scorned at his back. He was framed by the privacy curtain and wore a hospital gown which, mercifully, was of a more decent variety than normal.

Her father crossed his arms, causing the white ducks on his blue gown to crease in the fabric.

"Return where?" she asked.

He nodded his head to the window. "Resort. Any more brush-up work? Things need to be done?"

Adele shook her head. "I don't think so. Agent Marshall is actually bringing my things here."

"You'll leave then? Soon?"

Adele pushed herself up even more, leaning forward now, the cushions behind her dislodging. One of them fell to the floor where she left it.

John was still snoring. The paramedics had retreated to a safe distance from the Sergeant.

"I'll leave soon, yes," she said.

Adele thought of Angus—the talk she'd promised him. Roots? Would it finally be time to settle down? Was that what he wanted? Was that what *she* wanted?

She found herself glancing toward John, but just as quickly looked away. She looked out the window at the resort. She thought of the Benevetis; they had their own private chalet. All the security, all the money they could want. Married. And still... it all ended with a short six-foot trip.

Roots—perhaps roots were overrated? Or perhaps she hadn't found the place they'd be worth the sacrifice. Still, she would speak with Angus. But then... then what?

"You don't have to go back, you know," her father said, quiet again. He still stood, in defiance to his bed, but now stared out the window, no longer looking at his daughter. For a moment, a contemplative look crossed his face. "I know the thoughts," he said. "I made them, too, you know."

Adele smiled softly. Her father had settled. He'd married a French woman, and had left the US to settle in Germany. And yet... it had ended horribly.

The nagging thoughts she'd experienced came on her again. Memories of a vacation. Of family—of shouting, of another man?

Unbidden, the words spilled out. "Did Mom cheat on you?"

She winced the moment she spoke, wondering how it would be received.

Her father raised an eyebrow, glancing over at her, twisting but then wincing as his jaw strained against the bandages. He turned his whole

195

body now, instead, to acknowledge her. "Cheat? No. Why would you say this?"

Adele frowned. "I remember... not much... but I remember someone—not you, someone else coming to our hotel room when you were out. Someone in the room with Mom."

Her father frowned, but it seemed an expression of grief more than irritation. "No," he said, softly. "She didn't cheat. I... I remember," he said, quietly. So quietly, Adele had to lean forward to hear.

"It didn't have anything to do with mother's"—Adele swallowed, her throat dry, but managed to complete the thought—"her *murder,* did it?"

Her dad winced again. "The man in your mother's room was most likely her brother," he said. "That vacation, his family came with us. You likely don't remember them much. We didn't spend too much time with him. But he loved his sister... He saw how we would act and would console her, comfort her... a whispering snake in her ear," he started, growling, but then his shoulders slumped as some of his usual fire left him and he shook his head sadly. "Though, perhaps that's not fair... The truth, Adele... your mother and I grew distant. Simple as that. We loved each other—I know that. Once we did. But we'd been growing apart for years at that point. Different wants in life—different hopes for the future. She wanted more kids, did you know that?"

He laughed bitterly. "Perhaps I was a fool. But I wanted my career to improve... Never happened."

Adele glimpsed a spasm of pure, unfiltered grief and regret surge through her father. Her heart pained for him, but where he was, she couldn't go. His regrets were his own. So she listened, perhaps hoping to alleviate some of the pain through simply listening.

"The vacation you remember... just one of many. We would fight, yes. We would make up, yes. For your sake, though, Adele. Not for ours. Elise was wise—she saw it before I did. She knew the writing was on the wall."

He breathed again, shaking his head still. "It had nothing to do with her murder... no..."

He trailed off into contemplative, bitter silence, allowing it to swell around them. Adele didn't interrupt, didn't intrude. This wasn't her silence, nor was it her grief. She wouldn't rob her father of his feelings or his thoughts. Not now.

After a bit, though, some of the emotion seemed to fade. He seemed smaller, now, less threatening. Less scary. He looked at her and quietly said, "It had nothing to do with your mother's murder... But... Well... Perhaps this will help."

Adele frowned and watched as he pulled a small brown notebook from his pocket. He held it for a second, gripping it like a priest with a bible, but then, with the air of a man relinquishing something of deep value, he placed it on the table next to Adele's phone. Then he stepped back, distancing himself from it. He rubbed his hand on the side of his gown, as if cleaning it.

"What is it?" she asked.

"Notes," he said, softly. "You're right. If I was a better investigator, I would have found her killer. But that isn't to say I didn't try."

Adele felt her heart hammer.

Her father pointed a finger at the book, the same finger John was now missing. "I've been following leads for years—*years*. But it has all turned to dead ends for me... All of it." He sighed. "Perhaps it is time for me to let go. It's yours. All the notes. Maybe you'll find better luck. You know... you come here so often," he said, softly. "Have you considered moving back? Not to Germany—I'm not saying to Germany. But France? The Alps? You seem alive when you're here."

Adele said nothing, too stunned by the notebook to even truly hear anything else.

And with that, her father turned his back on the notebook and sat on his bed, staring at the privacy curtain and allowing the silence to return.

Adele blinked, staring. She half reached out for the notebook—a weathered, brown affair. Clearly it had seen use. But then she withdrew her hand and tucked it in her lap. Not now. Not yet.

But soon.

EPILOGUE

Angus sat across from her in the small restaurant two blocks from headquarters. He was nervous and twisting straws in his fingers as he looked at her.

Adele hadn't wanted to honor the meeting. But she'd given her word.

"Hey," he said, smiling and then speaking through the smile. "How are things?"

She leaned in her chair, looking at him. "I'm all right. Yourself?"

He nodded, bobbing his head, his brown curls shifting with the motion. "Fine, fine..." he said, distractedly. Angus had never been great at pleasantries when he had something on his mind.

"So," she said. "What can I do for you?"

"It's not... It's not a big deal," he said, quietly, carefully. "It's just..." He reached down, stirred his coffee with a straw, then returned his fingers to tapping against his knee beneath the table. "It's just, I've been thinking a lot. And... I know we left things strange last time we spoke. I know that."

"Angus," Adele said, gently. "I'm not sure I'm ready to commit to anything. I understand words were exchanged... but we're both in different places now. And—"

"Wait, hang on, no," he said quickly, shaking his head side to side. His cheeks flushed red and he winced. "Wow... No, sorry. I'm really bad at this, Adele. I'm not—I'm not asking—not *that*."

Adele frowned. "Oh?"

He puffed his cheeks and pressed his lips as if holding back a breath. Clearly, he wanted to say more, but just as clearly he seemed unsure how to say it. At last, he just came out with it. "Adele, I want our old apartment back..." He said it quickly, like tearing off a Band-Aid, and he winced at the conclusion and shrugged a shoulder. "I'm sorry. Really. No, I am. Just—things at work haven't been going as well as they could. To be actually honest—I... I lost my job. Or, well, the company is on hiatus for a bit. We're figuring things out." Hastily, he added, "It's all going to be fine. I'm sure of it." He repeated, with more

198

gusto, for himself rather than her, "It'll be fine!"

Adele stared, unsure whether to be furious or amused. She settled on humor, trying to suppress a smile. It didn't hurt—not this time. She'd never been good at reading Angus's intentions. Once, she'd thought he'd wanted to propose. Now, she'd thought he'd wanted to get back together.

But no... he was looking for a cheaper apartment. She coughed in her hand, disguising a sudden laugh.

"Well?" he said, earnestly. "Could you help me out? I miss that place... and... well, I just can't afford where I am now."

"Angus," Adele said, quietly, "I don't have the place anymore. I moved after we broke up."

Angus looked at her, stunned, his eyes widening. "Wait, really? Oh..." He slumped in his chair, staring at her. "The old place... do you know if they're renting it yet?"

Adele shrugged. "Probably. Location, location. You know."

Angus scratched his jaw and pushed his paper coffee cup toward a pile of brown napkins.

For a moment, Adele looked at him, trying to process her own thoughts. She wanted to be angry—but then why wasn't she?

Because you didn't want him back.

The voice in her head was clear, concise. And honest.

So why didn't she want him back? Would she ever settle down? Set roots? The more she thought, though... her mind strayed to France. To Robert. To John. She thought of her father... of his decision to settle in Germany. Of the small notebook, even now pressed against her thigh.

A strange kind of confidence fell on her. A reckless, careless confidence. She blurted out, "You can have my current apartment if you want."

Angus stared at her. "Your... like the new one? You're living there, right?"

"Yes. It's yours if you want it. Landlord won't care as long as bills are paid. Cheaper than the old place too. It's yours if you want it."

Angus seemed stunned. He opened his mouth, then closed it again. He frowned, tried to speak, but then seemed caught. "Are... are you sure?" he said, hesitantly.

Adele didn't think. She tapped her fingers against her leg, against the bulge of the brown notebook. She thought of France. "Yes," she said, simply. "I'm sure."

"But where will you live?" he asked, hesitant.

She sighed… She thought of Robert's mansion. Of John's bachelor pad. She thought of her father's house. She thought, most of all, of a small trail cutting through a garden in the middle of Paris. She thought of a decade ago, the discovery of her mother's body. She thought of the killer—out there even now, enjoying his freedom. Enjoying the pain he'd caused so many.

"I'll figure something out," she said. "Stop by tomorrow. I'll text you the address. We'll sort things out."

And with that, Adele pushed from the table and walked away, a spring in her step. She felt… all of a sudden… lighter. The only weight came in the small form of the notebook tucked in her pocket. She hadn't read it yet—not yet. But soon

.

NOW AVAILABLE!

LEFT TO KILL
(An Adele Sharp Mystery—Book 4)

"When you think that life cannot get better, Blake Pierce comes up with another masterpiece of thriller and mystery! This book is full of twists and the end brings a surprising revelation. I strongly recommend this book to the permanent library of any reader that enjoys a very well written thriller."
--Books and Movie Reviews, Roberto Mattos (re Almost Gone)

LEFT TO KILL is book #4 in a new FBI thriller series by USA Today bestselling author Blake Pierce, whose #1 bestseller Once Gone (Book #1) (a free download) has received over 1,000 five star reviews.

A young woman is found wandering, in a daze, on a rural road in Germany, having escaped her attacker. If she can talk, and remember, maybe she can lead authorities back to his lair—and save the other women there before it's too late.

As the sprawling international case begins to enmesh dozens of victims from many countries, authorities quickly realize there is only one way to solve this: to bring in FBI special agent Adele Sharp, triple citizen of the U.S., France and Germany.

But even with Adele's brilliant mind, this case, bringing up memories way too close to home, may be just out of her reach.

Can Adele save the other woman before it's too late?

Can she save herself?

An action-packed mystery series of international intrigue and riveting suspense, LEFT TO KILL will have you turning pages late into the night.

Book #5 in the series (LEFT TO MURDER) is now also available.

LEFT TO KILL
(An Adele Sharp Mystery—Book 4)

Blake Pierce

Blake Pierce is the USA Today bestselling author of the RILEY PAGE mystery series, which includes seventeen books. Blake Pierce is also the author of the MACKENZIE WHITE mystery series, comprising fourteen books; of the AVERY BLACK mystery series, comprising six books; of the KERI LOCKE mystery series, comprising five books; of the MAKING OF RILEY PAIGE mystery series, comprising six books; of the KATE WISE mystery series, comprising seven books; of the CHLOE FINE psychological suspense mystery, comprising six books; of the JESSE HUNT psychological suspense thriller series, comprising seven books (and counting); of the AU PAIR psychological suspense thriller series, comprising three books; of the ZOE PRIME mystery series, comprising three books (and counting); of the new ADELE SHARP mystery series; and of the new EUROPEAN VOYAGE cozy mystery series.

An avid reader and lifelong fan of the mystery and thriller genres, Blake loves to hear from you, so please feel free to visit www.blakepierceauthor.com to learn more and stay in touch.

BOOKS BY BLAKE PIERCE

EUROPEAN VOYAGE COZY MYSTERY SERIES
MURDER (AND BAKLAVA) (Book #1)
DEATH (AND APPLE STRUDEL) (Book #2)
CRIME (AND LAGER) (Book #3)

ADELE SHARP MYSTERY SERIES
LEFT TO DIE (Book #1)
LEFT TO RUN (Book #2)
LEFT TO HIDE (Book #3)
LEFT TO KILL (Book #4)
LEFT TO MURDER (Book #5)
LEFT TO ENVY (Book #6)
LEFT TO LAPSE (Book #7)

THE AU PAIR SERIES
ALMOST GONE (Book#1)
ALMOST LOST (Book #2)
ALMOST DEAD (Book #3)

ZOE PRIME MYSTERY SERIES
FACE OF DEATH (Book#1)
FACE OF MURDER (Book #2)
FACE OF FEAR (Book #3)
FACE OF MADNESS (Book #4)

A JESSIE HUNT PSYCHOLOGICAL SUSPENSE SERIES
THE PERFECT WIFE (Book #1)
THE PERFECT BLOCK (Book #2)
THE PERFECT HOUSE (Book #3)
THE PERFECT SMILE (Book #4)
THE PERFECT LIE (Book #5)
THE PERFECT LOOK (Book #6)
THE PERFECT AFFAIR (Book #7)
THE PERFECT ALIBI (Book #8)
THE PERFECT NEIGHBOR (Book #9)
THE PERFECT DISGUISE (Book #10)
THE PERFECT SECRET (Book #11)

Made in the USA
Columbia, SC
20 May 2022

60691743R00126